THE
COHORT

NATHANIEL SIZEMORE

The Cohort
By Nathaniel Sizemore

For information, contact
BDI Publishers, Atlanta, Georgia,
bdipublishers@gmail.com.

Cover Design and Layout: Tudor Maier
BDI Publishers

Atlanta, Georgia
ISBN: 978-0-9889330-3-3

Acknowledgments

To God, from whom all talents and blessings flow. And to my family, especially my wife and three children. You inspire me daily.

Finally, to the wonderful people who live and work on Kiawah Island, South Carolina. My family has enjoyed Kiawah for more than three decades and its beauty and mystique is second to none. Thanks for all the fantastic memories, Kiawah – this book is for *you*!

FACT:

Kiawah Island is a gated resort community located twenty-five miles from Charleston, South Carolina. *Kiawah* has been called "the Hamptons of the South," and a number of celebrities, business leaders, and politicians own homes on the island.

The Society of the Elect was a secret society founded in 1891 by English businessman and imperialist, Cecil Rhodes, for which the famous Rhodes Scholarship is named. The Society was the precursor to *The Round Table Group* which laid the foundation for America's Council on Foreign Relations – one of the most influential policy organizations in the world.

In his book, *The New Freedom: A Call for the Emancipation of the Generous Energies of a People* (1913), President Woodrow Wilson wrote: "Some of the biggest men in the U.S....are afraid of somebody, are afraid of something. They know that there is a power somewhere so organized, so subtle, so watchful, so interlocked, so complete, so pervasive, that they had better not speak above their breath when they speak in condemnation of it."

"For God will bring every deed into judgment, including every hidden thing, whether it is good or evil."
Ecclesiastes 12:14

Chapter 1

David Stoneman sprinted toward the conference room's exit as the wall of water raced toward him. His worn tennis shoes slipped on the patterned carpet as he tried to escape. David was frantic – if he didn't get out, he would be dead.

Just a few paces from the conference room door, David's worst fear was realized. The surge of water swept him off his feet. Like a phantom foe, it overtook him. The water moved as if it had a mind of its own and its sinister plan was to bury David in an unmarked watery grave.

David's arms flailed as his helpless body slammed into the unmoving cream-colored wall. The impact rattled him and he blinked several times to regain full consciousness as the room spun around him. The sound, like a raging river, was dampened by the pain of his rope-burned hands pushing against the wall. He clawed with all his might trying to avoid getting trapped. *Focus*, he thought. His life depended on it.

Despite his best efforts, the relentless surge continued to cascade over his head and shoulders, and all around him. His angled knees were pressed against the wall's baseboard and the expensive lights in the room flickered and then went completely dark. Just a sparse amount of natural light shone through the broken floor-to-ceiling window on the far wall.

David attempted to stand but the water's pressure was too great. He accepted the unfortunate fact that he would have to wait for the room to fully flood before he had any chance of escape.

The cold water was now chest high and lifted David off the ground. He floated away from the exit door and back toward the middle of the room. The tide was rising at what seemed like a foot every second. It wouldn't be long until he reached the top of the conference room's twelve-foot-tall ceiling. The murky water continued to churn like a whirlpool as it swirled around his battered body.

David screamed for help, but to no avail. The deafening sound of the hurricane's wind and torrential rain muted his desperate cries. Reality set in. *No one's coming.*

The room's once-grand feature was its floor-to-ceiling window abutting an elevated manmade lagoon. Today, however, it was a death trap.

David had to think fast. The water was muddy with zero visibility and the salty liquid caused David's eyes to burn. He could taste the salinity of the brackish water as he took a deep breath and plunged down into the darkness.

David visualized the room's layout, specifically, the location of the door and its handle; his only way out. He employed his best swim stroke and feverishly kicked his legs. With every passing second, he became more spatially disoriented. And with each kick and stroke his limbs grew heavier.

When David finally made it back to the wall, his exhausted, outstretched hands reached in all directions searching for the answer to his silent prayer – then he felt it. *The bronze door handle*. David clung to it for dear life with his right hand, but just as his left hand also found the handle, a blunt object barreled into David's face.

Pain shot like electricity through his nasal cavity and the shock of the blow caused him to lose his grip on the door. Without an anchor, the natural buoyancy of his body caused him to float upward.

He reached the surface and gasped. The salt air refilled his lungs with essential oxygen. He opened his eyes to find the item that had hit him – a bobbing wooden chain. David cursed under his breath and treaded water for a few precious seconds. The water continued to rise.

He wiped his face with the back of his hand and when he looked down, he saw blood and lots of it. David gently touched his nose with his right index finger and, again, pain shot through his head. But despite the discomfort, he didn't have a minute to lose. The small conference space would be completely filled with water in less than sixty seconds. It was now or never.

David huffed air into his aching lungs knowing he only had one more chance to dive and escape. He took a final glance around the room to determine if there were *any* other escape options he may have missed. The only other option was an unacceptably dangerous path through the broken floor-to-ceiling window. However, he immediately eliminated that option. After all, he didn't want to swim through an *alligator lagoon*. That's when he saw it.

Even in the room's darkness, David couldn't miss the unmistakable outline of dark green scales ominously floating toward him. A cold chill ran down his spine. David's muscles tensed and he wished he could stop his heart from beating so loudly in his bruised chest. It could only be one thing.

The partially submerged rounded snout emerged from the water. The slimy reptile floated toward its prey with open jaws showcasing eighty bone-crushing teeth above the hazy waterline. From tip to tail the alligator was thirteen feet and weighed seven-hundred pounds. The look in its menacing eyes demanded surrender.

David was paralyzed by fear, but he had to move. He took a final deep breath and dove down, one last time. The plunge was the most terrifying experience of David's life. He fully expected to feel sharp teeth tear into his flesh any second as he dove deeper and deeper. Still, he kept kicking and swam with all his might.

David touched the top of the doorframe and scratched feverishly down the door. Just as he felt the alligator's coarse skin brush his left arm, his hands found the bronze door handle. He grasped it tightly with both hands, turned it downward, and pushed.

Chapter 2

Four days earlier…

Tommy Felton was spending a relaxing afternoon fishing on the Stono River near James Island, South Carolina. His squatted frame was sitting in a blue and white, seventeen-foot Carolina Skiff JV boat, which he had purchased from a friend earlier that year. An impulse buy, for sure, but one that he didn't regret. At least *not yet*.

Tommy's casting rod rested securely in its holder as he cracked open a soft drink, took a swig, and placed the cold beverage in a spare cup holder. He belched and patted his growing gut which pushed up against his faded T-shirt.

Tommy had every intention of getting back into shape but, unfortunately, none of his favorite pastimes included significant physical exertion. As such, he was perfectly content with snug pants and an easy life.

The Stono River had been peaceful all day. Tommy sat back in his captain's chair as a cool breeze whipped across the calm water. It was September and the summer heat was beginning to give way to slightly cooler temperatures, which made for excellent trout fishing – Tommy's favorite catch. Within the last few weeks, Tommy had hooked half a dozen different types of fish, including, red fish, flounder, and tarpon. The diversity of his aquatic trophy case was a growing source of pride for the aging preacher. Of course, 'big fish' stories abounded.

The tourist season in Charleston was, thankfully, coming to an end as another school year was well underway. Tommy very much looked forward to a couple uninterrupted months on his boat before the weather turned too chilly.

He had stumbled upon a hidden alcove in a secluded section of the river which snaked back into a quiet inlet. At low tide, clusters of eastern oysters lined the banks of the inlet, showcasing the natural habitat for ecologically-important species of crab and shrimp.

The spot was perfect. Tommy could be alone with his thoughts for hours before seeing another passing vessel. It was a good thing, too. He had tried for months to let go of the horrific events he had experienced the previous year.

While he rarely spoke of it publicly, the preceding twelve months had been *dreadful*. The worst of his life. Tommy had tragically lost his wife, Marie, in a house fire, and went toe-to-toe with corrupt political officials in Washington, D.C. The silver lining, however, was that Tommy's daughter, Jenny, had moved back to Charleston from Oklahoma to be closer to him. In an odd way, his wife's death had brought Tommy and his daughter back together.

The sun was hot on the water and Tommy removed his dated *Chez Fish* hat and repositioned it on his sweating head. His thinning blonde hair had grown long and was nearly touching his shoulders. Jenny joked that her father was turning into Jimmy Buffett with his new look and laid-back lifestyle. Tommy wished he could be that relaxed, but the burden he had carried for the last year still weighed heavily on his troubled mind.

He flipped on the boat's radio to the local country music station. With his sandaled feet propped up on the side of his tiny fishing boat, he closed his eyes and placed his tanned hands behind his head. The methodic rhythm of the water's current gently rocked him to sleep.

Tommy's cat nap was interrupted by the unexpected sound of a boat engine. He slowly opened his eyes, dropped his feet to the deck, and sat up. Tommy was groggy from his snooze and was surprised to find what appeared to be a military boat coasting toward him.

Charleston was a naval town and many members of Tommy's church congregation were in the Navy. He had broken bread with dozens of military families and one of Tommy's favorite conversation topics was the types of watercrafts the Navy utilized to complete their missions. He was always fascinated with the newest state-of-the-art boats that ruled the high seas. As such, Tommy immediately recognized the ship cruising toward him as a small unit riverine craft, commonly called a *SURC*.

What's a SURC doing in this inlet? He wondered as he put his hands on his hips.

The SURC was carrying four passengers, all of whom were dressed in full military fatigues, which Tommy found odd. He started his own boat's engine to move out of their way. *Surely, they're in the area for a training exercise*, he surmised, as his engine hummed to life.

The SURC slowed and idled until it stopped next to Tommy. A muscular man in his late fifties with a military haircut and chiseled jawline leaned over the side of the SURC.

"Excuse me, sir?" The man said with a no-nonsense disposition.

"Yes? How can I help you?" Tommy replied with a warm smile and a subtle Southern accent. The sun was shining directly into Tommy's eyes which silhouetted the large military man. Tommy raised his right hand above his eyeline to see the man more clearly.

"I'm afraid I'm going to have to ask you to vacate these waters, sir...it's a protected wildlife preserve and fishing here can result in a fine or even jail time. Please follow us and we'll escort you to a safe location."

The muscular man was confident in his statement, but Tommy was skeptical. Before he had found his secret fishing spot, Tommy had done his due diligence to determine exactly where the restricted fishing waters were and made sure to avoid them. After all, it wouldn't look good if a minister was tossed in jail for hooking endangered fish in a restricted area. Believing the military man to be mistaken, Tommy prodded further.

"I'm sorry, sir, but can I get your name?" Tommy smiled again, not wanting to appear uncooperative.

"Sergeant James Henderson." The man responded coldly as he glanced at the three other men standing behind him.

"Sergeant Henderson, can you please tell me which law I'm breaking by being in *this* location? I have a permit and have been *fishin'* here for months, without issue."

Sergeant Henderson was annoyed by the question and covered his mouth with his large hand as he whispered to one of his boatmates.

"Yes, sir, Mr. Felton, we would be happy to give you that information once you vacate the area. Now, please come with us, sir. I don't want to ask you again." Sergeant Henderson was growing visibly agitated.

Tommy froze. He never gave the man his name, but he said it, nonetheless. *Something's not right.* Tommy's mind began to race. *Stay calm and everything will be fine*, he repeated silently to himself. Tommy intended to comply until he could figure out what was going on.

"Okay, if you insist. I'm happy to follow you. Just let me pack up my bait."

Tommy intentionally turned his back to the men, kneeled, and opened his rusty tackle box where he kept his cell phone. He couldn't make a phone call; that would be too obvious. A text would have to suffice. Tommy quickly scanned through his recent call list and located his daughter's phone number.

He glimpsed over his shoulder. The men were now huddled in a circle, deep in serious discussion. Tommy typed out a short distress message.

On Stono at usual spot. In trouble. Military here.

As he sent the message, he felt his boat rock. He looked up to see one of the men standing over him with a club in his left hand. The man raised it in the air and swung hard. Tommy was able to lift his shoulder just enough to take the brunt of the painful blow. Tommy heard a loud pop as his arm went numb. He howled in pain.

Tommy instinctively held his right shoulder as he fell backward on to the boat deck, writhing. The man swung again and this swing hit Tommy directly in the temple, instantly killing him.

"Make it look like an accident." Sergeant Henderson barked as the other two uniformed soldiers jumped into Tommy's boat and began pounding a hole in the boat's hull on the starboard side. Their metal battering ram sounded like a cannon going off every time it struck.

On the fifth hit, the vessel began to fill with water and one of the men tied Tommy's foot to the side with blue fishing line from his tackle box.

The men jumped back to the SURC and fled the scene. They had completed their mission. Tommy's lifeless body disappeared with his boat under the calm green water.

As the SURC whipped around the winding waterways of the Stono River, Sergeant Henderson had to make a phone call. Tommy Felton was dead and he had to report it to his boss. He pulled his secured cell phone from his pocket and dialed the most private number in his contacts list.

"*Prometheus*, it's Henderson. It's done. Felton is out of the picture."

The deep voice on the other end uttered a few foreboding words.

"Good…I'll see you on the island." Then the line went dead.

Chapter 3

David Stoneman was sprawling on a small couch in the waiting room of an independent radio station just outside of Washington, D.C. He was studying himself in the vanity mirror on the opposite wall. True to his overly critical personality, he was second-guessing his shirt and tie combination.

His internal debate centered on whether he should have selected a traditional blue tie rather than the vibrant pink one. David eventually made peace with his decision due, in large part, to the fact that he couldn't change it before his impending radio interview.

David's thick, black hair had grown longer in the summer months. Nevertheless, always sporting a polished, professional appearance, David had it neatly combed to one side and frozen in place with expensive molding clay.

While he still worked too much, David had made it a point to take some overdue time away from the grind. He had settled into a work schedule that was, by his standards, more balanced. His favorite non-work activity was sitting by his backyard pool with his girlfriend, Sarah Mercer, and her son, Mark.

Suddenly, the door flew open. The short, pudgy radio station manager barged into the room, flustered. The man studied his wooden clipboard and then glanced at the watch on his left wrist. He then looked up at David.

"Come on!!" The station manager frantically beckoned.

David shot up from the couch, buttoned the top button of his tailored suit jacket, sneaked one last look in the mirror, and followed the man through the open doorway. The long hallway was dark, and a red, illuminated 'On Air' sign was glowing above the door frame at the end of the hall. As they approached the sign, the station manager turned to David and gave him specific instructions.

"When I open the door, Jackson will already be live on the air. Quietly take your seat and put on the headset on the table in front of you. Speak into the hanging mic and do not mumble. Got it?"

David nodded and the station manager cautiously opened the door and peeked in. The room was brightly lit with mounted ring lights. The entire studio was barely larger than a walk-in closet. The host, Jackson Seymour, gave a thumbs up to the manager as he wrapped up a deeply political conversation with a loquacious caller.

Jackson was seated, but his bony knees protruded above the table signaling he was quite tall. David studied his host – his mannerisms and quirks. Force of habit for a Georgetown-educated lawyer.

One of David's many talents was his ability to read people in a matter of seconds. He was so skillful at the craft that his previous law firm's partners would ask him to sit in on their depositions just so David could read a deponent's tells and ticks. If he weren't a lawyer, David would have made a good living at the poker tables in Vegas.

After just a moment of careful observation, David had gathered everything he needed to know about his host, Jackson Seymour. He was ready for his interview.

Chapter 4

The brisk morning air felt pleasant as Bailey Thompson curled up on her front porch, eager to begin the day. Bailey's spacious Tudor-style home in Atlanta, Georgia's prestigious Druid Hills suburb was one of many surrounding mansions already bustling as the sun came up.

While her children dressed for school, the precious few moments of solitude Bailey enjoyed before the busyness of the workday began were therapeutic. She watched as her accomplished neighbors, many of whom were doctors, lawyers, and business leaders in Atlanta, headed to their fancy offices in pricey sports cars. Bailey and her husband, Hunter, would soon follow suit.

The seasonal weather was cooling, but a Vineyard Vines vest atop a comfortable undershirt, coupled with a cup of piping hot coffee yielded a perfect counterbalance.

Bailey was pushing forty, although her nearly wrinkleless face made her look ten years younger. Despite the perpetual bags nestled underneath her almond eyes from constant eighty-hour workweeks, she maintained an energetic and youthful exuberance that was magnetic. Her shoulder-length dark brown hair was pulled back into a tight pony tail and Bailey's high, prominent cheek bones were stunning.

She was in excellent shape even though she no longer had time for the long, planned jogs which she had enjoyed in her twenties. These days, she opted for a green diet and logged an hour on the stationary bike four times a week. The chiseled muscles in her arms and legs were evidence of her discipline in that regard.

As a mother of two, ages eight and five, Bailey often felt overwhelmed by the challenges of balancing a professional career and motherhood. However, she had heard the most chaotic child-rearing years were behind her. The kids were now old enough to be independent and were usually glued to a small screen.

Despite the kids' independence, Bailey had secured the services of a full-time nanny/housekeeper named Alice who was hired to clean, cook, and take care of the kids, as needed. Alice was expensive, but the expense paled in comparison to her value.

Alice arrived at 7 a.m. on schooldays to prepare breakfast and make sure the children were ready to go to school on time. She would then drive them to their elite private preparatory academy, which was just a few miles away, and then return to the house to handle whatever else was needed that day.

Bailey's husband, Hunter, was typically out of the house before Alice arrived, but not this morning. Today, he was running late. She heard his black Lincoln Navigator's engine roar in their detached garage as the garage door lifted. Hunter shot her a wave as he pulled out of their driveway and raced off to work.

Hunter was a partner at one of Atlanta's most reputable law firms, Townsend & Moore LLP. For a salary of nearly half a million dollars a year, plus bonuses, the firm expected Hunter to be at his desk billing clients well before the regular American workday began. Unsurprisingly, he was also required to work late into the evenings and most weekends. It was just part of the job.

However, Hunter actually enjoyed the daily slog. In truth, Hunter would have maintained that same schedule at *half* the salary. He loved to win and worked as hard as needed to crush his opponents.

Hunter was tall and athletically built, with neatly coiffed blonde hair which he combed back and to the side. He had blue eyes, which were captivating, and he oozed confidence. The female associates and support staff at the firm would stop and stare as he walked down the hall.

As a former Townsend & Moore attorney herself, Bailey was familiar with the grueling work schedule that a large law firm required. Among her unpleasant firm memories, Bailey recalled having to race back and forth from the bathroom to maximize her billable hours, which were recorded in short six-minute increments. She was glad those days were over.

However, despite the lack of any work/life balance, Bailey's *Big Law* experience did yield something positive – that's where she and Hunter had met nearly a decade earlier.

At first, Bailey didn't think she had a chance with Hunter. After all, he had his pick of any single woman in the firm, and that included divorcée senior partners who were often on the prowl for strapping young subordinates.

Bailey's chances improved, however, when she was assigned to one of Hunter's cases. She was a mid-level associate and he the junior partner working on a crucial litigation matter for one of the firm's top clients. As it turned out, Hunter found brains more attractive than anything else. Consequently, after less than a year of dating, Bailey and Hunter were married in a large, formal wedding in downtown Atlanta.

Within eighteen months, Bailey became pregnant and the honeymoon was over. Bailey's life of balancing her career and motherhood had begun. She suspected life would be predictable and formulaic from that point on – that was until she met her new boss, Damian Little.

Chapter 5

In the studio, radio host, Jackson Seymour, was wearing skinny jeans, a flannel shirt, and vintage sneakers with no socks. His greasy, light brown hair was parted in the middle and hung casually over his protruding ears. Jackson's sleeves were rolled up to his elbows, which revealed several animated tattoos that swirled down to his wrists.

Hello, Washington, D.C.! Welcome back to the Seymour Morning Show, America's favorite underground political talk show. This is your host, Jackson Seymour, coming to you live from Arlington, Virginia! My last guest this morning is Mr. David Stoneman, Esquire! David is an attorney who is earning quite the reputation in First Amendment circles here in town. Just in the last several months, he's flown on to the scene with numerous impressive articles, speaking engagements, and television spots. Most notably, his controversial article, titled: *How the Government Went Too Far: The Cautionary Tale of the Division Act and its Infringement on American Rights*, was featured on the Freedom Forum Institute's website just last week and received millions of views. Welcome, David, to the Seymour Show!

David settled into his seat and adjusted his headset to ensure it rested securely on his head. He leaned forward and spoke clearly into the hanging microphone, as instructed.

"Thanks, Jackson, happy to be here," David announced with a full smile. He was surprised when Jackson did not return the gesture.

"Tell us about yourself, Dave!" Jackson said as he waved over the short, stout station manager. He put his hand over his microphone and whispered something into the man's ear. The manager disappeared out the door and down the hall.

"I've been practicing law for about ten years. I started my career as a solo practitioner in Norfolk, Virginia. Then I transitioned to the D.C. office of Johnson, Allen, Peters & Branson for a while. I ultimately opened my own firm earlier this year which focuses on First Amendment, civil rights, and wrongful death cases."

David paused in case Jackson wanted to respond, but his host just sat and glared at him as if he had already said something wrong. *What's with this guy?* David wondered.

Not knowing what else to do, David carried on.

"Right now, it's just me, two eager young associates, and a receptionist, but we're having fun fighting the good fights."

David paused again to see if Jackson wanted to move on. He did.

"Now, you give lectures to organizations like the Freedom Forum Institute…tell us more about your work this year," Jackson asked without looking up as he thumbed through pages of notes.

"Sure, well, I've only been focused on this type of law for a short time, but I'm passionate about the subject matter and decided to dive-in, head first. I think people have the right to know what's going on in their world and given the opportunity to vocalize their support, criticism, or concerns in a free society." David stopped, satisfied with his answer.

Still, Seymour didn't look up from his notes, but moved his right hand in a hurried wheel motion prompting David to keep going. David was taken aback by Jackson's obvious disinterest in the interview, but continued.

"As you know, Jackson, the Freedom Forum Institute is a fantastic organization that houses both the *First Amendment Center* and *Religious Freedom Center,* so there's a lot of firepower there for lively debate and discussion. In fact, I was honored to speak at one of their recent events which was hosted at Vanderbilt University, and—"Jackson cut David off.

"You've churned out a ton of online content, but why the sudden change from a large law firm to going *gung-ho* on First Amendment issues?" Jackson's tone was surprisingly cross as he continued to rifle through his notes. The station manager reappeared with a steaming cup of tea, which he carefully handed to Jackson.

"I get that question a lot, actually, and I think my interests shifted when—"Jackson cut David off a second time.

"After you tried to tank the Division Act last year to serve your self-interests?" Jackson looked up at David with a 'got ya' smirk. David maintained his composure.

"Yes…I guess it was the Division Act that caused me to change directions." David was careful with his next comments.

"But, as I'm sure you've covered on this show, Jackson, there were many lawsuits filed against the Division Act last year – I just took a unique angle. The Supreme Court struck down most of its provisions as unconstitutional. But there were other reasons I—" Jackson interrupted for a third time.

"Tell us about Sarah Mercer." Again, Jackson glared at David. This was not an interview. It was an ambush. David's blood began to boil.

"Well, there's not much to say. Sarah had an interesting case that went into confidential mediation which prevents me from speaking about it further." David wasn't going to take the bait, but he could tell Jackson was far from finished.

"You're dating Ms. Mercer, aren't you? Isn't it unethical for lawyers to date their clients?" Jackson took a sip of his hot tea and sat back in his padded leather chair. David had gone up against the best litigators in Washington and he certainly wasn't scared of a second-rate radio host. He leaned in and put his elbows on the table, ready for battle.

"Yes. Sarah and I are dating, but we didn't start seeing each other until her case was closed. The bar says that's okay. And while we're on the subject of personal information, Jackson, I heard a rumor you're a peeping tom who likes to expose himself to his neighbors through the window at night, is *that* true?"

Jackson spit out his tea, which soaked his notes. The pudgy station manager was standing in the corner with his hand over his mouth trying to conceal his laughter. David doubled-down on his counterattack.

"What do you say we move away from personal issues and get back to the real issues? Does that work for you?" The question was rhetorical.

"Otherwise, I'd be happy to read aloud the other information my private investigator dug up on you, Jackson. I'm sure your listeners would be interested to hear more disturbing details." David smirked at his host who was wiping tea off the table. Jackson was mortified.

"Let's move on." Jackson swiftly responded as he stuttered over his next question. The interview continued with reasonable and relevant questions for the remaining ten minutes of the program.

After the interview ended, David removed his headset and tossed it on the table. He stood up and moved toward the door. Jackson stood too, his tall, lanky frame on full display. He extended his bony hand for a shake. David took Jackson's hand and yanked his arm, pulling Jackson in close. David was just inches from his elongated face.

"I know what you were trying to do and I don't appreciate it! Do something like that again and your name will be on a lawsuit." Jackson gulped and David continued.

"Then we can see how much of a tough guy you are in *my world*."

The host sheepishly nodded and avoided eye contact.

"Sorry, man. You pissed off the wrong people, including the folks who own this radio station."

"What do you mean?" David asked, loosening his death grip.

"My bosses pressured me to go there in the interview. But we're cool now. I backed off, didn't I?"

"Who are your bosses?" David squeezed Jackson's hand again.

"Look, dude, it's more than just my bosses. Please, just leave. I'm begging you."

Hearing fear in his voice, David released Jackson's hand and followed the station manager out of the studio and back down the dark hallway toward the building's exit.

Jackson collapsed into his chair. Out of the corner of his eye, he noticed his cell phone illuminate, indicating he had a text message. He stared at the phone, not wanting to read the message. After all, he didn't have to – he already knew what it said and it wasn't good.

Chapter 6

S arah Mercer had just received terrible news. Her friend, Pastor Tommy Felton, was found dead in the Stono River near Charleston. She sat motionless at David Stoneman's dining room table and wept. What had begun as a pleasant day in Northern Virginia quickly unraveled into deep emotional turmoil. Sarah's grief quickly turned to fear.

Was it really an accident? She wondered as she re-read the heartbreaking post Tommy's daughter, Jenny, had posted on social media earlier that morning. She glanced at the time on her cell phone. It was eleven. Sarah's stomach growled with hunger, but she was too upset to eat.

Sarah organized her thoughts and loathed having to break the sad news to David. He had an important radio interview that morning and likely had not checked his social media accounts for hours. Sarah was too distraught to tune-in and listen, but she expected David home any minute.

Sarah's massive lawsuit against the federal government had been settled the year prior, and the windfall was enough to allow her to quit her waitressing job and enjoy life for a while. After decades of working low-paying jobs, she was relishing some time off.

Her son, Mark, was enrolled at the prestigious St. Albans School in downtown Washington, and school was back in session. Sarah missed Mark but was glad to see him get a first-class education which is something she had never dreamed of just eighteen months earlier.

Mark's upbringing would, no doubt, be very different from her own. The recent settlement award had catapulted Sarah and Mark to the top of the social pecking order. They were now wealthy and Sarah hoped their newfound financial freedom would cause Mark's yoke to be lightened in life.

With Mark in school, Sarah spent most of her time at David's house in McLean, Virginia. She found it more comfortable than her small apartment in Fairfax, which she kept even though she could afford a serious upgrade. David, on the other hand, spared no expense on his home's high-end features, and Sarah was growing accustomed to the convenience they afforded.

Sarah and Mark had spent much of their summer enjoying David's swimming pool. Mark was usually focused on his tablet while Sarah soaked up the sun. Of course, David was often stationed nearby working on his laptop, but at least they were together.

Sarah gave up on the notion that David would *completely* unplug from work on the weekends – it simply was not in his DNA. It was a trait Sarah had come to greatly admire. David never quit.

However, all the summer's pleasant memories faded with the news of Tommy Felton's death. Sarah gazed out the large bay window in David's dining room. She felt numb. Blue birds danced on the branches of the trees in the front yard. Sarah envied the simplicity of their lives as they happily chirped and disappeared into the sky.

The grass was browning as the weather turned, and leaves on two of the trees were starting to change colors. As summer turned to fall, those birds would fly South and escape the cold, dreary months in Washington. That morning, Sarah wished she could escape with them.

Teary-eyed, she propped her elbows up on the long dining room table and looked around the quiet room.

David's dining room was elegant. The cream walls and tall ceilings were accented with light pink and green finishes. Natural light cascading in from the bay windows gave the room a serene ambiance which contrasted with Sarah's inner emotional storm. Even in the bright room she felt as if a dark cloud surrounded her. *If Tommy were murdered, will the people who killed him come for us next?* After all, they knew the same secrets.

Sarah's morose thoughts were broken by the sound of the garage door. David was home. The side door creaked open as David strolled into the kitchen. She immediately called him into the dining room.

"Did you catch the radio show this morning, babe? The host asked about *you*. Obviously, he had an ulterior motive, but I put him in his place as I'm sure you heard." David was in his own world and completely oblivious to Sarah's somber disposition. She hated to ruin his day but had to tell him the news.

"David…Tommy Felton is dead."

David froze.

"How? When?"

"Apparently, he died yesterday. Jenny posted on social media this morning. She said it was a boating accident."

David put his hands on his head. He let out a worried sigh.

"Sarah, we both know that was no accident."

Chapter 7

Jackson Seymour stared out his second-story office window at the D.C. traffic below. *I'm a dead man,* he thought as he awaited his inevitable fate.

Jackson spent most of his mornings in a dark studio. Consequently, it always took time for his eyes to adjust to his bright office. He squinted as the sunlight shone through a small section of stained-glass in the top right corner of his office window. The glass carried the studio's lightning bolt logo which had been added to all the building's exterior windows several years earlier.

Jackson heard a knock at the door. The chubby station manager barreled in, chomping on a pastry.

"Didn't go as planned, did it, Jackson?"

"No, no it didn't."

Jackson continued.

"*They* were listening. I already got a text and it's not good... for either of us." Jackson said as he pointed to the ceiling and turned from the window.

The station manager stopped chewing, leaned against the wall next to the door and threw the rest of his doughnut into a nearby trash can.

"I knew they wanted you to hit Stoneman hard, but never understood why. Care to share?" The manager asked, crossing his pudgy arms.

"You going to laugh again?"

The man shrugged and stared at the floor in embarrassment. Jackson filled him in.

> Last year, Stoneman filed a wrongful death lawsuit against the federal government on behalf of a gal named Sarah Mercer – the woman he's now dating. The Division Act legislation prohibited certain religious activities that, she claimed, contributed to her son's death. Stoneman went after some high-profile people and the case got pushed into confidential mediation to keep the whole thing quiet. According to my sources, Stoneman had dirt on major politicos and they settled the case as a result. I heard Stoneman and his girlfriend made millions on the settlement.

The station manager cocked his head to the side as he tried to absorb the juicy details.

"Alright, but what does that have to do with us?" The man asked, trying to string together the logic chain.

"Stoneman pissed on the shoes of the wrong folks, dummy." Again, Jackson emphatically pointed toward the ceiling.

"The power players in this town do not forget humiliation like that. This morning, I got a call from upstairs telling me to stick it to Stoneman in the interview. I mean, they wanted me to *go after him*."

"And?"

"Well, you were there. The guy turned it around on me. I wasn't about to go any deeper when he's making up lies about me on a live broadcast."

Satisfied with the explanation, the station manager opened the office door, "So, just to be clear, you don't flash your neighbors?" The man chuckled again, completely clueless as to the gravity of the dire situation. The manager waved a friendly goodbye and disappeared down the dark hallway.

He has no idea, Jackson concluded as he slouched his large frame in his small desk chair. *They won't let this go.*

Then his cell phone rang – it was *them*.

Chapter 8

Bailey Thompson had just started a new job with one of Townsend & Moore's top clients, Menda Industrial Corporation. Hunter had brought Menda Industrial in as a client a few years earlier and was elated to land one of the fastest-growing private companies in the Southeast. The residual bonuses he had generated from their massive billables easily earned Hunter an additional six-figures per year. Not to mention, social clout with the firm's equity partners.

Almost immediately after the engagement letter was signed, Townsend & Moore jumped into the fire and helped Menda Industrial handle some untimely international litigation which had become more than a nuisance. Hunter pulled Bailey in on the case and she, Hunter, and Menda's CEO, Damian Little, worked together to ensure the baseless claims disappeared.

Damian was so impressed with Bailey that he made her a generous offer to serve as Menda Industrial's General Counsel. Bailey was concerned Hunter would be offended that Damian made the offer to her and overlooked him. But it was quite the opposite. Hunter saw it as the perfect way to keep Menda Industrial's business for years to come.

Hesitant to step out of law firm life and transition in-house, Bailey requested a ridiculous compensation package, to which Damian readily agreed. As a result, Bailey was now the primary income earner in the Thompson household. That part *did* bother Hunter.

Bailey had her hands full, to say the least. Menda Industrial was on track to become one of the largest construction contractors in the United States and the business was only seven years old. The company had over five hundred employees scattered across nine offices, two of which were overseas. Menda worked in multiple industry subsectors, usually through wholly-owned subsidiaries with spotty paper trails – a legal liability that made Bailey uneasy.

Bailey was just four months into her new role and already felt like she was drowning. She never dreamed the transition from a large law firm to an in-house position would be *more* stressful, but that was the case most days. Bailey was slowly accepting the reality that all her legal experience had not prepared her for the rigors of the cutthroat business world. She had to learn fast, or get left behind.

Bailey glanced at her watch – it was time to go. She rose from her front porch rocking chair and opened her large wooden front door.

Her home's entryway was magnificent. The ceilings were tall, and a red imported Persian rug lay neatly on the floor at the foot of a grand staircase. The stairs split at its first landing in front of three transom windows which were regally dressed in idyllic crimson drapes.

Bailey climbed four steps but stopped when she heard voices in the kitchen. She trotted back down the stairs and continued from the entryway into the dining room, heading toward the kitchen. She wanted to see her kids before she left for work.

The blue, patterned oriental rug in the dining room lay flat underneath a formal table which sat carefully positioned below an antique crystal chandelier. In the middle of the table sat a decorated vase full of freshly-cut flowers.

Despite being one of the most elegant rooms in the house, the dining room sat empty most of the time. The busyness of Bailey and Hunter's schedules offered very little time for family meals. Consequently, the children usually ate with the nanny, Alice, in the kitchen, while Hunter and Bailey grabbed whatever was convenient between meetings and deadlines.

Bailey paused at a mirror and studied the bags under her eyes, which were becoming darker and more prominent by the minute. *Make-up will fix that*, Bailey thought as she continued to the kitchen, ignoring the obvious signs of unhealthy sleep deprivation.

Bailey pushed the swinging door connecting the dining room to the kitchen. The pleasant aroma of crisp bacon filled the air. Alice was in front of the large stove and turned to place the children's breakfast on glass plates which sat on the granite island in the center of the room.

Bailey's daughter, Emma, sat quietly at the kitchen table. Her plaid school uniform looked wrinkled as she hunched forward watching cartoons on the television in the corner.

Bailey's son, Daniel, was nowhere in sight. She turned to Alice.

"Where's Dan?"

Alice glanced over to the kitchen table, realizing Daniel had quietly snuck out while her back was turned.

"I assume he's down in the pool house again, ma'am."

Bailey rolled her eyes as Alice carried a steaming plate to Emma.

Bailey walked out of the back kitchen door, through the screened-in porch, and down the steps to the backyard to retrieve her obstinate child.

Bailey and Hunter's home sat in the middle of a gorgeous two-acre, wooded lot. After they moved in, the couple spent an additional four-hundred thousand dollars on upgrades to ensure their house was the "show house" in the neighborhood. The grounds were complete with an outdoor basketball court with overhead lights for night play, and a party barn that contained table-tennis, foosball tables, and a full bar, which was always stocked.

However, the jewel of the backyard was a lavish pool house that sat nestled adjacent to a pristine swimming pool. Bailey stomped through the damp grass and down the slate pool deck steps. She peeked in the pool house's front window and saw her son, Daniel, reclined on the white couch, watching Sports Center.

Bailey startled him when she banged on the window. *Come on!* Bailey mouthed as she pointed to her watch. Daniel begrudgingly flipped off the TV, slid on his shoes, and joined Bailey outside.

"What are you doing down here, Dan?! You're going to be late!" Bailey lectured as Daniel walked past her with his head down.

"Watching ESPN. Emma was getting on my nerves."

"If your father finds out you were late for school because you were watching ESPN, you'll be grounded for a week. Now, get up to the house, eat your breakfast, and get to school!"

Daniel threw a thumbs-up in the air, sarcastically acknowledging his mother's instructions, and meandered up the back steps and into the kitchen.

Not wanting to further disturb the breakfast routine, Bailey walked outside along the side of the house and re-entered through the front door. She then ascended the grand stairwell and into the master bedroom.

Bailey turned on the shower and noticed her phone illuminating on the nearby counter – it was a text from her boss, Damian.

Need you here early, want to introduce you to someone. You close?

"Oh, crap!" Bailey blurted. She had received these last-minute 'where are you?' text messages from Damian before, and they wouldn't stop until she responded. This one had come in over twenty minutes ago, which meant her response was already way overdue.

Bailey jumped in-and-out of the shower and dressed in record time. She hollered to Alice and the kids to have a great day as she flew out the door and jumped into her navy-blue Mercedes-Benz SUV. As the engine roared to life, her phone rang; it was Damian. Bailey answered, hoping she could shave several minutes off her usual morning commute. At this point, every minute was crucial.

"Bailey?! Where have you been?! I sent you a text that said I needed you here early today. Where are you?!"

"Good morning, Damian...yes, I'm right around the corner."

Chapter 9

Sergeant James Henderson was silent in the backseat of a black sedan in the parking lot of Bohicket Marina near Seabrook Island, South Carolina. His large, muscular frame caused his knees to cramp under his civilian khakis as he repositioned himself. The back of his tight, black T-shirt was soaked with sweat as the seat's leather refused to breathe. He had been there for over an hour waiting for a phone call. *The* phone call.

The car's windows were tinted and there were only a handful of other vehicles in the lot. Sergeant Henderson performed another overly cautious panoramic scan of the area. Seeing no imminent threat, Sergeant Henderson sat back and continued to wait. His contact was late.

As the leader of the FEDERATION AGAINST RELIGIOUS COERCION AND OPPRESSION (FARCO), Sergeant Henderson met frequently with high-profile people in secret locations. This liaison, however, was different.

FARCO was founded as an "off-the-books" government security group developed to eliminate religious-backed terrorism overseas, or at least that was the story. Lately, however, FARCO had emerged as the enforcement arm of a much more powerful organization.

Sergeant Henderson traveled with FARCO operatives for security. There were hundreds of dangerous people who wanted him dead and, like a pack of wolves, there was strength in numbers. Over the years, many had tried, and failed, to kill him. To date, they were the ones who ended up in body bags.

Today, Sergeant Henderson's two accompanying operatives were statuesque in the sedan's front seats waiting for orders from their commanding officer. Most of the FARCO operatives were ex-special forces, turned mercenaries. All of them had been dishonorably discharged and jumped at any chance to use their special skills once again. Some even hailed from the intelligence community. Those operatives had technological skill-sets which, in the digital age, were just as lethal as direct combat, if not more so.

FARCO's numbers were growing and Sergeant Henderson was honored to lead their deadly ranks. It is what *they* commissioned him to do.

He ran his hand along the back of his gray hair and pursed his lips.

"Should only be a couple more minutes, boys."

"Copy that, sir," both operatives robotically replied.

Just then, Sergeant Henderson's phone vibrated – he had a text message.

> *I'm here. End of Boat Dock C. Come alone.*

Sergeant Henderson sprang into action. He did not want to keep his VIP contact waiting.

"Stay here," he commanded. "If I'm not back in thirty minutes, come find me at *Boat Dock C*. Make sure you're armed at all times."

The operatives acknowledged their orders as Sergeant Henderson opened his car door and headed toward the marina.

He walked between two buildings that opened into an outdoor seating area and courtyard near the water's edge. The turquoise umbrellas stood upright in the center of a half-dozen black metal tables. Sergeant Henderson weaved through their gauntlet as the late morning sun beat down.

To his right, local fishermen were unloading their early catch beneath the marina's iconic *Bohicket Charter Dock* sign. In a way, he envied them. They had been on the water since the crack of dawn and were bringing home the fruit of their honest labor. Their only enemies were sunburn, broken fishing lines, and choppy waters.

Sergeant Henderson could never be like them. His skills were too unique. His talent was taking human lives and he could not deny his true nature, no matter how much he wanted to.

Sergeant Henderson turned left at the marina's fountain and looked up at the American flag which hung gallantly from the top of a large silver flagpole. There was a time when he proudly saluted the flag. That was until he met a number of Washington insiders who showed him the ugly underbelly of American politics. *If only the military called the shots*, he thought, *maybe this country would have a chance.*

Sergeant Henderson had grown jaded by the usual talking points of phony political oration. He had been to too many rallies where candidates stirred up the hollow, patriotic emotions of their large crowds. Like him, most politicians were just mercenaries masquerading as patriots. After a while, Sergeant Henderson lost his star-spangled passion and started taking the money. After that, he never looked back.

He arrived at *Boat Dock C*, opened the gate, and ambled down the ramp to the end of the deck. Before he reached the end, he was met by a muscular security guard with a shaved head and a goatee.

"Arms out!" The man barked as Sergeant Henderson reluctantly accommodated his request and put his arms out for a routine pat down. Sergeant Henderson could not pass up an opportunity to belittle the rent-a-cop.

"He won't need you hired guns this week, you know? He's got us; the big dogs."

The man gave him a nasty look and continued his body search.

As the security guard patted down both legs, Sergeant Henderson looked up at the enormous, white yacht floating in front of him. The name *Just Jurisprudence* was written on the side in prominent, shiny black letters.

When the security guard finished his check and stepped back, Sergeant Henderson frowned at him with cold eyes. The man returned the gesture in an uncomfortable stare down. Sergeant Henderson broke the silence and put the security guard in his place, once and for all.

"You're lucky you work for *him*. Otherwise, I'd shoot you between your beady eyes and dump you in the ocean."

The security guard huffed, crossed his arms, and defiantly turned his back as Sergeant Henderson climbed aboard the yacht and onto the swim platform. He then climbed the outdoor stairwell to the aft deck and into the main salon which was spacious and adorned with high-end features.

Two L-shaped couches sat in the middle of the room with a round coffee table bolted to the floor on the near side. At the far end of the salon was a wet bar, above which sat a television displaying the day's weather report.

Perched like a twig on one of the bar stools was a slight man with a green patterned blazer, light brown pants, and matching green boat shoes. His mostly white hair had hints of its original red color and curled just above the gentleman's frail shoulders. Hearing Sergeant Henderson's footsteps, the thin man turned to greet his guest.

"Hello, *Sawgeant*!" The man said with a thick, genteel Southern accent. Sergeant Henderson smiled.

"Good to see you, *Your Honor*."

Chapter 10

Bailey Thompson gazed blankly at her computer screen as she stooped, defeated in her oversized leather desk chair. A redlined legal document was on the computer screen in front of her, but she was not reading a word of it. She was too distracted, trying to make sense of what had just happened. Her mind wandered to the morning's uncomfortable fiasco.

It all started when Bailey told her boss, Damian Little, that she was just around the corner from the office when, in reality, she was pulling out of her driveway in Druid Hills. When it became clear that her lengthy commute would be even longer due to heavy Atlanta traffic, Bailey chose to screen Damian's repeated phone calls. She couldn't answer. If she did, she would have to admit she had lied. A mistake she was regretting more with each passing minute.

Bailey flew into Menda Industrial Corporation's parking lot and screeched her luxury SUV to an abrupt halt in one of the visitor parking spaces closest to the building. An unexpected gust of wind blew her hair into her face as she raced up the sidewalk, causing her to misstep on the uneven pavement and fall clumsily to the ground.

Her computer bag hit the ground with equal force and sprang open. Confidential company documents whirled in the air like confetti. *Perfect*, Bailey thought as she crawled into the bushes to retrieve loose pages.

She scanned the area hoping no one had seen her blunder. Bailey then looked up at the four-story office building.

Menda Industrial's new corporate headquarters was grand and modern. The company had moved into the renovated space a year earlier and was still settling in. Damian insisted on new, contemporary offices to reflect the company's focus on the future. It was cliché, but effective.

As Bailey barreled through the front doors, she was immediately met by her angry boss who was standing on the far side of the lobby with his arms folded. *He's pissed*, Bailey concluded by the scowl on his face.

Damian was leaning against the receptionist's desk roughly a hundred feet away, but Bailey was still terrified of him.

"There she is, Mr. Little." The receptionist timidly announced as she pointed at Bailey.

Damian raced toward her. Bailey could tell by the furious cadence of his expensive brown shoes on the polished ceramic tile floor that she was in for a severe reprimand. She would have to fall on her proverbial sword and apologize for her tardiness. However, if Bailey knew what was to follow, she would have run out of the office and never returned.

Chapter 11

H unter Thompson slammed the phone receiver down. He thought he had broken it as he huffed and nervously paced in his plush, downtown law office.

A whistleblower had contacted their firm, Townsend & Moore, claiming to have damning evidence against one of the firm's largest clients, Menda Industrial. To make matters worse, the whistleblower was a *current* Menda employee.

According to Hunter's law partner, the employee claimed to have proof the company was illegally laundering money and bribing public officials overseas. Unfortunately, that wasn't even the worst part. The whistleblower also claimed to have witnessed *a murder* at one of their facilities.

Hunter impatiently tapped his fingers on his expensive desk.

He needed more details in order to devise a plan. That's what Hunter did best – he was the 'plan man.' His mind ran to the rigid provisions of the Anti-Money Laundering Act and the Foreign Corrupt Practices Act. Violations of either were serious, but violations of both could spell disaster for Menda Industrial.

Hunter was a nationally-renowned litigator, but international white-collar crime was not his forte. Nor was international criminal law. Luckily, he had recently attended a continuing legal education (CLE) class which focused on the increased scrutiny the government was placing on domestic, privately-held companies with robust international operations. That was Menda Industrial in a nutshell.

He opened a filing cabinet and retrieved the CLE materials for a quick reference guide and tossed the materials on his desk. He would have to become a quick study in order to extinguish this legal fire.

Hunter remembered the CLE presenter's main talking points and was confident Menda Industrial had stepped on a couple of landmines. Of course, as Menda's lead outside counsel, Hunter conveniently ignored the questionable activity while it was underway. A strategy that likely would come back to bite him.

While he did not publicly condone his client's illegal activity, he also didn't want to stifle their financial growth. After all, larger clients meant greater attorney's fees and bigger bonuses for Hunter and his partners.

Hunter closed his eyes as his mind went back to the room at the local law school where the CLE was held.

Hunter had a memory that defied logic. He remembered minute details from books, classes, television shows, events, and even casual conversations, *years* after they happened. This talent made him an academic juggernaut. Consequently, he sailed through Stanford Law School where he earned a coveted position on the prestigious *Stanford Law Review*.

After law school, he used his photographic memory to skyrocket his promising legal career at Townsend & Moore, one of the top law firms in the Southeast. By the time he was a mid-level associate, he was universally feared in the Atlanta legal community.

His reputation for questionable, but effective, trial tactics generated recruiting calls from some of the best firms in New York, Los Angeles, and Washington, D.C. But he wasn't interested in going anywhere. His upward mobility at Townsend & Moore was virtually limitless.

Further, Hunter's athletic build, handsome features, and charismatic personality won juries' hearts, as his keen intellect and sharp wit dazzled their minds. He was unstoppable in the courtroom and his work ethic and grit made him nearly bulletproof. *Nearly*.

Hunter's Achilles heel, however, came in situations which were out of his control. He did not do well on the fly without time to adequately prepare, and this whistleblower's allegations represented that blind spot.

Hunter closed his eyes for a second time and remembered a conversation he had with a partner *years* earlier regarding a Japanese client in a similar sticky situation.

"The Corporate Transparency Act is part of the National Defense Authorization Act of 2021. It was updated to bolster anti-money laundering legislation." The partner read aloud with his nose just inches from his computer screen. He continued reading silently, and then turned to Hunter.

"This is not good, Hunter. The Treasury Department Financial Crimes Enforcement Network, or *FinCEN*, has a national registry of corporate owners."

"What's that mean for us?" Hunter had asked.

"It means our client's shell companies in the APAC region won't have their shell for much longer!" The partner responded.

"But there are twenty-three exemptions to the Corporate Transparency Act, aren't there? Let's make the case that our client falls into one of those exemptions…"

Hunter snapped back to the present and opened his eyes. *I've got it. We can claim Menda Industrial is exempt from making corporate disclosures the whistleblower claims were intentionally kept secret.*

It wasn't perfect and certainly didn't fully address the criminality concerns, but it was a solid initial response to buy them some time to develop a more robust defense. Hunter called his favorite associate attorney and asked him to draft a memorandum addressing that strategy. He then turned his attention to the greater concern – the firm's exposure.

Townsend & Moore was privy to a significant amount of information related to the whistleblower's claims of illegality. Of course, both Menda Industrial and Townsend & Moore still enjoyed the protection of attorney-client privilege, but that protection grayed in cases of criminal activity, especially if the firm was possibly a co-conspirator in the wrongdoing.

Hunter turned in his chair and rubbed the growing stubble on his chiseled jaw line as his blue eyes stared out the window of his twenty-sixth-floor office. Hunter usually enjoyed observing the hustle and bustle of the busy Atlanta streets below, but not today. His mind was assessing the endless catastrophic possibilities if the whistleblower's claims were actually true.

To complicate matters, bad news spread like wildfire amongst the firm's staff. With over three-hundred lawyers and nearly one-hundred support staff in the Atlanta office alone, the news had likely already circulated. It would only be a matter of time before the firm's six-person attorney team assigned to the Menda account would be called into an emergency meeting to address the issue.

Such meetings always took place in the second-floor conference room. It was the most private conference space in the building and was reserved for only the most confidential matters. There, the team would brainstorm how to address these claims quickly and quietly.

However, before that happened, Hunter needed answers to important lingering questions. He left his suit jacket hanging on the back of his office door and headed toward Menda Industrial's dedicated war room which was just down the hall. He had to get there before anyone else did.

Chapter 12

Damian Little's short frame marched toward Bailey Thompson in the lobby of Menda Industrial's headquarters. His Napoleon complex was on full display. In his mid-forties, Damian had pep in his step and a chip on his shoulder.

Growing up as an African-American who was dragged by his overbearing, social-climbing stepfather to the outskirts of predominantly white, upper-class neighborhoods, Damian constantly fought for respect. He battled negative stereotypes and, sometimes, literally fist fought silver-spooned bullies. But Damian was a fighter by nature.

After months of backyard beatings, Damian finally retaliated against one of the bullies, breaking his nose. Unfortunately, for Damian, the bully was the son of a prominent investment banker in town. Not surprisingly, Damian and his family were permanently expelled from the community under threat of criminal prosecution.

Damian's stepfather took out his anger on Damian and his mother with a leather belt, usually after a night of binge-drinking. One day, however, to Damian's delight, his stepfather put a gun in his own mouth and ended everyone's suffering with one bullet. After that, Damian and his mother started over.

However, those years on the fringe of wealthy society had left an indelible impact on Damian. He witnessed, firsthand, the protection and security wealth could provide and he wanted it for himself. As a result, Damian clawed his way into an Ivy League college on a need-based scholarship and, subsequently, was admitted to an elite business school. All the while, Damian's chip remained firmly perched on his shoulder.

He pined for the opportunity to thumb his nose at those who had made life so miserable in his youth. As such, Damian's cutthroat business reputation preceded him. He gladly burned bridges on his way to the top and enjoyed de-throning the social elite. In his mind, it was poetic justice for the hardships of his childhood.

And, when he had the money, he spared no expense on a top-shelf wardrobe to match his success. Even in informal settings, Damian sported bespoke suits from London's famous Saville Row. He hid the extent of his deep receding hairline with a close-cropped haircut and would frequently get his teeth whitened to boast a fluorescent smile.

While Damian had not yet taken a life, he often employed killer instincts in his business dealings. To Damian, all activity was a zero-sum game with winners and losers, and Damian would rather die than lose.

Bailey had been forewarned that Damian's temper mirrored his stature – short.

The look on Damian's face as he stormed toward Bailey sent chills down her spine. She spoke up, hoping to mitigate his irritation before the volcano erupted in front of her.

"Damian, I'm *so sorry*, traffic was—" Damian interrupted, mid-sentence.

"No, no, no! I don't want to hear it, Bailey! I've waited for you for forty-five minutes!" Damian's raised voice echoed loudly through the large, vacant lobby.

"I pay you a small fortune, and if I need you at work early, I expect you to be here with bells on, got it?!" Damian barked.

An awkward silence hung in the air for, what seemed like, an eternity. Sensing the seriousness of the situation, the receptionist took a fake phone call and pretended not to hear the humiliating public reprimand.

"You're right, Damian, I'm sorry. It won't happen again." Bailey responded, red-faced. Damian studied her to see if the remorse was genuine. Bailey grew more anxious by the second, but her years working at the law firm had taught her to always remain professional, no matter how she felt.

Eventually, Damian rolled his eyes, shook his head, and waved for Bailey to follow him.

She sheepishly trailed her boss through the foyer. The tall cathedral ceilings were more than thirty-feet high with spacious skylights which allowed natural light to cast angled shadows on the furniture in the seating area next to the receptionist's desk.

The building was an old soap factory and much of the original brick was salvaged in the renovation. Consequently, faded red brick lined the walls of the foyer and complimented the new, progressive architecture.

Damian always walked with a purpose, almost aggressively, and rarely stopped until he reached his destination. Most days, Bailey literally could not keep up with him. Today was worse; he was walking faster than usual.

After passing reception, Damian removed a key-fob from his right pants pocket and swiped it across a tech sensor on the door frame. The door beeped and slid open to reveal the hallway leading to the executive offices.

As Damian and Bailey funneled down the corridor, Bailey glanced at the company's recent awards and accolades which hung proudly on the wall, carefully spaced and at Damian's lower eye level.

Menda Industrial had done extremely well in the last half-decade, and was even included on *Fortune's Fastest-Growing Company* list. Menda's recent exponential growth was a major factor as to why Bailey chose to move in-house with them in the first place. The company had doubled in size in each of the last three years, and she was convinced Menda Industrial would soon go public, causing the value of her shares of company stock to skyrocket.

However, that golden IPO now seemed lightyears away. The company was disorganized, scaling too fast, and comprised of an aggregate of disjointed subsidiary companies around the world. As a result, corners were cut, business processes were soft, and very little attention was paid to legal matters. It was a recipe for corporate disaster.

Damian pointed further down the hallway toward Bailey's office.

"I have someone I want you to meet, but because you were late, I had to shuffle my morning schedule. Wait in your office until I come get you." Damian commanded as he bolted down an adjacent hallway.

That interaction had been hours ago and Bailey had not dared to leave her office, not even to use the restroom, until Damian came to collect her.

The sound of a new email in Bailey's inbox broke her reflective daydream. She then heard the rapid footstep cadence coming down the hall – it had to be Damian. She glanced up from her computer and saw him standing in her doorway.

"Come on, we're ready for you in the conference room," he announced and then disappeared back down the hall.

Bailey's mind was spinning. *Am I being fired?* She could not help but think the worst as she rose from her desk and followed her boss.

Chapter 13

Menda Industrial's war room at the Townsend & Moore law office was massive. It housed all hard copy case documents from the company's recent litigation matters. Boxes-upon-boxes of old depositions, expert reports, and financial statements were stacked to the ceiling.

Menda's caseload had increased significantly in the last two years. And for the current year they had seven figures budgeted for outside legal support. Menda was now nearly a billion-dollar business and Townsend & Moore was enjoying the benefits of that growth as well. After all, more business meant more lawsuits, bigger contracts, and more legal issues to resolve.

In addition to having its own war room, Menda Industrial was also assigned its own project assistant, which was rare at the firm. The assistant's desk was buried in a dusty dark corner of the war room. His entire job was to review, catalogue, organize, and disseminate case files and electronically stored information to the attorneys, paralegals, and other support staff assigned to Menda Industrial's account. Not a glamorous detail, by any stretch.

Hunter barged in to find the young project assistant listening to indie rock music and enjoying his lunch. The young man's pale, freckled skin and bright orange hair could not be missed, even in the dimly lit room. He stopped chewing and dropped his sandwich on the paper plate the second he saw Hunter. Hunter's unannounced presence in the war room was as infrequent as Haley's Comet.

"Hello, Mr. Thompson. What can I do for you, sir?"

Hunter looked around the rectangular room like a caged animal. He finally saw what he was looking for and marched toward a shelf on the far wall.

"*These*…these boxes labeled *Asia* and *Middle East*. I need to pull all project financing documentation from Menda's active projects in those regions, got it?" Hunter ordered as he pointed to a stack of white banker's boxes.

"Yes, sir. Obviously, we have those in digital format as well, but the files are password protected. Do you want me to pull both digital and hard copy versions for you, Mr. Thompson?" The young project assistant turned to his computer and logged in to his document management software.

"Yeah, pull both and put the originals in labeled binders in my office ASAP, okay?" Hunter did not wait for the young man to respond. He retreated as quickly as he had entered and flew down the hall.

As he approached his office, Hunter could hear his phone ringing. He raced in and saw the words Conference Room – 2nd Floor on the caller ID. He pressed the phone's speaker button.

"Hunter Thompson." He answered in a pleasant, professional voice.

It was one of his partners. "Hunter, the Menda team is meeting on the second floor in ten minutes. We need you down here right away."

"I'll be down in five."

Hunter ended the call and bit his lip – a nasty habit he formed as a collegiate rower getting ready for a big race. It calmed his nerves to literally have something to gnaw on as he prepared for a *high-stakes* competition. And this matter would certainly be high-stakes.

Still, Hunter was conflicted. This challenge was not as simple as humiliating an opposing counsel in open court, as he had done so many times before. This was personal.

He had to avoid saying anything that could throw his wife, Bailey, under the proverbial bus, and he didn't want to risk implicating himself in a criminal cover-up either.

Hunter racked his gifted brain trying to recollect recent conversations and email communications he had with his wife or other members of Menda Industrial's executive team that may be incriminating and discoverable. Nothing immediately came to mind.

Hunter inhaled deeply and exhaled with equal vigor. He glanced down at his expensive diver's watch. He needed to get to the second floor. As he grabbed his suit jacket off the back of his door, his office phone rang again – it was the project assistant. Hunter answered.

"I'm running late to a meeting. What's up?"

"Yes, sir, quick question. Who else needs copies of the binders you requested? The whole Menda team, I presume?"

Hunter shimmied his shoulders allowing his blue suit jacket to settle nicely on his muscular torso. He lowered his voice and leaned down toward his desk phone, almost to a whisper.

"No…just me, for now."

"Uh, okay. Will do. I'll have everything in your office by close of business."

The call ended and Hunter headed for the elevators. Before anyone else saw the documents he needed time to review them, in private, and assess the extent of the potential exposure for Menda Industrial, Townsend & Moore and, especially, his family. He had no doubt one of the three parties would bear the brunt of the whistleblower's ire. He intended to make sure it wasn't the Thompsons.

Chapter 14

"It's been a while, my friend."

S ergeant James Henderson said to the retired judge as the subtle rhythm of the waves rocked the massive yacht, back-and-forth, in *Boat Dock C* at Bohicket Marina.

"*Faahve* years, *Aah* suspect." The judge said as he turned off the television which sat over the bar. He wrapped his bony hands around his strong cocktail – an old fashioned with a carved orange peel and garnished with a maraschino cherry. The drink's condensation sweated and pooled on the marble bar top.

The judge slid off his stool, eager to greet his guest.

Sergeant Henderson was taken aback by the judge's ghostly disposition, which had become noticeably worse. The judge's cheeks were sunken with a yellowish tint which contrasted with his long, curly hair.

Sergeant Henderson and the judge were the same age, but the jurist's haggard appearance made him look twenty years older. Cigarettes, booze, and women had certainly taken their toll.

The judge's breathing was shallow as he moved across the room. His tall torso was hunched over and his elongated nose and protruding chin led the way. To the unassuming passersby, his appearance was almost frightening. Hard to believe, given the judge's nearly unlimited financial resources.

The aging jurist crumpled into one of the couches in the center of the room. He extended his shaky hand offering Sergeant Henderson a seat as well.

The judge opened a humidor sitting on a small circular table adjacent to the sofa and grabbed a short, pre-cut cigar from the box. He held the stogie up in the air, studying it as if it were a rare artifact. He then removed the cigar's shiny sleeve and bit down on its end with his yellowed teeth. The stogie quickly became saturated with saliva which dripped down his chin and onto the floor.

Sergeant Henderson was waiting for the judge to light the cigar, but the thin man seemed satisfied simply gnawing on the tobacco stick.

"New boat?" Sergeant Henderson finally asked as he scanned the room.

"Yes, sir, it is. This is a one-hundred twenty foot tri-deck motor yacht. It has six state rooms and ten flat screens. *Aah'm* told *Aah* can go two-thousand nautical miles on this beauty – and it certainly impresses the lady-folk!" The slim judge boasted as his purple lips drew up into a deviant smile. He continued.

"But enough about my boat, give *meah* status update." The judge's countenance turned serious and his cigar chomping became more pronounced.

"To start, Tommy Felton is dead…"

"Good, *Aah'l* be sure to tell the others." The judge took a big gulp of his drink, "may he rest in peace," he said as he held his glass in the air.

"I already informed *Prometheus*. Called him right after it was done." Sergeant Henderson said.

"As *Aah'm* sure you heard, everyone is thrilled to see *Prometheus* on the island this week. We're taking extra security measures. *Aah'm* sure you've been told, haven't *ya?*"

"Yes, sir. The event is still on schedule, I assume?"

"Yeah, we are. Felton was the last item that needed to be dealt with." The judge spotted a silver tray full of cashews on the coffee table in front of him. He rested his gamey cigar on the lid of the humidor as he grabbed a handful.

"As you know, Felton's death was essential for our plan, but may have complicated matters as well." Sergeant Henderson said as he leaned back in his seat and crossed one leg over the other.

"Felton was lucky to make it this long, *Sawgeant*." The judge grabbed another handful of cashews and continued munching. Like a squirrel, he shoveled the nuts into his wrinkled mouth and chewed feverishly.

"We made it look like an accident, but it wasn't as clean as I would have liked." Sergeant Henderson admitted.

The judge stopped chewing.

"What do you mean?"

"Well, one of my guys hit Felton in the shoulder before the death blow to the head. We tried to make it look like an accident, but if forensics looks more closely, they may suspect foul play with blunt trauma bruising in two different spots." The judge glared at Sergeant Henderson.

"*Aah* hope for your sake, *Sawgeant*, they don't."

Sergeant Henderson feared no one, but he certainly did not want to upset the judge. It was not the man himself that scared Sergeant Henderson, it was *the family* he represented. The family that started it all – the Cathpert family.

"You run this county, Your Honor. Can't we make the boat evidence disappear?" Sergeant Henderson questioned as he moved up to the edge of his seat with his leg nervously bouncing up and down.

"*Aah've* owned this town for some time now. But it depends who gets involved. Hopefully, this doesn't become a *fedral* issue. Then it gets *challengin'*."

The judge slowly rose to his unsure feet. He extended his bony arm toward the door indicating the meeting was over. As Sergeant Henderson exited the boat's main salon, the judge had a final comment.

"One more thing, *Sawgeant*. *Aah* understand Stoneman is en route as we speak?"

Sergeant Henderson nodded.

"We're sure he's *goin'* to Felton's funeral tomorrow?"

"Yes, sir."

"Good."

The judge looked at Sergeant Henderson and cocked his head to the side. He enjoyed making the alpha-male FARCO leader uncomfortable.

"Just let me know what *Prometheus* and the rest of Council want me to do. I'm here to serve." Sergeant Henderson offered.

"*Aah'l* see *ya* on the island." The slight judge said as he ambled back to the bar.

Chapter 15

David Stoneman flipped the light switch near his home's front door which lit the chandelier hanging from the ceiling. He then climbed the winding staircase up to his second floor but paused halfway up when he realized Sarah wasn't following.

David glanced back to find her standing at the bottom of the stairs clutching the banister with tears rolling down her face.

"Honey, are you okay?" David asked as he descended to console her.

"No, Dave, I'm not," she managed, "they're going to come for us, too, I just know it!"

David put his arm around Sarah as they sat on the third step.

"Sweetheart, our ordeal with FARCO is over. The ringleaders went to jail, remember? What happened to Tommy was probably just an accident." David claimed, although he wasn't so sure.

However, David *was* confident the government would not make the same mistake they had made the year prior. If those same powerbrokers came after David and Sarah again, their most closely-held secrets would be leading the news within an hour. They wouldn't risk that – *would they?*

Sarah leaned into David as he embraced her.

Tommy's visitation and funeral were the following day in Charleston and David and Sarah planned to attend. David would call off of work for the rest of the week, and Sarah made special arrangements for her son, Mark, to stay in the boarding facilities at St. Albans School through the weekend.

After a minute of quiet consolation, David ushered Sarah up the stairs and began discussing their travel plans as a distraction.

"It's probably too late to get seats together on a commercial flight. Are you okay flying private? A private charter could leave tonight if we wanted to head that way."

Sarah always preferred the less expensive option, but this was an extenuating circumstance.

"Private is fine." Sarah responded.

"I'll have my staff make the arrangements."

David retrieved his cell phone and called his office.

"Stoneman Law Office, how may I help you?" The young receptionist pleasantly answered.

"Katie, it's David. How's it going?"

"Doing great, Mr. Stoneman. Two new prospective clients called today. Said they were referred from—" David politely interjected.

"Excellent! But, Katie, I need you to do me a favor. Call the team together, I have a quick announcement."

David could hear his receptionist hollering for the two young associates who worked for him.

"Okay, Mr. Stoneman, we're all here, and I have you on speakerphone."

"Hey, everybody. I just received news that one of my friends passed away this week. Sarah and I are going to his funeral tomorrow in South Carolina. So, I'll be out of the office until next Monday."

General words of condolences were offered and David continued.

"I'll have my laptop with me and will be available by cell if something is urgent. Call me if you need me. Katie, do I have anything on the calendar this week?"

"No, sir. You had the *Seymour Show* interview today. Great job, by the way! And you have a motion filing deadline next Wednesday."

"I can handle that filing for you, Mr. Stoneman." One of the associates announced.

"Sounds good. Again, call me if you need me. Katie, can you hang on the line for a sec? I need your help booking a private charter for this evening."

David pulled his new roll-aboard suitcase from under the bed, along with Sarah's dated, off-brand suitcase. As David polished and packed his black dress shoes, along with a variety of outfits, he noticed Sarah was uncharacteristically packing light.

"Do you need anything from your place, babe?" He asked as he shuffled through his white and blue button-down shirts which were meticulously pressed and hanging neatly in the closet.

"Nope, I have plenty of clothes here." Sarah said as she folded a blouse and placed it at the foot of David's bed.

David's phone buzzed indicating he had an email. It was the private charter confirmation.

"Our flight is wheel's up in four hours. You about ready to head that way so we can beat rush hour traffic?" David asked as he looked over his shoulder.

"Yeah, let's go."

Within minutes, they were taking an Uber to a private charter parking lot at Dulles Airport. Little did they know, someone else knew about David and Sarah's last-minute flight plans as well. Everything was going according to *their* plan.

Chapter 16

Bailey Thompson followed Damian Little into Menda Industrial's executive conference room. The spacious room had a huge window on the far wall which offered a magnificent view of the dense green foliage surrounding the secluded building.

Bailey was surprised to see a slender, attractive woman with her hands folded neatly in front of her seated at the end of the long, cherry wood conference table. Without saying a word, the woman rose from her chair and walked toward Damian. *She's beautiful*, Bailey thought as the woman drew closer.

Bailey found it odd that the mystery woman did not even acknowledge her presence. Bailey had grown accustomed to cultural norms in the South, which generally included pleasant introductions. Not this time.

Damian circled the conference table and met the woman halfway. They shared a brief, hushed verbal exchange and then both sat down next to one another and faced Bailey.

"Have a seat, Bailey." Damian instructed as he unbuttoned his top jacket button and extended his arm to a chair on the opposite side of the table. Bailey did as she was told, fearing the worst.

They are firing me. I knew it! She grew anxious. Still, Bailey remained poised and professional – she would not let them see her sweat.

The emotionless mystery woman stared at her. Bailey leaned forward and asked a preemptive question.

"Damian, who is this?" She pointed at the new girl.

"This is Tara...she's a consultant." Damian smiled at the attractive young woman who stared stoically back at Bailey as if she were a statue.

Bailey studied Tara. The woman's long, jet-black hair, piercing blue eyes, and blood-red lips perfectly accented her caramel skin. Her light gray pantsuit and white blouse looked expensive, and her carefully manicured fingernails and silver jewelry showcased her attention to her wardrobe's every detail.

"Okay...is she a consultant, or is she *our* consultant?" Bailey was confused.

"She's *my* consultant." Damian clarified. He leaned back in his chair and crossed his hands which rested on his silk tie. Bailey grew annoyed, "...and what is she consulting on?"

Again, Damian looked at Tara. He wanted her to answer the question directly. She complied.

"Ms. Thompson, it's best if you're unaware of the exact nature of my business here." She mechanically responded with an air of elitism. Bailey was dumbfounded by the answer.

"I'm sorry? Miss, I'm Menda Industrial's chief legal officer. I'm entitled to know the details related to your business with this company." Bailey glared back at Tara. She wanted it to be crystal clear she was a force to be reckoned with. The woman seemed totally unphased by Bailey's retort.

"I know who you are, Ms. Thompson. I can't, however, imagine why you think I would care."

"I'm sorry, who do you th—" Tara cut Bailey off.

"I may not be an attorney, Ms. Thompson, but I've worked with enough of them to know how you all operate. Let me guess, you thought you could jump in-house to secure a better work-life balance and dodge the billable hours requirement until the company went public. Am I close?"

"Well, no, actually, you—" Again, Tara interrupted.

"You probably read some *American Bar Association* article about the day-to-day duties of a General Counsel and felt confident you could babysit a team of corporate drones and delegate most of the work until you were able to race home at five o'clock. Right?" She briefly paused, and continued.

"God forbid you ever had any litigation. Well, in that case, you would just farm it out to your husband, Hunter, at the law firm from whence you came and he would make a fortune in origination bonuses. Tell me I'm wrong, Ms. Thompson." Tara smirked. Bailey was shocked by the woman's brazenness.

Damian tried to ease the tension in the room.

"Look, Bailey, Tara is working with me on some potential growth areas of the business. Nothing illegal or untoward, I assure you. Tara's more like a *career coach* for me than a consultant for the company. I'm not sure why this is getting nasty, ladies." He shot a reproving look at Tara and continued.

"Bailey, I just wanted to introduce you to Tara because she'll be attending our executive meetings for the foreseeable future." Damian glanced at Tara who had not blinked an eyelash as she continued to stare daggers at Bailey. Believing no additional conversation was necessary, Damian glanced at his expensive gold watch.

"As you know, we have a board meeting later this afternoon. Bailey, why don't you grab a quick bite and we'll see you back here in a bit."

Bailey had been dismissed. She closed the conference room door on her way out and walked back down the hall to her office.

Bailey peeked back through the conference room door's sidelights and found Damian and Tara talking intently. They were sitting awfully close to one another. *Maybe it's an affair*, Bailey speculated. Unfortunately, that would be the *best-case* scenario. Bailey wasn't sure what was going on, but she was determined to find out.

Damian dialed the most confidential number in his cell phone's contact list. He was calling *Prometheus*.

Tara had instructed him to make the call before the afternoon board meeting. *Please don't pick up*, he prayed as the phone rang.

"Yes?" A deep voice answered.

"*Prometheus*? It's Damian, sir. Tara's here as well. We just want to let you know that we'll be rolling out Menda's strategic plan to the board this afternoon, just like we drew it up."

The voice was silent. Damian could hear the muffled sound of busyness in the background. Damian glanced at Tara and then returned his focus to the call, "...we don't anticipate any issues from our end, sir. I'm confident the board will rubberstamp our initiatives and remain blissfully ignorant."

The voice responded.

"Good. As you know, Mr. Little, we have no patience for excuses or delays."

"Yes, sir, I understand."

"I'll see you on the island." The voice said and then hung up.

Damian put his phone into his left jacket pocket and took a deep breath. He was usually calm and collected even when dealing with the most cutthroat business tycoons. However, he tensed up whenever he spoke to *Prometheus*. He was *that* powerful.

Tara sensed Damian was flustered and she could not have the company CEO out of sorts heading into an important board meeting. Years of hard work hinged on the board signing off on the strategic plan and they had to execute their plan to perfection.

Chapter 17

It was 3:45 p.m. and Menda Industrial's board of directors trickled in one-by-one for Menda's quarterly board meeting. Damian plastered on a fake smile and started shaking hands.

Menda Industrial's board was comprised of eight illustrious male members, all of whom were influential in the Atlanta business community. Each member donned bespoke clothing from the finest men's stores in the Southeast. Like peacocks showcasing their vibrant feathers, the attire at the quarterly board meetings never disappointed.

Menda's board meetings often started late due to members' small chat. Typical conversations revolved around golf handicaps, mistresses, and tall tales of former business conquests.

Bailey quietly snuck into the room and took an open seat in the back. She attended the executive meetings just in case any legal topics arose. Early on, it became clear that Bailey was not to give her legal opinion in board meetings, but rather, to assuage the members that the company's actions were legally appropriate, even if that was not the case.

Bailey settled into her seat and flipped to a blank page in a notebook to take notes. She eyed Tara from across the room. It also didn't take long for Tara's beauty to catch the attention of a couple easily-distracted board members. But Tara was cold with them too.

Tired of the ogling, Tara relocated to a spare chair in the corner and instructed Damian to sit at the head of the table. It was obvious she was calling the shots, regardless of where she sat. Damian dutifully complied.

"Gentlemen, welcome back! I trust everyone had a pleasant summer and is ready to get back to business." Unenthusiastic nods, groans, and snickers came from around the table.

"I believe all of you received the board packet that includes meeting minutes from our previous meeting. If there are no questions, I would like to make a motion to approve the minutes from last quarter's meeting. All those in favor raise your hand."

Eight hands shot up. Damian moved on.

"The meeting minutes have been approved. However, before we jump into the P&L statement from second quarter, I would like to introduce you to our company's newest consulting resource, Tara." Damian extended his arm to formally present Tara to the members. She nodded.

"Well...does she have a *last name*?" The question came from one of the board's senior members. Tara curtly responded.

"You don't need to know my last name. I work for Mr. Little, and Mr. Little *alone*."

The icy response caused the air to immediately drain from the room. Damian hung his head in embarrassment. Tara's rude comment would, no doubt, spark vicious retribution.

Damian held his breath waiting for the board member's reply. The older gentleman was initially flabbergasted. However, in seconds, his grumpy frown turned into a smile.

"Sounds like my ex-wife," he joked. The room roared with laughter and Damian took the opportunity to offer a believable lie to cover up the truth.

"Tara is here on my dime. She's an executive coach and, as you can see, she utilizes a bootcamp consulting style."

Damian's comment was met with nods and chuckles. He shuffled the papers in front of him to determine what was next on the agenda. The senior board member added a final remark.

"I think I could use a little discipline, myself if you know what I mean…" He said with a wink to Tara.

"Do you do house calls, sweetheart?"

Tara ignored the inappropriate catcall and Damian continued.

"Anyway, Tara signed a non-disclosure agreement with us, so, we can speak freely around her. The next item on the agenda is the quarterly P&L statement…"

The board meeting continued for two hours. Not surprisingly, Bailey was not called on once. She might as well have been a potted plant. Damian, on the other hand, dazzled the board with his charts and graphs which highlighted skyrocketing revenues, impressive profit margins, and a healthy project backlog. Damian stood tall and triumphant as the compliments cascaded over him. He lived for that applause.

Of course, he also reminded the board members of the financial perks afforded to them, personally, as a result of the company's strong financial performance. After he had laid the positive primer, Damian delved into Menda's strategic plans for the remainder of the fiscal year. This was the moment of truth.

At a high level, the strategy was simple: Menda Industrial would cease new customer acquisition efforts and focus *exclusively* on large-scale projects for a handful of companies with international operations. And, Damian would have unilateral financial authority over the company's capital and global assets.

Still elated over the company's strong financial performance, the board unanimously accepted the path forward when the motion to approve the plan was presented. With each board member having an equity stake in the company, they weren't about to do anything to derail Menda's meteoric upward trajectory.

The meeting adjourned just before dinner. Many of the board members scurried off to their private clubs. On his way out, the senior board member, again, tried to make a pass at Tara. For the second time she rebuffed his advances and sent him away with shoulders slumped.

Bailey raced out of the conference room and back to her office. She placed her empty coffee cup on a small *Georgia Law* coaster, settled back into her desk chair, and logged into her computer. Bailey wouldn't rest until she learned more about the beautiful mystery puppet master who was, obviously, running her company.

Chapter 18

Hunter Thompson exited the elevator on the firm's second floor. The conference room was just a few steps from the elevator bank across from a small, glassed-in sitting area with four wooden chairs positioned around a rectangular table.

Hunter noticed the latest business magazines fanned out in the center of the table, inviting waiting clients to thumb through their pages. Menda Industrial Corporation was featured on the cover of one of the national magazines. *If they only knew the truth*, Hunter thought as he glanced at his watch and quickened his pace. He was late.

The second-floor conference room's door was ajar and Hunter overheard lively conversation. He entered and recognized five of the six people sitting around the long conference table. The familiar faces were the Townsend & Moore attorneys assigned to Menda's account. However, a stranger was in the table's middle seat.

Senior partner and head of the firm's litigation practice group, Matthew Phillips, was leading the meeting and sitting across from the new face. Hunter had always admired Matthew. He was the quintessential big firm partner, but without the usual negative stereotypes.

Unlike other senior partners, Matthew exuded poise and humility, rare traits for trial attorneys of his credentials and experience. Matthew's unparalleled ability to settle complex cases without utilizing fear or intimidation tactics was admirable. By doing so, he achieved something very few big city litigators ever accomplished – opposing counsels actually *liked* working with him.

In addition to his top-notch trial skills, Matthew was also known for his impeccable personal style. Today, for example, he was wearing a light gray suit with subtle blue pinstripes which perfectly complimented his blue shirt. His sleeve carried a navy stitching with two V's, which Hunter assumed represented the shirt's exclusive brand. Of course, the stitching's thread color matched his navy, polka-dotted tie, which rested in a half-Windsor knot in the middle of his neck. Matthew's meticulously combed graying hair did not move an inch and his kind brown eyes were warm and reassuring.

"Ah, Hunter, come in. We are just getting started." Matthew invited as he patted the open seat next to him.

"Hunter, this is Dominic Harkness, the young man who came forward with some information about Menda Industrial. He was walking us through the details."

Matthew turned his attention back to Dominic.

"Dom, if you don't mind, please start again from the beginning."

This is the whistleblower, Hunter concluded as he sat and opened his binder.

Hunter studied Dominic. He was just a kid in his twenties with an average build, short, disheveled blonde hair and juvenile stubble on his chin. He wore a neon green Menda Industrial branded T-shirt, which was too small, and a pair of blue jeans.

Dominic shuffled in his chair. Aside from Matthew, he avoided eye contact with the other attorneys in the room and was therapeutically wringing his hands on the table. He was nervous, or *scared*.

"Take your time, son. You're doing great." Matthew encouraged.

> Yeah, so, like I was saying…I have been a superintendent at Menda for about three years and started right out of school. I liked the idea of working on large projects and Menda was getting a ton of business. I also liked Damian, the CEO. He promised pay increases and bonuses to folks working on my project. That's when the problems started.

Dominic paused for a moment, put his head down and coughed.

"Can I get some water, please?" The young man requested as he cleared his throat.

Matthew instructed one of the associates to retrieve a bottle of water from the nearby kitchen. Within seconds, the associate reappeared and handed Dominic a bottle of sparkling water. He took two large gulps and continued.

> After a couple months, my project manager asked me to do some things which seemed sketchy. He said he needed me to pick up black duffle bags which were going to be dropped off at the jobsite in the middle of the night. A mark would be left on

the job trailer's door and that's how I'd know the bags were there. I was supposed to load the bags into one of the company trucks and take them to an official at the airport.

Matthew paused from taking notes and asked clarifying questions.

"How many times did you do this, Dom?"

"At least four, maybe five times."

"Did you ever look in the bags?"

Dominic nodded, "Unfortunately, yes. But I wish I hadn't."

Everyone in the room was quiet. Dominic was staring blankly at the middle of the table. Matthew prodded.

"What was in the bags?"

"Cash. A ton of it. I don't know how they got the bags into the U.S. with all that money in them, and I didn't ask. I just gave the bags to the guy at the airport and left."

The attorneys shot concerned looks at one another. It was never a good sign when off-the-books bags of money crossed international borders. Matthew flipped the page of his legal pad and continued.

"Why did you keep delivering the bags after you discovered they were full of money?"

"After the first couple times, I finally mustered up the courage to ask my boss about it. He scared me to death. I—" Dominic stopped. His hands began to shake. Matthew put down his pen and gently knocked his knuckles on the table to get Dominic's attention. The kid looked up with tears in his eyes. Again, Matthew smiled at him.

"Dom, we *will* protect you. But you have to tell us what happened, bud."

Dominic believed him. Matthew had one of those trustworthy faces. *Anyone* would believe him. Dom took another sip of his sparkling water and continued.

"My boss told me the money was for some very powerful people and they would have me arrested or killed if I blew the operation. They paid me twenty-thousand dollars, per delivery, to keep my mouth shut."

Hunter's heart dropped in his chest. He hoped Bailey was not involved in this.

Dominic shook his head in regret, "I knew it was wrong, but I had a ton of student loans and I didn't think anyone would get hurt." He put his head in his hands and wept.

Matthew rose from his chair and relocated to the open seat next to Dominic, "It's going to be okay, Dom. Tell us who got hurt?"

Dominic wiped his runny nose on his shirt's sleeve.

> A couple days ago, I was in the job trailer with another employee. It was late. We heard voices outside. I looked out the window and saw a group of guys unloading the bags from an armored truck. They were dressed in military gear. One of the men saw me and told the others. They ran into the trailer and dragged both of us out, threw us on the ground, and stuck guns in our faces.

Matthew looked at Hunter. His look of alarm sent chills down Hunter's spine. Hunter had never seen Matthew *that* concerned. The story was getting worse by the minute.

"They asked which one of us takes the bags to the airport. I raised my hand. To confirm I wasn't lying, they asked me what symbol was left on the trailer door when the bags were ready for pick up. I told them and they calmed down."

Again, Dominic's eyes welled with tears, "…that's when it happened."

"What happened, Dom?" Matthew asked.

"They shot the guy I was working with."

The room remained silent. Dominic continued, his face red.

> One of the military guys asked me when the next concrete pour was. I told him it was the following morning. He instructed me to go home for a couple hours and then come back to get the bags, as usual. So, I obeyed. When I came back, the symbol was on the trailer door, as it always was. Not knowing what else to do, I took the bags to the airport. But, this time, I saw a white envelope sticking out of one of the bags. It had a name on it. When I saw the name, I decided, then and there, I was done with Menda. I took off for the airport and caught the first plane stateside.

"Have you spoken to the authorities about this?" One of the associates asked.

"How could I? I don't want to go to jail! I didn't know where else to turn. I knew you all were the company's lawyers. I saw your firm's name on a bunch of contract documents in the job trailer. That's why I'm here."

Matthew chimed in and suggested next steps.

"Dom, you did the right thing. Our team will handle this." Matthew patted Dominic's sweaty back.

"Before we take a break, can you draw the symbol that was on the trailer door?" Matthew asked as he slid a legal pad and a pen in front of the young man.

Dominic drew the symbol and returned the notepad to Matthew, who cocked his head to the side as he looked at the scribble. He held the legal pad up for the other attorneys to see.

"It looks like a sideways N," one of the associates commented. Hunter squinted, puzzled by the image. Dominic clarified.

"It's not an *N*...it's a *lightning bolt*."

"How do you know?" Matthew asked.

"The same image was in the corner of the white envelope hanging out of the duffle bag. It was yellow and everything." Dominic sniffled and asked if he could use the restroom. Matthew gave him instructions on where to find it.

"We'll break for an early dinner after your return, Dom. We need your help this evening to dig a little deeper." Matthew explained as the associates pulled their phones from their pockets to alert their spouses and significant others they would be working late.

As Dominic walked toward the conference room door, Hunter had one final question.

"Real quick, Dominic, what was *the name* on the white envelope sticking out of the bag? I don't think you mentioned it."

Dominic wiped his nose again as he turned back to the group, "The name was Damian Little."

Chapter 19

B ailey Thompson sat in traffic on her way home thinking about the day's perplexing events.

As Bailey collected her things at the end of the workday, Damian had unexpectedly dropped by her office. Out of nowhere, he insisted she accompany him and Tara on a last-minute business trip to Charleston, South Carolina. Of course, he wanted to leave the very next day.

Before Bailey could object, or even ask any questions, Damian scurried down the hall to meet Tara. He informed Bailey she could expect the flight details within the hour. *Ugh*, she thought, *now we have to take this circus on the road?*

Bailey had taken the in-house role in order to improve her work-life balance, not make it more lopsided. Moreover, the disconcerting behavior she had witnessed that afternoon in the board meeting was pushing her to the limit. If it continued, she would be putting in her two weeks' notice as soon as they returned from Charleston.

Bailey pulled into her home's circle driveway and was surprised to see her husband, Hunter, sitting, comatose, in his black Lincoln Navigator. His vehicle was uncharacteristically parked in front of the house instead of in the garage. The digital clock on the dashboard read 7:00

p.m., but Hunter was never home before eight. *Something's wrong*.

Bailey wheeled her SUV alongside Hunter's vehicle and rolled down the passenger-side window. Hunter was in a daze. So much so, that he did not even notice Bailey pull beside him. She lightly tapped her horn to get his attention.

Hunter jumped; his eyes wide. He rolled down his window.

"You okay? What are you doing home so early?" Bailey questioned.

Hunter started to answer, but paused. He held his hand up in the air and cautiously scoped the surrounding area as if someone were watching them.

"Let's talk in the pool house," Hunter requested as he rolled up his driver's side window and followed the driveway to the back of their property. Bailey followed.

She joined her husband in the pool house and he shut the door behind them. He then paced in front of the stone fireplace before saying a word. Bailey sat on the white couch, waiting for her husband to speak. The words that came out of his mouth sent a shockwave through the room.

"I think we're in danger, Bail!" He exclaimed.

"What are you talking about?!"

"Menda Industrial. You have *serious* issues going on over there. When were you going to tell me?" Hunter seemed rattled.

Bailey's heart skipped a beat. *How does he know about what happened today?* Bailey played dumb.

"Again, what are you talking about? Menda doesn't have any issues. We had a board meeting this afternoon and the company is doing great. What kind of issues are *you* talking about?" Bailey moved to the edge of her seat.

"Is this about a woman named Tara?!" Bailey eagerly asked, hoping Hunter could shed light on the mystery consultant.

"Who?! No! this is bigger than just one person, Bailey! The entire company is caught up in very shady business."

Hunter was in one of his hyper-analytical moods. When this happened, he babbled to himself until he, inevitably, solved the problem and shared his brilliant conclusion with everyone else. Bailey waited for that moment, but it never came.

"I pulled some old files from the Menda war room at the firm, and I have hard copy documents which show questionable financial transactions overseas. I didn't say anything to you or Matthew because our billables have been so strong lately and I didn't want to put you, personally, under the microscope." Hunter continued to pace. Suddenly, he stopped and turned to his wife as if something had just dawned on him.

"Bailey..." He drew closer and kneeled to meet her eyeline.

"We had a whistleblower in the office today."

Bailey's spine-tingling feeling returned; this time accompanied by nausea.

"He was just a kid. He told us Menda was involved in a variety of international crimes, and even murder! *Murder*, Bailey!!" Hunter's veins protruded from his muscular neck.

His last comment caused Bailey to chuckle, which exacerbated Hunter's irritation. She owed him an explanation.

"Are you kidding me, Hunter? Murder? You think we have hitmen on the payroll? We're a construction company for goodness sakes!" Hunter was silent. Bailey continued.

"I've seen Damian bludgeon people in a business negotiation, but he would never actually hurt anyone. It's not his style."

Wanting to learn more, Bailey played along.

"Okay...who is this whistleblower and what did they say?" Bailey crossed her arms, skeptical, and leaned back on the couch.

"Do you know a *Dominic Harkness*, by any chance?" Hunter asked.

Bailey searched her memory, but shook her head.

"He was a superintendent for Menda's Middle East project. He claimed he was an accomplice to a plan which filtered millions of dollars into the country in unmarked bags." Hunter sat down next to Bailey and took her hand.

"...he said he witnessed one of his colleagues get murdered at the jobsite for seeing too much."

Bailey looked into her husband's blue eyes for any hint he may be kidding – but he was dead serious.

"I don't know anything about that, Hunter." She said as the gravity of the situation began to sink in.

"Bail, it's only a matter of time before this whole thing hits the fan. We have only *days* to fix this. Is there anything you need to tell me?!" His tone was firm.

"Isn't it too late? I mean, the whistleblower will go public with what he knows, won't he?"

Hunter stood and shook his head.

"That's why I raced home to talk with you, Bailey. The whistleblower is *dead*."

The comment caused Bailey's skin to crawl.

"What?! How?!"

Hunter gave her the rundown.

> We were meeting with him at the office and broke for an early dinner. Matthew suggested we go across the street for a quick steak and take the kid with us. You know, to make him more comfortable. As we crossed the street, Harkness was hit by a car. And it was no accident. They veered to hit him, Bail. The car sped off and no one got the license plate. The cops took statements and released us. Then I raced home.

Hunter walked into the pool house's kitchen, retrieved a glass from an overhead cabinet, and filled it with tap water. After he took a sip he leaned against the counter and waited for his wife to respond to the bombshell news.

"I can't get into this now, Hunter. Damian wants me to go to Charleston with him tomorrow. He just told me this afternoon. We're taking a private jet."

Hunter put down his glass as anger built inside him.

"Bailey, you can't go to Charleston with that man! I just told you your company is having people killed! It's not safe!"

"Think about it, Hunter. If I cancel now, won't that just raise red flags?"

Hunter took a minute and acknowledged the risk.

"I promise to keep my eyes and ears open for anything fishy. We can discuss our next move when I return." Bailey stood up and moved toward the door.

"I'll pay Alice double to stay with the kids this week. That way you can focus on the issues at your office. Are you going back tonight?"

Hunter stared out the window.

Yeah, I have to review a mountain of documents. Aside from the murder allegations, Matthew thinks Menda violated the Foreign Corrupt Practices Act too. Which, as you know, carries both civil and criminal penalties. It'll be an all-nighter for me, for sure. Remember, if you see anything odd with Damian, just get out of there, okay?

"Will do. Love you, and I'll text you tomorrow when we land." Bailey left the pool house and headed toward the main house's back door. It was getting dark outside.

Hunter stayed in the pool house thinking through his predicament. He exhaled a sigh of frustration as he put his empty glass in the sink. He then flipped off the lights and locked the door's deadbolt behind him as he exited.

Hunter removed his cell phone from his pocket and scrolled through his phone's contacts list as he circled the swimming pool. Just then, he heard a loud rustling from the nearby bushes. *Probably just an animal.* However, his curiosity got the better of him and he decided to investigate.

Hunter engaged his cell phone's flashlight feature and held the phone in front of him. Light cascaded over the dense green foliage. *Nothing.* Yet, the sound continued. He approached the back fence and the rustling stopped. Hunter leaned down and slowly pulled the shrubbery back. Again, nothing.

Suddenly, a bag whipped over Hunter's head. He felt strong hands grab his arms and yank him backwards. Before Hunter could call for help, he absorbed a strong, painful punch to his abdomen. Then another, followed by a blunt punch to the face. The blows caused him to collapse on the wet grass. He couldn't speak and he couldn't breathe.

Hunter tried to fight his attackers, but to no avail. The punches caused him to become dizzy and disoriented. In that moment, all Hunter could think about was Bailey and his kids as he slowly lost consciousness.

Chapter 20

David Stoneman's hand tightly clenched Sarah Mercer's arm as the white Cessna Citation Mustang jet took off from a private charter runway at Dulles Airport, near Washington, D.C. Sarah turned in her seat to find David holding his breath, teeth gritted, with his eyes shut tightly. She found it humorous that the man who was fearless in the face of giants turned into a scaredy-cat when it came to heights.

Simply put, David disliked flying altogether. He found it especially distasteful in small airplanes. But David hated waiting in lines at the airport even more. So, he usually chose the more convenient travel option and just toughed it out. Once he got past take off, David was able to remain calm enough for the remainder of the flight. That is, until the plane began its descent.

"You okay, hun?" Sarah asked as she rubbed David's knee.

"Uh huh." David muttered as he released her arm from his death grip. He inhaled two deep breaths and his shoulders softened.

The private jet was well-appointed. The cabin was nearly ten feet long and the six oval windows caused the late afternoon sun to illuminate the four taupe, leather club seats which lined the cabin's aisle. David and Sarah were in the rear of the cabin facing the cockpit.

David retrieved his bottled water from the cupholder and a sudden patch of rough air caused him to drop the bottle on the floor. Sensing he was not comfortable unbuckling his seatbelt to collect his beverage, Sarah leaned over and grabbed the rolling bottle for her boyfriend.

She uncapped it and handed it to him. David took several hearty gulps before placing it back in the shiny silver cupholder. Sarah made a joke to try and ease the tension.

"You know, you really don't have a fear of *flying*." She exclaimed as she turned toward him.

"No?"

"No. You have a fear of *crashing*." Sarah laughed out loud as she playfully squeezed his shoulder. David was unamused.

As the Cessna leveled out above the clouds, they heard the pilot's voice.

> Okay folks, we are now at cruising altitude, so, please feel free to unbuckle your seatbelt, if you'd like. Just a reminder, FAA regulations prevent passengers from sitting up here with me during the flight and, yes, that rule applies even in a privately chartered aircraft. However, there are some perks in flying with us. For starters, I'll be happy to answer any questions you may have about the aircraft, your destination, or any other topic you would like to discuss. Flight time today is just under one hour and thirty minutes, so, sit back, relax, and enjoy.

There was no door separating the cabin from the cockpit. As such, after the pilot completed his announcements, he glanced back at David and Sarah.

"Another perk is that we can chat face-to-face!" He said with a warm smile. David just wanted the pilot to focus on flying the plane.

"What was your name again?" Sarah asked as she leaned forward in her seat.

"Randy, ma'am." After giving his name, Randy flipped a few switches on the large computerized controls in the cockpit. Thereafter, Sarah realized her simple question had triggered an unsolicited and detailed account of Randy's entire life story.

Randy appeared to be in his mid-forties. He wore a black baseball cap with large aviator glasses perched on top of his hat. His cheap golf shirt carried a dated aviation symbol on the sleeve.

Sarah and David learned that Randy had graduated from the Citadel, the military college of South Carolina. His consistent references to his alma mater indicated he was a proud alumnus. Randy had broad shoulders, hairy arms, and a thick brown mustache. He was long-winded, but had a friendly disposition.

After Randy concluded the fifteen-minute monologue about his background, he paused to take a breath and asked why David and Sarah were traveling to Charleston.

"A friend of ours passed away. His funeral is tomorrow." Sarah responded.

"Oh, I'm sorry to hear that, ma'am. How long are y'all staying down here?"

"Just a few days." Sarah replied, realizing she and David had not yet finalized their return travel plans.

"Very good. Just FYI, there's a hurricane brewing off the coast. Weatherman says it's likely headed for the Carolinas and will make landfall sometime *this week*. Just keep that in mind."

Randy turned his attention to David who had been quiet the entire flight.

"Do you have a place to stay down here, Mr. Stoneman?" Randy asked, trying to engage David in the conversation. David was not in the mood for small talk, but suspected the rest of the flight would be terribly awkward if he was not, at least, cordial.

"Not yet. This trip was kind of last minute. We'll figure something out."

Randy asked a follow-up question, "Is this y'all's first time in Charleston?"

Sarah glanced at David who was looking out the plane's small window, attempting to extract himself from the conversation entirely.

"No, actually. We were here last year to visit this same friend; the guy who passed away." Sarah replied.

"Well, then y'all must know about the fantastic barrier islands, just outside the city, right?"

Sarah smacked David's arm, urging him to respond.

"Sorry, what was the question?" David sat up and took another swig of his bottled water. Randy asked again.

"Have you been to the barrier islands around Charleston?"

"Not personally, no. Although I've had a number of clients with second homes near Kiawah Island." David replied.

"Are you able to tell me their names?" Randy's odd question caused both Sarah and David to look at each other.

"Unfortunately, no. Attorney-client confidentiality prevents me from sharing any information about my clients." David lied.

Randy realized he may have overstepped and tried to recover.

"The only reason I ask is because the islands are home to many high-profile folks, and I thought one of your clients might be a movie star, or something."

"Nothing like that, unfortunately. Just good ole' fashioned rich people." David sarcastically responded.

"You know it's pretty secretive out there on those islands. Kiawah, for example, has guard gates and everything. There's only one road in and out. They also have alligators just walking around on the golf courses. Can you believe that?" Randy chuckled and continued.

"I have a buddy who works out there – he's a golf professional." Randy lowered his voice, almost to a whisper, as if someone could be eavesdropping on their conversation. David and Sarah could barely hear him over the hum of the airplane's engine.

"My pal can get you a discount at one of the nicest private hotels out there. And, I get a ten percent referral fee. Interested?"

David recognized the polite thing was to simply say *yes*, if for no other reason than to get Randy to stop talking.

"Sure. We're happy to consider that option. I'll get his contact information from you when we're safely on the ground," David replied with a not-so-subtle hint that Randy should return his attention to the controls.

After more than an hour of conversation, Randy prepared for landing. David breathed a sigh of relief and Sarah closed her eyes to rest. David watched the darkening clouds dart past his oval window as the plane began its descent into Charleston Executive Airport (JZI), roughly ten miles from downtown.

In the cockpit, Randy pulled out his cell phone and held it to the left side of his seat and out of view of his passengers. With one hand still on the plane's yoke, he typed a simple text message:

> *They're either playing dumb, or they don't know anything. We're landing now.*

Chapter 21

The following morning, the mood was somber as David and Sarah sat stoically in a wooden pew at the New Beginnings Baptist Church. Tommy Felton's daughter, Jenny, was ceremoniously delivering her father's eulogy.

The sanctuary was packed with hundreds of members of Tommy's congregation and other prominent citizens from Charleston County. The crowd was older and many were dressed in their Sunday best. David expected nothing less in the Deep South.

Crimson roses lined the base of Tommy's white casket and complemented the red carpet which decorated the sanctuary's center aisle.

David and Sarah were sitting near the back of the church. It had been roughly a year since they had surprised Tommy at one of his Sunday night services. That was the last time they were all together. It seemed like a lifetime ago.

David watched Jenny at the front of the church. Tears streamed down her porcelain face as she uttered her final, emotional farewell to her beloved father. The morning sunlight cascading through the church's colorful stained-glass windows created a beautiful rainbow hue at the base of Tommy's casket.

At the end of the service, one-by-one, each row was invited to pay their final respects. When it was their turn, David and Sarah ambled down the side aisle to meet Jenny in the receiving line. Jenny had never met David and Sarah, in-person, but as David introduced himself, Jenny gave him a big, tearful hug as if they had known each other for years.

"He talked about you often, you know? He called you his *D.C. folks.*" Jenny said as her red face managed a smile.

"Is that right? Well, he was a great guy. We're so sorry for your loss." David sympathetically responded.

"Let us know if you need anything." Sarah added, as she, too, embraced Jenny.

"There is one thing…" Jenny announced. David leaned in.

"Dad sent me a text message on the day he died. He said 'the military' was with him at his fishing spot. I told the local authorities about the text, but they dismissed it. Does that make any sense to you?"

"No, it doesn't, but I'll see what I can find out." David promised as he moved down the line and toward the casket. He wiped a tear from his eye as he took Sarah's hand and followed the crowd up the center aisle, out of the sanctuary, and into the church foyer.

Jenny and her family requested privacy at the burial site. As a result, most of the attendees had dissipated from the church. David and Sarah lingered.

As he scanned the remaining faces in the crowd, David noticed a man standing in the corner with his hands in his pockets, staring back at him. He looked out of place and his gaze was unpleasant.

The man was tall and thin, with high cheek bones, pale skin, and a buzzed haircut. His lineless face indicated he was younger, likely in his early thirties, and his outfit was wrinkled and thrown together.

David pretended not to see him and turned back around. However, curiosity caused him to look once again in the man's direction. The stranger continued to stare. He was not even blinking. David turned his back and lowered his face to Sarah's ear.

"Psst, Sarah." David called in a hushed tone. She looked up.

"There's a creepy guy in the corner behind me. Is he still looking this way?"

Sarah cautiously glanced over David's shoulder, then darted her eyes around in confusion.

"Who are you talking about, Dave?"

David spun around – the man was gone. He scanned the room, but there was no sign of the stranger.

"Forget it. He must have left. I'm going to the restroom before we head out. You okay for a second?"

Sarah nodded and pulled her cell phone from her purse to check emails and text her son, Mark. David saw the men's room sign hanging above a door just past the sanctuary's side aisle entrance. He made his way through the small crowd and into the lavatory.

The bathroom was empty except for an older gentleman drying his hands. David nestled up to one of the two urinals, faced the taupe wall, and relieved himself. When he finished, he turned toward the sink and froze. The tall mystery man was standing just a few feet in front of him with his arms crossed over his chest. David recoiled in shock.

He was tempted to yell and, perhaps, someone would rush to his aid. David's adrenaline continued to pump.

"What do you want?!" David blurted.

The man did not say a word. He simply grinned and reached inside his left jacket pocket. *He's got a gun!* David feared, as he gritted his teeth and clenched his fists. He was ready for a fight.

Just as David was about to lunge forward and take a swing, the man pulled out a black folding wallet which he flipped open to reveal an FBI badge and ID card.

"Mr. Stoneman, I'm Special Agent Joseph Manheim with the FBI. Can I have a minute of your time?"

Relief flooded over David and he exhaled a massive sigh. He was lucky he used the restroom *before* the encounter, otherwise, he would have needed a change of clothes.

"You couldn't wait until I was out of the bathroom?!"

David walked past the agent, turned on the sink, and filled his hands with liquid soap.

"What can I do for you?" David asked as he lathered his palms under the cool water.

"I'm based in our Columbia field office, but was sent to Charleston this week to investigate Tommy Felton's death. Do you know anything about it, Mr. Stoneman?" The man asked as he frowned at David in the mirror.

"How do you know who I am? Have we met before?"

"No. You're just famous at the bureau. *David Stoneman, Senator slayer.* The man said, with a hint of condescension.

"That was last year. What's that have to do with Tommy's death? I was in D.C. when he died—"

"You have an alibi to corroborate that?" Special Agent Manheim interrupted. David was offended by the implication.

"I don't know what you're getting at, but I was told Tommy died in a *boating accident*. Obviously, you suspect foul play. And, yes, I have an airtight alibi." David turned off the sink and retrieved a white paper towel.

"So, unless I'm missing something, I'm not sure I can help you, Agent Manheim. Excuse me…" David dried his hands and headed for the bathroom door.

"You don't think his death had anything to do with what he knew about the Division Act, do you?"

The agent's words stopped David in his tracks. He turned and looked at the man.

"I don't know what you're talking about."

"Sure, sure. You don't know anything about Felton's connection to a major government cover-up that landed your former boss and a United States Senator in jail last year. Or, perhaps, it's because the details of that case are confidential and you don't want to risk jeopardizing Sarah Mercer's case settlement. She looks good today, by the way." The man's piercing eyes were trained on David.

"How do you know—"

The man anticipated David's question and finished his sentence.

"How do I know about your *sealed, confidential* Division Act settlement? Come on, Mr. Stoneman, I work for the FBI. You think a rinky-dink confidentiality agreement is going to stop us from getting the information we want? Why do you think I'm talking to you instead of the local cops? There are bigger issues at play here." Special Agent Manheim coolly responded.

"Okay, let me ask you a better question, Mr. FBI...why are you looking into this at all? Like you said, the bad guys went to prison. Case closed." David took two steps forward.

"It's more complicated than that, Mr. Stoneman. Does the term *FARCO* mean anything to you?"

David was surprised to hear that word again. His mind drifted nearly every day to the unpleasant encounter he had with that militant group the year before. Special Agent Manheim added additional context.

"I hear you were very popular with them last year when they were trying to kill you in Washington. Ring any bells?"

David feigned a half-smile. "Yeah, I know who they are. So what? They're just a group of hired guns. I heard they left D.C. altogether."

"Not quite. The FBI believes FARCO is still alive and well." The agent replied.

"What's that got to do with me? And why is it so urgent that you have to disrupt me while I'm taking a piss?" David was growing impatient with the circular conversation.

"It's just very suspicious, Mr. Stoneman, that one of the only people on the planet to have seen a FARCO operative in action and lived to talk about it, is now lying in a casket in the other room. Killed under mysterious circumstances, might I add." Agent Manheim continued.

"After studying this group, I know they rarely leave witnesses. Yet, here *you* are. Which means you could be working with them." Agent Manheim moved his six-foot-four-inch frame toward David, hoping to intimidate him. "Your dad was a veteran, right?"

David didn't respond. Agent Manheim took his silence as confirmation.

"Yeah, I pulled his service records…maybe you were looking for some combat action to live up to your old man's tough guy standards, huh?"

David had had enough.

"This conversation is over. So, unless you're arresting me, I'm out of here." David scurried out of the restroom, gathered Sarah in the foyer, and hurried out of the church.

As they descended the church's steps, Special Agent Manheim emerged from the front doors behind them.

"Mr. Stoneman…" He yelled.

David paused halfway down the steps and turned, wanting to avoid a public scene. The agent dug into his coat pocket and retrieved a white business card.

"Here's my card. Call me if you have something you want to tell me." Special Agent Manheim put on his sunglasses and continued down the steps, past Sarah, who was confused by the strange interaction.

"Oh, and one more thing," Agent Manheim announced as he hit the sidewalk, "the damage to Tommy Felton's boat came from *inside* the boat. Felton also had bruising on his shoulder and a contusion on his head. Interesting for a drowning victim, don't you think?"

"What's he talking about, David?" Sarah asked.

"Tell her, Mr. Stoneman. She deserves to know. By the way, whoever wanted Tommy Felton dead probably has you on the same list. They could be watching you right now, for all I know. If I were you, I'm not sure I'd be walking around the busy streets of downtown Charleston without security. We'll be in touch."

With that, Special Agent Manheim disappeared into an unmarked vehicle and sped away. Sarah demanded an explanation and David reassured her she would get the full download once they were alone.

To the agent's point, their existing luxury hotel accommodations in the middle of downtown were likely unsafe. Between Jenny's comment regarding the suspicious text she received from Tommy the day he died, coupled with the bizarre interaction with the FBI agent, David concluded they needed a place to hide out until he could figure out what was going on.

"Do you still have the information that pilot gave you about the private hotel outside of town?" David asked.

"Yeah, why?"

"We're going to take a little detour."

Chapter 22

Despite his prickly demeanor, Special Agent Joseph Manheim was a legend in South Carolina. His local stardom stemmed, not from his law enforcement activity, but from a storied college basketball career at Clemson University.

Joseph was a four-star point guard in high school and earned a full athletic scholarship to Clemson. He was most famous for hitting a last-second shot to win an *Atlantic Coast Conference* Championship over the Duke Blue Devils during his senior year. After making that shot, he never again paid for a drink in the Palmetto state.

While he briefly considered playing professionally, an untimely knee injury limited his options and he joined the FBI soon thereafter.

Joseph was smart and always laser-focused on the task before him. The same grit and determination that propelled his sports career, also catapulted his career with the bureau. Joseph became known as the 'go-to' agent in South Carolina and, consequently, was highly sought after for complex cases in the region.

The favoritism made him unpopular with the other field agents, but Joseph didn't care, he was out for number one.

Ironically, that had always been his problem on and off the basketball court – he wasn't a good *team player*.

However, despite his colleagues' ire, Joseph's attention to detail and innate ability to analyze strings of incomplete information and form accurate conclusions were unmatched in the South. But it was not his investigative insight that ruffled feathers, it was his lack of tact.

With all his talent, Joseph was rude, cutting, and accusatory when his fellow agents missed key pieces of evidence, or botched an investigation. As a result, he spent most of his time working alone, which he preferred, and usually communicated with his superiors via email or text message, and only as needed.

After making his not-so-veiled threats to David Stoneman at Tommy Felton's funeral, Joseph decided to pursue an anonymous tip the Charleston field office had received earlier that week regarding a missing military boat.

Special Agent Manheim had a hunch.

Chapter 23

The National Hurricane Center (NHC), which is part of the National Oceanic and Atmospheric Administration (NOAA), tracks weather patterns in the Atlantic Ocean. Within the NHC, the Hurricane Specialist Unit (HSU) employs some of the world's most highly-trained meteorologists whose primary job is to track tropical storm activity.

When a storm or hurricane threatens land, public advisories are issued and public offices are alerted in order to prepare for the storm's potentially deadly impact.

For stubborn residents who choose to remain hunkered in their homes, they are left to the mercy of Mother Nature. Unfortunately, not all of them make it out alive.

The NHC had been tracking *Tropical Storm Mary* as it passed the U.S. Virgin Islands and Puerto Rico. With winds of over 105 mph, *Mary* had just graduated to a Category 3 hurricane as it moved toward Florida.

The first wave of storm-related winds would hit the Carolinas within days. Thereafter, weather conditions would become incredibly dangerous, almost overnight. The NHC had already sent alerts to local officials and mandatory evacuations were imminent.

North and South Carolina had weathered their fair share of hurricanes in the past century. However, every few decades a storm hit with such merciless force that it took years for the affected communities to recover.

One such storm was *Hurricane Hugo*, which pummeled Charleston in September 1989. *Hugo* made landfall in Charleston County with windspeeds exceeding 100 mph and a storm surge of over ten feet. *Hugo* was responsible for dozens of local deaths, thousands left homeless, and billions of dollars in property damage. More recently, *Hurricanes Helene* and *Milton* riveled *Hugo's* destruction in the Carolinas and were responsible for some of the most severe wind and water damage on record in the Southeast.

Hurricane Mary was predicted to be even worse.

Nevertheless, unsuspecting, oiled-up tourists blissfully lounged on the beaches of Charleston's surrounding Sea Islands as the ocean's waves grew choppier.

Hurricane Mary was coming.

Chapter 24

As he pulled up to the guard gate at Joint Base Charleston, Special Agent Joseph Manheim flashed his credentials to the stern-faced Security Forces Squadron entry controller. He had made an appointment with an investigator in the Naval Criminal Investigative Service (NCIS) office, which was a secret Lowcountry extension for NCIS's Carolinas Field Office based in Camp Lejeune, North Carolina. The local office was so clandestine that those outside of the intelligence community were unaware of its existence.

As a whole, Joint Base Charleston is one of twelve Department of Defense Joint Bases, and home to over sixty Department of Defense and federal agencies. It maintains $7.5 billion in base property and assets throughout three seaports and two airfields. Needless to say, it was well-guarded.

The entry controller gave Joseph directions and returned to his post.

Once Agent Manheim was in the correct building, an administrative employee escorted Joseph to a tiny makeshift office where he was met by a small, older man with a brown beard who greeted him with a wilted handshake.

"You must be Special Agent Manheim. I'm one of the NCIS investigators." The man was finishing a chocolate doughnut, half of which was still glued to his beard. As the man settled into his dated desk chair, Joseph got right to the point.

"My office received a tip that y'all have information about a missing watercraft, is that correct?"

"Uh, yessir, that's right. The SURC disappeared after a routine training exercise two weeks ago. No witnesses and no leads. Probably at the bottom of the river by now." The man laughed at his own joke and put his hands on his cluttered metal desk.

"Frankly, Agent Manheim, this is very low on my priority list. I have a dozen other cases which are more important. There were no weapons onboard the SURC and no one is pressing me to find it. So, if it turns up, great! If not, we'll have another one here next month."

The man consumed the last bite of his doughnut and squinted at his desktop computer screen. Joseph was not thrilled by the man's apparent lack of concern, but saw an opportunity to do what he did best – take control of the situation. The fact that Tommy Felton died on the river and a small riverine watercraft just happened to go missing around the same time, was too coincidental for Joseph to ignore.

"Can I get copies of the case file?" Joseph curtly requested.

"Sure. The secretary can give you copies to take with you. I would love it if the FBI would take this off my hands, especially with the bad weather coming this week." The man tossed a thin manila folder across the desk to Joseph.

A pink sticky-note was pasted on the file. Joseph read it out loud.

"Dr. Kenneth Lyons, Department of Engineering at Citadel. How is this relevant?"

The investigator squinted as Joseph held up the note.

"Oh, yeah…when we began our investigation someone said that guy was on base asking about the SURC training schedules. I was going to call him, but just haven't gotten to it."

While it certainly was not the smoking gun Joseph was hoping for, it was a solid lead.

"Do you mind if I follow-up with Dr. Lyons, myself? I can swing by the Citadel this afternoon." Joseph asked as he rose from his chair and extended his hand for a shake.

"Sure, no problem. Let us know if you find anything." The man returned the handshake and turned his attention to the other files on his desk.

Joseph hurried off Joint Base – he had business at the Citadel.

Chapter 25

Kiawah Island is twenty-five miles from Charleston and remains one of the most exclusive private resorts in America. Kiawah's commercial appeal dates back to 1802, when General Arnoldus Vanderhost, a Revolutionary War hero and twice mayor of Charleston, built his home on the island. Subsequently, the Vanderhorst family occupied Kiawah, in some capacity, for the next two-hundred years.

In 1974, the island was sold to a development company. Thereafter, Kiawah began its quiet rise to premium resort status.

In present day, prominent business leaders, celebrities, and politicians visit Kiawah each year, and many own second homes on the island. VIPs can be seen enjoying Kiawah's nature-filled walking trails which are buried deep within the island's dense, green foliage; or riding bicycles on the island's pristine beach.

David drove his rented, silver C-300 Mercedes-Benz down Betsy Kerrison Parkway toward Kiawah. Sarah was leaning back in the passenger seat with her feet propped up on the dashboard. They had been traveling on the understated two-lane road for miles. Sarah turned to David.

"Where in the world are you taking us, Dave?" Sarah asked, skeptical that the long thoroughfare would, at some point, present the resort community she had been promised.

"Randy's golf buddy gave me an address where he wanted to meet…this is the way the navigation is taking us."

David, too, was skeptical.

Eventually, David entered a roundabout. Signs for *Seabrook Island*, *Freshfields Village*, and *Kiawah Island* indicated they were close.

As the car circled, Sarah looked back and over her right shoulder to get a better view of the inviting shops and boutiques *Freshfields Village* had to offer. She saw pastel-clad families clinging to their new purchases and lapping up melting ice cream. *It's like a scene out of a movie*, Sara thought.

"This place looks amazing." Sara announced as David kept his eyes on the roundabout to ensure they took the correct turn.

The car's navigation feature directed them to exit onto Kiawah Island Parkway. *Kiawah Island* was stenciled in large letters on a sign surrounded by beautiful red and yellow flowers – they had arrived.

Within minutes, a golden marsh appeared on both sides of the road. It extended for miles and lay prostrate before dense, green tree lines in the distance. Narrow emerald waterways snaked through the marsh and David noticed small fishing boats bobbing in the water, hoping for a lucky catch. The blue afternoon sky contrasting with the marsh was nature's way of showcasing the majestic scenery of the Lowcountry.

As the car followed the posted 35 mph speed limit, David rolled down his window and let the sunshine hit his face. His black hair flew back.

While he would never admit it, David needed time away from the hustle and bustle of Washington. *This* is what he needed. The ambiance of Kiawah Island was already causing David's stress to melt away as the sweet aroma of the island filled his nostrils. He gave himself permission to deprioritize anxious thoughts and just enjoy. He had certainly earned it.

They passed a family bicycling with bags of groceries in baskets. The patriarch of the family was pulling a wheeled carriage with two smiling toddlers wearing matching, bright pink outfits. They were having the time of their lives.

"Looks like a family place. We'll have to come back with Mark." Sarah noted as she extended her arm out the passenger-side window. She opened her hand to catch the fresh, salty breeze in her palm.

"Hey, look over there!" David pointed as a snowy egret took flight from a salt shrub thicket and landed on the branch of a nearby live oak tree.

They passed another *Kiawah Island* sign on the left which sat below three resolute flagpoles. Just beyond the flags was a large security checkpoint.

"I didn't know we were staying at Area 51." David joked as he steered to the left lane, following the sign's explicit instructions to do so. He rolled his window down and was greeted by a pleasant female security guard wearing a green shirt and cap.

"Checking in?" The guard asked.

"Yes, I'm meeting *Jacob Blake*. He should be expecting us."

David swiftly retrieved the hand scribbled note Randy, the pilot, had written for them to ensure he had said the name correctly.

The guard carefully studied her computer screen and then looked up at David.

"What's your name, sir?"

"David Stoneman."

"Yes, sir, I have special instructions for you to meet Mr. Blake at the Cougar Point Clubhouse. You'll take your first right onto Kiawah Beach Drive." The guard said as she pointed down the road. She then handed David a paper parking pass and instructed him to keep the pass visible on his car's dashboard at all times.

Sarah noticed a second gate lane on her right, near a smaller guard shack. Vehicles in that lane breezed through automatically, which piqued her curiosity. She leaned over David.

"Excuse me, ma'am? Why are some of the cars allowed to go in without being stopped?"

"Property owners are given special RFID decals so they can come and go as they please. The decals digitally register."

"Looks like residents get extra perks, huh?" Sarah offered.

"Oh, yes, ma'am. More than you know..." The lady guard said with a sly grin as she opened the gate.

Chapter 26

Jacob Blake sat alone at the Players' Pub at Cougar Point Golf Course. He was drinking a tall glass of sweet tea and watching the golf channel on one of the bar's mounted televisions. His white ball cap, baby blue golf shirt, and sailor's red shorts made him hard to miss as he sat hunched with his tanned forearms resting on the bar's edge.

David and Sarah had heeded FBI Special Agent Joseph Manheim's warning about their safety and took their charter pilot's recommendation to stay outside of Charleston at an 'exclusive private hotel.' David and Sarah were instructed to meet the pilot's buddy, Jacob Blake, a local golf pro, for discounted room rates.

"Mr. Blake?" David asked as he and Sarah approached the bar.

"That's me. You must be the Stonemans. I'm glad you made it!" Jacob responded as he pushed his tea to the bartender with a wink.

"I'm David Stoneman and this is my girlfriend, Sarah *Mercer*." David corrected.

"Oh, I'm so sorry." Jacob apologized, "Honest mistake. Nevertheless, welcome!" He said as he energetically shook

David and Sarah's hands.

"Did you have any trouble getting past the gate?" Jacob asked as he glanced at his watch and motioned for the couple to follow him.

"Not at all. But I was surprised by the amount of security. Is it always like that?" David asked as they tried to keep up.

Jacob led them through the clubhouse lobby, out the large front doors, and into the parking lot. They could hear the crashing ocean waves in the distance. *So nice.* The pleasant salt air was calming as they followed their hurried host.

"Yeah, actually, it is. We have a ton of celebs on the island who like their privacy, *ya* know? Which one is yours?" Jacob asked as he pointed to the line of parked cars.

"The silver Benz."

"Good deal. My apologies for the rush, but I have to escort you to the hotel for you to get *my* discount, and I have plans this evening. I can find my own ride back, but is it cool if I ride over with y'all?"

David and Sarah looked at each other, surprised by the odd request. However, they acquiesced and Jacob piled in the backseat.

"You'll have to tell me where we're going; it's our first time here." David said as he put the car in reverse.

"Head back to the Parkway, the main road you came in on, and then make a right." Jacob looked out the window and up at the gray clouds in the sky.

124

"By the way, looks like y'all got here just in time. A hurricane is coming up the coast as we speak. If it stays its course, this place could get really soggy, real fast." Jacob chuckled and scooted into the middle seat.

"So, did y'all have a nice flight with Randy?" Jacob asked with a snicker.

"We did. How do you know each other again?" Sarah asked as she buckled her seatbelt and rolled down the window.

"We go *way back*, Randy and me. I've known him for years! Make a right here." Jacob reminded as David dutifully turned onto Kiawah Island Parkway. Sarah found it strange that Jacob didn't answer her question. David asked another.

"You two have a referral arrangement, is that right?"

"Uh, kind of...he refers people to me and I get them discounts at a super-secret hotel." He smirked. "The hotel pays me for referrals and I kick back ten percent of my take to Randy. It's a very sophisticated operation." Jacob laughed again as he removed his white cap to reveal a tan line across the middle of his forehead.

"So, where are we staying?" Sarah asked, intrigued by Jacob's 'super-secret' comment. Jacob leaned forward and smiled.

"I don't want to ruin the surprise! But I guarantee you've never even *heard* of this place before. It's *that* secretive."

Chapter 27

The Military College of South Carolina, better known as *The Citadel*, was founded in 1842 as one of six senior military colleges in the United States. Special Agent Joseph Manheim had a unique connection to The Citadel. His father was an alumnus and desperately wanted Joseph to play basketball for the Bulldogs.

However, the academic rigor and military environment was of no interest to Joseph as an obstinate teenager. He preferred late party nights over early morning push-ups.

Using an online campus map, Joseph found the building he was looking for. It resembled a shining white fortress sitting confidently in the warm Charleston sunshine. Joseph hoped to find Dr. Kenneth Lyons in his office. It would be better to catch him off guard.

Dr. Lyons was one of a handful of adjunct faculty members who had an office on campus. Fortunately, that made him easy to locate.

After several minutes of hall roaming, Joseph was standing outside Dr. Lyon's office door. He knocked twice. No answer. Joseph turned the door handle – it was unlocked. True to his personality, he barged in.

Dr. Lyons was meeting with a student cadet. Both professor and cadet were startled by the intrusion and jumped in their seats.

"Excuse me, sir, but I'm in the middle of a—" Joseph interrupted by waiving his FBI badge in the air. The cadet immediately excused himself and Joseph took his seat.

Dr. Lyons was fit for a man in his late fifties. He had short hair, which was mostly gray, low cheek bones, and a prominent, pug nose which expanded the length of his upper lip. His office was tidy and his posture impeccable.

"Dr. Lyons, I'll get right to the point. I'm investigating the disappearance of a SURC from Joint Base a couple weeks ago. Do you know anything about that?"

"No, sir, I don't." Dr. Lyons lied as he shrugged his shoulders. Joseph asked a follow-up question.

"Have you been to Joint Base within the past month, sir?

"No, it's been a while." Again, he shrugged his shoulders.

Joseph asked the second question to discover the professor's lying tell. Which, in this case, was a shoulder shrug.

"Okay, Dr. Lyons…you're not telling me the truth, so, let me give *you* some truth. A man was killed this week on the Stono River. I have reason to believe that incident may be connected to a stolen SURC which disappeared from Joint Base and I think you helped steal the SURC."

Dr. Lyon's hands began to shake.

"Some of the damage inside the dead guy's boat looked like it had been caused by military-grade hardware." Joseph paused, giving the professor one last chance to come clean. He didn't, so Joseph carried on.

"From what I've been told, a SURC is one of the only military watercrafts able to navigate the marshy inlets where the death occurred. So, I know you're withholding information and as a result, I'm going to charge you with conspiracy to commit murder." Joseph was now leaning forward with his elbows resting on his long thighs.

Dr. Lyons remained silent but his hands continued to shake. That, plus the subtle twitch in his eyelid told Joseph the professor was panicking internally. Special Agent Manheim lowered his voice, nearly to a whisper.

"I'll ask you one more time, you little pissant…what do you know about the missing SURC?"

Dr. Lyons was taken aback by the offensive comment from a federal agent and awkwardly repositioned himself in his desk chair.

"I think you should leave, sir. I want to speak to an attorney." Dr. Lyons slowly moved his hand down toward his desk drawer. His eyes remained trained on Joseph. Suspecting the worst, Joseph made his move.

He sprung from his chair and swiftly circled the desk. He grabbed Dr. Lyon's hand as he tried to open his desk drawer and smashed it into the side of the desk.

"You reaching for a weapon? Huh?" Joseph asked as he put Dr. Lyons in an unsanctioned choke hold. Dr. Lyons sloshed in his chair, trying to claw away from Joseph's constricting grip.

"You only have seconds left and then you're going to die. You want to die?" He whispered in Dr. Lyon's ear. The professor squirmed in desperation.

"You have one chance to save yourself!" Joseph growled.

After several tense seconds, Dr. Lyons tapped Joseph's forearm, signaling his surrender. As usual, the questionable interrogation tactic had worked. Joseph released the professor and tossed him, gasping, onto the floor. Joseph then opened Dr. Lyon's desk drawer.

To his surprise, he did not find a gun; just a cell phone. He grabbed the phone, leaned down, and held it up to the professor's face.

"Why were you reaching for *this*?"

Dr. Lyons, still coughing, shook his head. Joseph hit the man in the back which caused him to recoil in pain. He then put up his right index finger signifying he needed a minute to compose himself.

"Last chance, doc. Truth time. Why is this phone important?"

"Alright, alright! I'll tell you!" Dr. Lyons exclaimed as he rose to his knees, then to his feet, and plopped down into his desk chair. He rubbed his bruised neck. Joseph resumed his seat as well, waiting for the confession.

"About a month ago, an old friend of mine unexpectedly showed up at my door. When I say *unexpectedly*, I mean everyone thought he was dead. He told me he ran a private sector security group, but didn't say much else."

Joseph interrupted, "Did he give you the name of the group?"

Dr. Lyons shook his head.

"He brought a bag full of cash with him. One-hundred thousand dollars. He told me it was mine if I just went to Joint Base and retrieved the SURC training schedule for him. That's it, I swear!" Dr. Lyons unbuttoned one of his shirt's top buttons, still flustered by the altercation. Joseph had more questions.

"Did you take the money?"

"Of course I took the money. I didn't know he was going to steal the boat for crying out loud!"

"So, what's with the phone?" Joseph asked as he pointed to the cell phone lying on the desk.

"He gave me this burner phone and told me to call him on the only saved number when I had the schedule. He also told me to *immediately* destroy the phone if someone, like you, showed up asking questions."

Dr. Lyons continued.

"Look, I still have the money at home. I'll give it to you, just don't arrest me." Dr. Lyons pleaded with Joseph as the gravity of his situation bore down on him.

Special Agent Manheim saw Dr. Lyon's vulnerability and pushed even harder.

"The man who came to see you. What's his name?"

Dr. Lyons winced, knowing he had no choice but to identify his secret contact. It was either that, or go to jail. He turned and faced the windowsill behind his desk and lifted a small 5x7 framed photograph and handed it to Joseph.

It was an old graduation photo. In the picture, a handful of cadets were donning their Class A Dress Blue uniforms. Each of the pictured cadet's names were scribbled in pencil at the bottom of the photo. Joseph looked up at Dr. Lyons as he pointed to the picture.

"That's me on the far right. The guy on the left is the person who came to see me. His name is James Henderson."

"Henderson, huh?"

"Yeah, Henderson. As you can see from his plain clothes, he wasn't a Citadel cadet. He was a townie who had enlisted, but liked to hang out with us cadets. Made him forget he was from the wrong side of the tracks, I guess." Dr. Lyons said as he rubbed his aching neck.

"Rumor was that Henderson made it all the way up to Sergeant First Class, but was demoted for bad behavior before eventually being dishonorably discharged. But I'd be careful if I were you," Dr. Lyons warned.

"He's the smartest guy I've ever met; the most ruthless too."

Joseph scanned the rest of the cadets in the picture. Suddenly, something caught his eye. *No, it can't be.* He did a double-take.

"Is that who I think it is?" Joseph asked. Dr. Lyons nodded.

"I'm taking this picture and the phone with me as evidence," Special Agent Manheim declared. Dr. Lyons had no choice but to acquiesce. Joseph pulled the photograph out of the metal picture frame and headed for the door.

"Keep the money, doc. Use it to get your family out of town."

As Joseph left, a crowd of curious cadets had formed outside the office. He pushed his way through the students and heard Dr. Lyons reassuring them that everything was okay as Joseph disappeared down the hall.

Once he reached his car, Joseph tossed the burner phone in the center console, confident its saved number had long been disconnected. Instead, Joseph studied the photograph for a second time. He froze.

There was something else. Something he had not seen earlier. *This just keeps getting better and better.*

He definitely recognized one of the cadets in the picture. Everyone in town knew *him*. He was one of the biggest names in Charleston.

But now, Special Agent Manheim realized he, actually, recognized *two* names stenciled below the photograph. *It can't be…*

One thing was for certain; this case had just gotten a lot more interesting. He planned to chase the bigger fish first, then he'd track down David Stoneman and ask him why his father was in this photograph.

Chapter 28

J acob Blake playfully patted David's shoulder as he leaned forward from the car's backseat. David continued to chauffeur as the silver rental car sped down Kiawah Island Parkway toward their destination.

Jacob blabbered on and on about his golf career and his unmatched expertise on the various degrees of pitching wedges that were ideal to get 'up-and-down' on tough golf courses. David and Sarah couldn't have cared less. They were too mesmerized by the beauty surrounding them. Kiawah was breathtaking – an elegant jungle.

When Jacob realized David and Sarah had all but tuned him out, he tried to recapture their attention with local trivia.

"You folks probably want to know a little more about the island, huh? I know of ton of useless info about this place." Jacob said as he looked at Sarah, beaming with Southern charm.

"That'd be great, but just tell me where I need to turn." David reminded as he glanced to his right to find Jacob's head uncomfortably close to his.

Let's see, where to begin…well, way back in the 1600s, Captain George Raynor, a suspected pirate, owned part of Kiawah. Some folks 'round here even believe there's buried treasure on the island somewhere. It sure would be nice to stumble upon a treasure chest on the golf course, am I right?"

Jacob said, chuckling at his own joke. He continued.

"Anyway, the island is nearly fifteen miles long, depending on if you count the marsh, and is home to about 1,400 full-time residents. The tourists and part-timers hover around 10,000 during vacation season."

"Wow, that's a lot more than I thought," Sarah said. "I don't see that many houses."

She looked out the driver's side window, searching for hidden structures.

"Good point, ma'am. That's the neat thing about Kiawah; hundreds of massive mansions are buried in little nooks and crannies. Only a small portion are visible from the main roads. That's part of the appeal. Very private." Jacob commented with a cheeky grin.

He saw a couple fly by on a golf cart which gave him an excuse to veer the conversation back to his own interest.

"Of course, with the big houses come big golfers. I make my money giving private lessons during the summer months. I also lose about twenty pounds just from being outside in the ungodly heat all day." Jacob snorted and, again, slapped David's arm.

"Are you folks golfers?" He optimistically asked as he leaned back.

"Not really," Sarah replied, "David works too much, and I've never played."

"Well, shoot! We may just have to get you out and teach *ya* a thing or two. I can't believe Randy sent me two non-golfers. I'm *gonna* talk with him about that."

Jacob was silent for several pleasant seconds. Unfortunately, the silence was too much for him to bear.

"But man, I tell *ya* what…Randy carts the high-rollers in here like he's running a full-time air shuttle service. He must make a killing on private charters." Jacob said as they passed an *East Beach* sign on their left.

"As I said, this place is crawling with VIPs." He then looked out the right side of the car as they passed Sea Forest Drive.

"To the right, there; that's *Night Heron Park*. It's fun for big family events. They have a great Fourth of July party, too! Tons of folks come out to have a few beers and grab some grub. Good times!"

David and Sarah noticed dozens of children playing in the park. Their pastel swimwear and sun-bleached hair could be seen from the road. Polo-wearing parents congregated in small groups, no doubt intensely debating which fine dining option they would patronize that evening. David turned his attention back to the road, but Sarah's gaze lingered.

This is the life I want for Mark, she thought. Sarah reflected on the hardships she and her son had endured before David was in the picture. But now, they had turned a new leaf. She had David to thank for that. It was the American dream – she had won a lawsuit.

David was curious about Jacob's connection with the hotel they were staying at and inquired further.

"So, do you work for this hotel?"

Jacob beamed, "I work for *me*, Dave! I'm an independent contractor. The hotel has me on retainer and I take their guests out on the links." Jacob continued.

"I hire my own caddies, too. I've been running my own little operation here for a while."

"So, you do work for the hotel?" David clarified.

"Well, *kinda*, yeah, but as a contractor. Seven years ago, a development company from Atlanta bought up a bunch of residential sections of the local islands. They purchased all the homes in one area called *Rhett's Bluff*. There, they built a small, members-only hotel. That's where we're headed!" Jacob announced as he lit up with excitement.

"*Rhett's Bluff*?" Sarah asked.

"Yes, Rhett's Bluff. It was one of the oldest parts of Kiawah, sheltered from the rest of the island. Like I said, some development group, *Menda something*, came in with a handful of investors and wanted to build a private hotel, but there was just one problem..." Jacob paused, hoping either David or Sarah would ask the obvious question. Sarah indulged him.

"What was the problem?"

"The land was *already developed*. Dozens and dozens of million-dollar homes were already on Rhett's Bluff. So, what do you think the development company did? You won't believe it." Again, Jacob stopped, waiting for the suspense to build.

By now, David and Sarah were intrigued. Jacob continued.

"They made offers to *every* homeowner asking to buy their property outright, in cash. From what I hear, the offers were ridiculous. All but one of the homeowners sold."

David believed it. He had heard rumblings of institutional investors spending tens of billions of dollars to purchase entire residential neighborhoods throughout the United States. At one point, he read that those purchases accounted for nearly twenty percent of all of the homes purchased in the country. As such, it came as no surprise that the trend had extended to resort communities as well.

"Who was the holdout?" Sarah asked.

"A local judge. A big name in these parts." Jacob answered as he returned to his story.

"Anyway, the developers demolished all those mansions to make space for their new hotel. They called it *the Rhett's Bluff Inn*. That's where we're headed. See, I told you you've never heard of it. Hardly anyone has. It's a members-only spot and doesn't even have a website."

"That's amazing!" Sarah responded as she glanced over at David, excited.

"But it's still part of Kiawah Island?" David asked, trying to connect the dots.

"No, actually. The developers successfully petitioned to be formally separated from Kiawah. How they govern themselves is still a big mystery. Some think it's a cult, or something. Others think it's just another exclusive club. Who really knows?" Jacob peeked down at his phone which had buzzed in his pocket, indicating he had a new text message.

"Believe it or not, that's not even the craziest part. There's a lesser-known eleven-acre enclave on the back side of Rhett's Bluff called *Captain Maynard's Island*. The developers bought that too. You can't make this stuff up! A private place within a private place!" Jacob grinned as if he had just told them the location of the lost city of Atlantis. Knowing David and Sarah were a captive audience, he deepened the mystery.

"There was only one home on *Captain Maynard's*. The developers bulldozed it and built a handful of high-end cottages on the plot. A private trust holds the deeds to those cottages, so, no one knows, for sure, who owns them. Very mysterious…"

The car approached a second security gate and David slowed. The guard studied their guest pass, which was visibly displayed on their car's dashboard and waved them through.

The silver car hummed over a bass pond and down a long road which seemed to disappear into a line of condensed trees. David could barely see the dimly-lit entrance to the Rhett's Bluff Inn in the distance. It looked like a castle hidden deep in an enchanted forest.

Jacob had quieted in the backseat. He pulled out his cell phone and read the text message he had received.

Are you close? We're ready for them.

Chapter 29

It was less than an hour flight time from Atlanta to Charleston. Bailey peered out the tiny window of the privately-chartered Cessna Citation Mustang jet. The plane descended through ominous storm clouds.

Even on the small airplane Bailey felt like an outsider. Damian and Tara were in the back of the cabin facing the cockpit. They had whispered the entire flight. Bailey attempted to eavesdrop but was only able to hear parts of their conversation.

She was relegated to the seat nearest to the cockpit and, unfortunately, close enough to be forced to answer the loquacious pilot's barrage of unusual questions. The pilot said his name was Randy.

Randy told Bailey his clients paid good money to fly directly into Charleston Executive Airport (JZI) from all over the country. He said he had taken a young couple from Washington, D.C. into JZI just the day before. Randy then proceeded to tell Bailey his entire life story. He eventually quieted down in order to land the plane.

As they taxied on the tarmac, Randy asked Bailey one final question. Knowing her escape was imminent, Bailey indulged the curious pilot.

"Do y'all have a place to stay in town?" Randy inquired. He then mumbled something into his headset to air traffic control.

As Damian collected his personal items and prepared to deplane, he answered for the group.

"We do. Why do you ask?" Damian seemed irritated by the pilot's innocent question. Sensing that inquiry may not have been well-received, Randy backtracked.

"No particular reason, Mr. Little. My apologies for being nosey. I only mention it because if y'all don't have a place to stay, I have a buddy who can get you an incredible discount at an exclusive hotel out on one of the barrier islands."

That comment caused Damian to look back at Tara, then back at the pilot.

"What did you say your name was?"

"Randy, sir."

"And which hotel are you talking about?"

"The Rhett's Bluff Inn, sir."

"How do *you* know about the Inn?" Damian's tone grew serious.

"A buddy of mine. He's a golf pro and—" Randy was interrupted by further instructions from air traffic control.

Outside one of the plane's oval windows, Damian recognized Sergeant James Henderson's muscular physique leaning against an unmarked black sedan – he was waiting for them. Two other hulking men donning military fatigues and security earpieces loitered near a second black car parked behind the first. Damian grabbed the handle of his laptop bag, moved past Bailey, and leaned into the cockpit.

"Our driver is outside. We need to get out *here*."

"Sure thing, Mr. Little."

The plane came to a sudden halt.

"Okay, ladies, let's go. Our security detail is outside. They'll take us to the Inn."

Security detail? Bailey wondered. *Since when do we need security on a business trip?*

"The Inn?! So, y'all are staying at the Rhett's Bluff Inn! How long have y'all known about it?!" Randy excitedly asked.

Damian ignored him. The affront was blatant and caused Randy's smile to wane as he sunk back into the cockpit.

Seconds later, the outer cabin door opened and one of the security guards took Damian's computer bag as he stepped out of the small plane. The other guard assisted Tara and Bailey with their things as well. Bailey was the last one off and the only person who thanked Randy for the safe flight. Randy sheepishly nodded. He looked uneasy.

The military men retrieved the remaining luggage from the plane's cargo hold and escorted Tara and Bailey to one of the black vehicles. The windows were tinted, and with night falling, Bailey could barely see out the dark windows.

But, even with limited visibility, Bailey noticed something strange. One of the members of the security team was unloading large black duffle bags from the plane's luggage compartment. Those bags were then placed in the trunk of the car behind them. Damian was still outside talking to the leader of the security detail.

Curious, Bailey turned to Tara who was sitting silently to her left.

"Hey, do you know what's in those black bags? Apparently, they were on our flight."

Tara looked past Bailey, but Bailey's eyes remained fixed on Tara. She studied her facial expressions searching for any hint of genuine surprise at the bags' presence. Tara showed no emotion whatsoever.

"Don't know." Tara lied as she turned away from Bailey. She then opened her door and yelled to Damian that it was time to leave. Bailey did not appreciate the blowoff and asked a second question.

"Well, can you at least tell me who Damian is talking with?"

Without even looking, Tara answered.

"That's James Henderson. He's retired military." Again, Tara opened the door and hollered at Damian, this time with greater urgency. It was obvious the barrage of questions was making Tara uncomfortable.

Damian pointed to the plane's cockpit as he headed toward the car. Sergeant Henderson nodded as Damian retreated to the front seat. One of the security guards settled into the driver's seat and revved the engine as the car began to move.

Sergeant Henderson watched the first black car speed away. After it was out of sight, he and the other guard approached the jet's door, which was still ajar. Randy was watching them from the cockpit and knew he was in trouble.

Sergeant Henderson waved to the pilot, indicating he wanted a word. Randy nodded, removed his headset, and disappeared from view. Sergeant Henderson scanned the area – not another soul around.

As Randy appeared in the cabin's doorway, Sergeant Henderson drew a silenced sidearm and fired two shots into the middle of Randy's chest. A look of horror was frozen on Randy's face as his fell onto the tarmac, *dead*.

"Clean this up, then meet us at the Inn." Sergeant Henderson instructed as he walked back to the remaining vehicle. A tracking signal on his phone showed the other car was just a few miles ahead of them and heading for the boat dock, as planned.

Chapter 30

The circle driveway leading to the Rhett's Bluff Inn showcased the charm and sophistication of a top-tier Southern hotel. The 50,000 square foot, fifty-key antebellum resort was nestled atop a lush knoll and nearly hidden in a thicket of live oaks and cabbage palms. Surrounded by sweetgrass, the grounds oozed of old-world allure.

The Inn was tastefully lit with hanging gas lanterns on either side of the tall, wooden entryway doors. The building's cream exterior, thick white columns, and large windows teased at the first-class interior décor.

Jacob jumped out of the backseat of David's rental car and muttered something to the young valet as he slipped him a large bill. In seconds, Jacob received a valet ticket, held it up, and beckoned for David and Sarah to join him.

"We're all good. Here's your ticket," Jacob handed David the claim ticket. "They'll make sure your luggage gets to your room. Just leave the keys in the car."

Two doormen wearing white gloves and crimson uniforms slowly opened the Inn's front doors to reveal a massive crystal chandelier hanging from the seventeen-foot lobby ceiling. An enormous patterned oriental rug sat settled over a pristinely polished hardwood floor.

The lobby's open floor plan revealed a stunning sitting room just beyond the check-in counter, complete with a crackling fire burning in the white stone fireplace. Guests were seated in the oxblood leather couches and surrounded by pictures of Greek and Roman deities which regally hung on the walls in golden frames.

The smell of freshly cut flowers wafted through the lobby. The front doors, which were still open, caused a cool coastal breeze to blow through allowing the flowers' fragrances to circulate nicely in the open space.

The windows on the lobby's far wall displayed the hotel's pristine back lawn which included an immaculate pool deck. And the Kiawah River created a dream-like scene in the distance.

Jacob gravitated to the concierge desk where a well-dressed man with a slight build and tortoise-shell glasses greeted him with a hearty handshake. The man wore a blue herringbone sport coat, yellow tie, and matching pocket handkerchief. He eagerly circled his desk to meet David and Sarah who were aimlessly wandering under the lobby's massive chandelier, still caught up in the hotel's grandeur.

"David Stoneman and Sarah Mercer, I would like to introduce you to the Inn's concierge, Mr. Simon Seifert." Jacob announced as he opened his hand to present his guests to their host.

"It is my sincere pleasure, folks! Welcome to the Rhett's Bluff Inn." Simon said as he clasped Sarah's right hand in his manicured grip. He slightly bowed as if he were greeting royalty. Sarah blushed at the genteel gesture.

David noticed a gold lapel pin on his jacket – it was a hollow circle with a small lightning bolt in the center. *Interesting.* The pin didn't fit with the rest of his impeccable ensemble, which David found curious for a man who was, obviously, meticulous about every detail of his wardrobe. David perished the thought.

"Mr. Seifert, I must say, this place is amazing!" David complimented as he took in the room's beauty, yet again.

"I hadn't heard of the Rhett's Bluff Inn before today. This has to be the best-kept secret in the South."

Simon smiled at Jacob.

"Actually, Mr. Stoneman, we *are* a secret. Jacob hasn't been entirely forthcoming with you. You see, this is an *invitation-only* hotel. Each member goes through a rigorous, multi-year screening process before an invitation is extended." Simon's tone was polite, but carried a shade of elitism. He casually rested his hand on Jacob's shoulder.

"I choose to overlook the fact that Jacob uses his connections with a chartered jet pilot to invite guests, like yourself, to stay with us in order to earn a small kick-back." Simon playfully commented and continued.

"If Jacob weren't so popular with our members, we would be stricter with him."

David grew uncomfortable when he realized their presence was a slight imposition.

"How does someone become a member?" Sarah asked.

Simon adjusted his glasses, "We operate on an annual subscription model where members and their *approved guests* enjoy an all-inclusive experience which includes boating, dining, golf, pool and beach access, bar service, private events, and other *special* amenities." Simon said as he waved at another couple walking through the lobby. David couldn't help but notice that Simon dodged Sarah's question.

"Any famous members we would know?"

"Unfortunately, Ms. Mercer, we are not at liberty to share the names of our more prominent members, but I can tell you that many are quite recognizable."

"Do *guests* have to pay to stay here?"

"Yes, ma'am. Our guest fee is five-thousand per night."

Sarah's jaw dropped.

"You've got to be kidding me!" Sarah blurted. Her face reddened and David shot her a reproving look. Simon smirked.

"Fortunately, Ms. Mercer, you're in luck. As I mentioned, we have a special arrangement with Mr. Blake that allows his guests to stay for just one-thousand dollars per night." Simon said, as if he was giving them a huge concession.

"Still…" Sarah mumbled under her breath.

David asked if he and Sarah could be excused for a moment. David pulled Sarah away to speak to her privately.

"Please don't do this here, Sarah."

"Look, Dave, I'm sorry, but we could stay at another hotel for *ten* nights for a thousand bucks!" Sarah protested, her frugality on full display.

"You're right, it's expensive. But it's also a once-in-a-lifetime opportunity. When else are we going to be invited to stay at a member-only, luxury hotel at the beach?"

David continued, "It's only a few nights – let's live a little!" David put his hands on Sarah's shoulders.

Sensing this was important to him, Sarah agreed and they rejoined Jacob and Simon.

"Mr. Seifert, we'll plan to stay for three nights. Thank you again for the opportunity to do so." David said as he shook Simon's hand.

Simon directed them to the check-in desk behind him. After a few short minutes they received their room key and were briefed on the Inn's dress code which required business attire in the dining room and business casual attire in all other areas, except the pool deck. Simon glanced at the number on David's key card.

"You're in Room Six. It's here on the first floor, just down the hall to your right." Simon said as he pointed.

"Also, I want to make sure you're aware that, unfortunately, it looks like Hurricane Mary is headed our way. Heavy rain is supposed to begin sometime tomorrow. If there are any notable weather updates, a member of the Inn's staff will let you know right away."

David and Sarah thanked Simon, bid farewell to Jacob, and walked down the first-floor hallway to their room. Once they disappeared down the hall, Simon's demeanor changed.

"Who are they?" Simon coldly asked Jacob.

"You didn't recognize *him*? That's David Stoneman."

Simon stared blankly at Jacob.

"He's the one Sergeant Henderson wanted down here this weekend. Remember?"

That triggered Simon's recollection.

"Oh, that's *Stoneman*?"

"Uh-huh." Jacob replied as he headed toward the front doors to hail a ride back to Cougar Point Clubhouse. Simon scurried after him and twirled Jacob around, commanding his full attention.

"Jacob…listen! You know *they* expect perfection. Stoneman won't screw anything up, will he?" Simon asked in a hushed tone.

"No, Simon. It's all under control. Plus, it's not your call. *They* wanted Stoneman here." Jacob shrugged off Simon's grip.

Just then, one of the on-island shuttles pulled into the Inn's circle driveway. Jacob boarded and gave Simon a thumb's up through the shuttle's window as it departed down the Inn's long, dark driveway.

Just then, the front desk clerk frantically ran up to Simon. She was out of breath. Between belabored gasps, she was able to relay the important message.

"Mr. Seifert, Sergeant Henderson will be arriving at the boat landing shortly. He wants to meet with you when he arrives, sir."

Simon straightened his yellow tie and hurried to gather his materials – the week's important events were about to begin.

Chapter 31

Something's off, Bailey feared as she sat quietly with her hands folded in her lap.

Within the last twenty minutes, she had been escorted to a suspicious car by security guards and witnessed unmarked duffle bags being loaded into the trunk of the vehicle behind her. Now, she was riding in a military watercraft through the dark South Carolina marsh.

The most unsettling part, however, was the fact that both Damian and Tara seemed completely at ease, as if they had done this before. As the boat puttered along in the darkness, Bailey had to know what was going on.

"Damian, why are we in an army boat?"

"This is called a *SURC*, and I think it actually belongs to the Navy, not the Army." Damian joked as he exchanged haughty glances with Tara and Sergeant Henderson. Bailey was dissatisfied with the tongue-in-cheek answer. So, she asked again.

"Okay...then why are we in a *SURC* in the middle of a marsh?" Her rebuttal was direct.

"I told you, Bailey, we're going to an island for a business meeting. The easiest ingress option is by boat."

Bailey realized she needed to ask specific questions in order to receive better answers. A skill she had developed as a litigator.

"You're telling me this island is unreachable except by SURC-shuttle?" Her irritation was palpable.

"Of course not, but we're going to a hotel that has its own boat landing. The SURC is the fastest way, trust me." Damian smirked at Sergeant Henderson who sat stoically with his eyes trained on the waters ahead.

Recognizing Damian was a captive audience, Bailey asked another question.

"Well, what's in the black bags? You didn't mention we were toting extra cargo."

That question caused Sergeant Henderson to turn around. His cold, disapproving glare was haunting.

"We're transporting the bags for a friend at the hotel. He assured me it's not drugs, if that's what you're worried about. Look up ahead...we're close!" Bailey could sense Damian was relieved they had reached their destination. He wouldn't have to answer any more questions, at least for now.

As the salt air whipped Bailey's brown hair into her face, her eyes wandered to glimmering lights in the distance. As the SURC drew closer, Bailey saw the back of a large, palatial Southern estate.

Bailey's mind mapped out possible nefarious scenarios. After all, Damian was the CEO of Menda Industrial and Bailey would, inevitably, have to answer for his actions if the bags contained some kind of contraband. Or worse, she would be forced to prove she was not willfully ignorant of the bags' contents. *What a mess.*

Damian turned back to Bailey and smiled.

"Welcome to the Rhett's Bluff Inn."

Chapter 32

The following morning, the sun slowly rose over Charleston Harbor as Special Agent Manheim banged on the door of a historic home on the most celebrated street in town.

Rainbow Row was the colloquial term given to a set of brightly-colored, Georgian row houses on East Bay Street. The renowned thoroughfare was purchased in 1931 by Judge Lionel Legge and his wife, Dorothy. Wanting to gentrify the area, Dorothy painted the homes an inviting shade of pink. The color scheme stuck and, as the homes sold, subsequent homeowners followed suit by also coating their homes in a variety of pastel colors. To this day, Charleston city ordinances require the structures maintain their vibrant appearance.

As Joseph pounded repeatedly on the fragile doorframe, he couldn't have cared less about the historical significance of the home. He was on a mission.

New information had come to light which significantly complicated his investigation of the missing SURC and Tommy Felton's death. The photograph he had taken from Dr. Lyon's office the day before at The Citadel led his investigation in an entirely new direction – a more dangerous direction. One minor misstep could land him in a world of hurt. However, Joseph was like a blood hound – he had picked up a scent and no one could stop him until he found what he was looking for.

He banged on the door more loudly. Joseph was confident the next piece to his puzzle was just beyond this threshold. He could feel it.

As he drew his clenched fist back for another fierce round of knocking, the doorknob turned and opened a few inches to reveal a well-dressed, older woman peering out at him.

The woman's demeanor was cautious, but warm. Her lime green knit sweater, khaki pants, and string of expensive neck pearls screamed of blue blood wealth. The woman's flowing white hair was fluorescent as rays of sunshine shone through the door's crack.

"Can *Aah* help *ya* young man?" She asked in a thick Southern accent.

Joseph could be charming when the occasion called for it, especially when the audience was someone who reminded him of his grandmother. He was, after all, raised in the South.

"Yes, ma'am, I'm so sorry to bother you this morning. I'm Special Agent Joseph Manheim with the FBI. Is Judge Cathpert available, by any chance? It's rather urgent." Joseph conveyed as he raised his credentials for the woman's review. She took a silent moment to examine the badge to ensure its authenticity.

"*Aah'm* afraid Holton took the boat up to Rhett's Bluff this week. *Aah'm* Barbara, Holton's wife. Please come in." The woman invited as she swung open the door.

Retired Judge Holton Cathpert was a household name in South Carolina. The Cathpert family had settled in the area in the late seventeenth century and were recognized as one of the most powerful families in the region.

The Cathpert's history had always been shrouded in mystery. Lowcountry folklore told that the family's rise was expedited by a series of illegal activities which were buried in blood.

One such story said that Judge Holton Cathpert's great-great grandfather was friends with a local legend, George Raynor. Raynor was a suspected pirate who, allegedly, used his fortune to ascend in the ranks of Charleston's polite society. In 1699, the Lords Proprietors gave Raynor ownership of Kiawah Island. Of course, rumors circulated that Raynor kept treasure on Kiawah, where some say it could remain to this day.

As a result, the prevailing gossip was that the Cathpert family lined their pockets by colluding with *pirates*. However, the city's top-brass knew better than to make such remarks publicly. In doing so, they would find themselves on the wrong side of the Cathpert family's fury, and the family's bite was much worse than their bark.

Joseph was well-aware of the Cathpert's reputation as he accepted the invitation to enter Judge Cathpert's residence.

The interior décor was steeped in old world luxury. Barbara Cathpert ushered Joseph from the grand entrance hall into the adjoining parlor. The parlor's crown moldings were as brilliantly white as Barbara's hair. The detailed ceiling frieze told a story of its own as it wrapped around the top of the room. The Iron Leaf Roman bronze chandelier hung from the ceiling in the center of the space, above the expensive furniture.

You've seen one mansion, you've seen them all, Joseph thought, unimpressed as he refocused.

A portrait of two generations of the Cathpert family hung regally above the marble fireplace. The portrait was dated because in it Barbara had black, permed hair. Joseph recognized a more athletic Judge Cathpert behind his wife, and he could only assume the little girl standing in front of them was their daughter.

"*Aah've* always loved that portrait of us." Barbara exclaimed as she followed his gaze.

"Is that your daughter?" Joseph clarified as he pointed to the girl in the picture.

"It is. Her name is Margaret. Margaret married a big city *fella* and moved away. Doesn't have much to do with us these days." Barbara quickly changed the subject.

"Would you like a cup of coffee, hun?" She asked as she stood next to the fireplace with her hands clasped behind her frail back.

"No ma'am, I'm fine," Joseph politely responded.

Barbara extended her arm to a silk couch, suggesting Joseph take a seat. She positioned herself in a high-back, green chair near the room's antique grand piano.

"So...what has Holton done this time?"

Joseph was surprised by the brazen comment as he sunk deep into the couch. He was fascinated by how quickly Barbara had assumed her husband was in trouble.

"Well, ma'am, I just want to talk to him about a photograph, that's all." Joseph pulled out the picture he had taken from Dr. Lyon's office and handed it to Barbara. He continued.

"That's a young Judge Cathpert in the picture, isn't it?"

"Oh yes, it most certainly is. Look how *handsum* he looks in his cadet uniform. Hard to believe he would turn out *lahk* he did." Barbara said as she studied the photo.

"He's just skin and bones now."

"Mrs. Cathpert, another gentleman in that picture, James Henderson. Do you see his name written there at the bottom of the photo?" It took Barbara a second to match the names at the bottom of the dated picture with the corresponding person.

"Yes, sir, *Aah* do."

"Do you recognize him?" Joseph asked.

The elderly woman held the picture up into the light, "He looks familiar, but with all the folks Holton knows, *Aah* can't be sure."

Barbara handed the photograph back to Joseph and gingerly rose from her chair.

"He may be one of the island crew." Barbara walked over to a wooden bookcase next to the fireplace and thumbed through some of the leather-bound books on one of the shelves.

"Island crew, ma'am?"

"It's a whole different world, son. One they *lahk* to keep hidden from the rest of us."

"Would you care to elaborate?" Joseph requested, curious to hear more.

"Ah, here it is!" She exclaimed with excitement. Barbara blew dust off the fragile spine of a book and returned to her chair and opened the book on her lap.

Barbara turned to a chapter and handed the book to Joseph. The phrase THE BARRIER ISLANDS AND THE CATHPERT FAMILY was stenciled in fine calligraphy in the center of the yellowed page.

Joseph was confused, "I'm sorry, Mrs. Cathpert, I don't understand."

Barbara was surprised by Joseph's ignorance.

"You're *swimmin'* with sharks, son, and you don't even know it."

Chapter 33

David and Sarah awoke to sunny skies outside the double stacked windows of their hotel room at the Rhett's Bluff Inn. The blinds hung halfway down the wall and gave way to the picturesque view of the majestic Kiawah River, just beyond the Inn's back lawn. The white wood ceiling brightened the space and a pair of lemon-colored chairs added a splash of citrus to the sitting area which sat adjacent to a mounted television.

Sarah yawned as she stretched her arms high in the air. She rolled out of the soft bed leaving her body's image embedded in the mattress and meandered into the sitting room. Sarah turned on the in-room coffee machine for a quick caffeine kick.

The pleasant aroma of coffee roused David from a deep, dreamless sleep. Sarah was disappointed when she saw him put the pillow over his head and roll over instead of joining her. She flipped on the television to nudge him in the right direction.

With the sound of the national news as an alarm clock, David begrudgingly let his feet hit the carpet and sat on the edge of the bed as he moved his neck in a rolling motion. The cracks and pops that followed helped loosen the tightness that had developed overnight.

Although David had successfully distanced himself from the non-stop billable hour grind that his former large law firm demanded, he still had trouble stopping himself from making to-do lists each morning as he woke up. Usually, he'd have his entire day mapped out before he even brushed his teeth.

David asked Sarah to make him a cup of black coffee as he wandered over to his laptop bag, removed his computer, and planted himself in one of the yellow chairs. Sarah obliged as she set the piping hot coffee mug on a side table next to David's chair along with a judgmental look.

"What?" David asked as he fired up his computer.

"You know *what*. You said you'd take a few days off." Sarah reminded as she sat on the other lemon chair.

"I'm just checking emails. No conference calls, I promise."

Truth be told, Sarah had come to respect David's insatiable work ethic. As such, she gave him significant latitude in that department. But there had to be a line and sitting in a hotel room hunched over a computer screen at the beach was *the line*.

"Hey, babe, you up for going to the beach around lunch?"

"Maybe." David responded, half-listening.

"With the hurricane headed our way this may be our only day to enjoy the ocean."

"Oh, yeah, the hurricane. Any updates on that?" David asked as he deleted several spam emails.

"The news said we're directly in its path. Not looking good. So, let's redeem today and get outside. What do you say?"

David nodded as he put up his email's out-of-office message and closed his laptop.

"Done already?" Sarah was shocked.

"No…but like you said, we may only have one beach day. Emails can wait."

As David and Sarah scampered out of their hotel room, they inadvertently left the television on. The news turned its coverage from the weather to a developing story out of the nation's capital. The anchor grew solemn as she reported the tragedy.

"In other news, controversial Washington, D.C. radio talk show host, Jackson Seymour, was found dead this morning in his Arlington, Virginia, apartment. Local authorities suspect foul play…"

Chapter 34

Industrial fishing occurs in over fifty percent of the world's oceans. The captain of the rickety fishing vessel, the *Elizabeth-Grace*, intended to push the limits of that statistic. The captain had ignored repeated warnings from the boat's South Georgia headquarters regarding the severity of Hurricane Mary.

The captain was a legend in the Georgian fishing community. He had developed his reputation by consistently sailing into port with two or three times the fresh catch his competitors delivered. As such, he wasn't about to have his good name tarnished by some wind.

Just a little longer, then we'll be out of it, was the mantra he repeated to himself as the waters grew choppier around the vessel's rusted hull. The captain's ego would never let him admit it, but he had made a grave miscalculation regarding the hurricane's trajectory, speed, and severity. He should have listened when he had the chance; now, it was too late. They were in the thick of it.

The captain was alone at the ship's helm and the bridge was eerily quiet. He had ordered the other six members of his crew to remain below deck and hunker down, preparing for the worst. The captain reassured them the nastiest bits would pass within the hour. But that was just wishful thinking.

Not only did the captain want to shelter his crew from the elements, but also from the reality of their bleak situation. If they saw the size of the waves towering over the *Elizabeth-Grace*, they would panic.

This was the worst hurricane the captain had seen in his three decades at sea. The waves were as large as mountains and the wind was more punishing than a tornado. Even the raindrops seemed to have sinister intentions as they continually pounded the ship's deck. At one point, the captain could have sworn he even heard the hurricane *growl*, like a caged beast hellbent on destruction.

The *Elizabeth-Grace* was eighteen nautical miles east of Cumberland Island, off the Georgia coast. The captain had sent out the distress signal and repeated the ship's last known coordinates into the black radio receiver. No answer. He tried again and again.

"Mayday, mayday! I repeat, the *Elizabeth-Grace* is at 30.771583 and 81.112617, do you copy?! Over!!"

Only static came back as the vessel's bow suddenly tilted toward the heavens. For a second, the captain caught a brief glimpse of the dark clouds as they swirled in the sky, like marble. The visual psychedelic euphoria snapped back to reality as the boat dropped down the backside of a massive wave.

As the bow of the ship blasted into the water, the centrifugal force caused the captain to lose his footing and jolt forward, face first. The sound of his nose breaking on the ship's wheel was the last thing he heard before the world went black.

With the captain unconscious on the floor and blood pouring from his broken nose, the unmanned fishing vessel thrashed wildly in the open sea. It was now at the mercy of Mary.

Below deck the crew knew something was wrong. One of the crew members jumped down from his elevated berth and balanced himself on the flooded floor. Disobeying the captain's direct orders to stay below deck, he headed for the cabin's stairs toward the bridge.

Water cascaded down the steps as he ascended. The courageous crew member took two steps forward holding on to the wall for balance. The other crew helplessly looked on from their bunks, praying their boatmate would make it to the bridge safely. Sadly, he would not.

Without warning, the crew member felt his feet leave the ground as he floated, suspended in midair. His body slammed into the wall and somersaulted on to, what once was, the ceiling. The boat had capsized.

After several panicked seconds, the crew members accepted their fate – the *Elizabeth-Grace* was upside-down in the Atlantic Ocean and sinking fast. There was nothing they could do now but make their peace with God.

In minutes, the *Elizabeth-Grace* was completely submerged, plummeting to the bottom of the sea. Hurricane Mary had claimed another victim and her next stop was Charleston.

Chapter 35

David's arm was casually draped around Sarah's shoulder as they exchanged romantic glances in the backseat of the on-island shuttle. The Inn wisely offered bathing suits and beach towel service that members and guests could use, free of charge. As such, David and Sarah both donned the Inn's complimentary swimsuits and looked forward to a couple uninterrupted hours of beach time.

David and Sarah were finally able to relax. Tommy Felton's suspicious death and the warning from the stern FBI agent were slowly fading into the recesses of their minds. The Lowcountry had that calming effect. It was the perfect place to recharge a weary soul.

As the shuttle approached the boardwalk, the driver suggested they set up camp near the world-renowned Ocean Course Clubhouse.

"If *yuah* hungry, *dey* have *da* best *burgahs* on *da* island!" The driver informed in his Jamaican accent.

A juicy cheeseburger and a cold draft beer sounded great to David and Sarah.

"*Da* shuttle stops by *dis* boardwalk every *tirty* minutes. Enjoy!" David slid the driver a twenty and he and Sarah wandered down the wooden boardwalk toward the sound of crashing waves. The scent of the ocean air filled their lungs as they made their way past sand dunes and onto the beach.

The mid-morning tide was moving out which made the extent of the shoreline visible to the naked eye. They walked down the beach toward the Ocean Course Clubhouse as happy families sped by on bicycles. Above them, seagulls squawked and floated, almost frozen in the sky, waiting for generous beachgoers to share their snacks.

Just offshore, a Brown Pelican dove into the water for its lunch. *It's lovely here*, David thought as he listened to the gentle roar of the methodic waves tumbling onto one another.

Eager to soak up some rays, Sarah laid the blue and yellow beach towels on the soft sand. She retrieved a small bottle of SPF 30 sunscreen from her purse, another gift from the Inn, and began slathering it on her porcelain face. She encouraged David to do the same.

"I've got to use the men's room and I don't feel like peeing in the ocean," David crudely announced as he studied his surroundings for the nearest restroom. Sarah rolled her eyes, placed her knock-off sunglasses on her lotioned face, and reclined on her towels.

David trudged through thick sand, which became heavier with every step. He finally reached a paved pathway leading past three prominent flagpoles adjacent to a pristine putting green on the backside of the Ocean Course Clubhouse. Beyond the putting green was the large brick and wood-shingled gray building where he would, no doubt, find a restroom.

David passed a foursome of golfers on the practice green as he snuck past a standing Rolex clock which stood grandly for all to see. He then quietly dipped into one of the clubhouses' open side doors which led straight into the men's locker room.

After David finished his business, he wandered through the golf pro shop and emerged to find another sitting area with oversized windows, a massive fireplace, and wood-beamed ceiling.

A glance down a side hall revealed two dining options, the more formal, *Atlantic Room*, and the less formal, *Ryder Cup Bar*. It was probably too early for a cocktail, but David was tempted.

He strolled onto the Ryder Cup Bar's immaculate wraparound porch which sat below the structure's dormers. He paused for a moment to watch a confident golfer sink his final putt on the 18th green and celebrate with high-fives to his friends. Sitting just a hundred feet to his left, David recognized a familiar face – it was the golf pro, Jacob Blake.

"Hey Jacob, is that you?" David hollered as he walked down the porch steps.

Jacob was on his cell phone and put up his index finger, signaling it would only be a minute. Jacob then hurriedly relocated to the far side of the putting green to finish his private conversation.

Surprised by Jacob's speedy exodus, David settled into one of the Adirondack chairs on the back lawn. Obviously, Jacob was discussing something he didn't want David to overhear.

"…I have to go. Stoneman's here and he may have heard me talking to you." Jacob listened intently to the instructions on the other end of the phone.

"I know we're running out of time. I'll take care of it." He assured the person on the other end of the line.

Jacob ended the call and walked back across the putting green and resumed his seat.

"Sorry, about that, Dave! That was my mother, it's her birthday today!" Jacob lied.

Just keep smiling and keep your stories straight, Jacob reminded himself. One slip up and the whole jig is up.

Chapter 36

The dusty Cathpert family history book rested on Special Agent Joseph Manheim's lap as he sat in the parlor of the Cathpert's home. Barbara Cathpert had been a pleasant host for, what Joseph had thought would be a routine spousal interview. But it was turning into something more.

"You see, Agent Manheim, *Aah* grew up in *Chaahs-tun*, but was from the wrong side of the tracks." Barbara said as she shifted in her chair.

"*Aah* married into privilege with the Cathpert family, but was told not to ask too many questions about the family's business." Barbara said as she folded her hands.

"*Aah* had always suspected they had made their fortune by unsavory means..." Barbara looked Joseph in the eye. "Piracy, to be exact."

Joseph was stunned. She had to be joking.

"Pirates, huh? Well, the judge is a *lawyer*." Joseph said with a smirk as he began to thumb through the old pages of the Cathpert family history book. He glanced up and found Barbara staring at him. She didn't even crack a smile.

"Oh, *you are* serious."

"Why are you telling me this, Mrs. Cathpert? I'm not here to solve piracy crimes from a century ago, I'm here to—" Barbara interrupted.

"Because, Agent Manheim, *Aah* was recently diagnosed with stage four cancer and only have a few months left. *Aah've* covered for my husband and his family for decades and just don't want to leave this world living a lie."

Joseph just received a pseudo-confession from the matriarch of one of the most powerful families in the South – and he didn't even ask for it! Barbara continued.

"My husband has silenced many people for airing the Cathpert's dirty laundry. Members of the house staff, Holton's mistresses, even the family lawyer went missing some years back. All of them paid off or, more likely, at the bottom of the ocean."

She looked out the parlor's window and up at the bright blue sky as if she could see into heaven.

"*Aah* guess *Aah'm* saying that whatever it is you suspect Holton may be caught up in...he probably did it." The words floated in the air like thick volcanic ash.

She's willing to cooperate. What now? Joseph bounced his right heel anxiously on the two-hundred-year-old hardwood floors.

"Do you know when Judge Cathpert will be home, ma'am? I'd love to bring him into this conversation."

"He won't be home for days. *Aah'm* sure Holton's with one of his lady friends. *Aah'm* happy to give you the address of the beach house, if you think that would help."

Barbara retrieved a pen and small notepad from a side table and jotted down the address. She then disappeared into the kitchen and returned with a rectangular paper guest pass for Joseph to display on his car's dashboard when he arrived at Kiawah Island's security gates.

"You'll need this to get in." After handing Joseph the pass, Barbara remained standing. It was her polite way to signal that it was time for him to leave. Joseph took the cue.

Barbara escorted him to the front door. As she opened it, Joseph realized he was still holding the family's book.

"Oops, almost walked out with this," Joseph acknowledged as he tried to return the book to its owner.

"Keep it for a while, hun…and read some of it. You look *lahk* a smart young man. *Aah'm* sure you'll be able to put the pieces together." She smiled.

Joseph stepped out onto the front porch and into the warm Charleston weather. He turned and thanked his host. As he did, a golden glimmer caught his eye above the doorframe. It was a stained-glass transom window. He hadn't noticed it when he arrived, but now the sun was at high-noon, the stained-glass was on full display. The color patterns were intricate, displaying two white magnolia plants on either side of the rectangular window with a yellow lightning bolt in the center.

"Beautiful window," he said as he pointed above Barbara's head.

"I recognize the magnolia but, just curious, what's the significance of the lightning bolt?"

The pleasant woman turned serious almost instantly. Barbara leaned out her front door and looked like a hawk down the street to the left then to the right.

"That's the best question you've asked all *mornin'*. Have a nice day." She said as she abruptly shut the door in Joseph's face.

Weird, Joseph thought as he walked on the sidewalk of East Bay Street. Joseph glanced back at the Cathpert's house and, again, studied the curious lightning bolt above the door.

He noticed the blinds inside the house aggressively being drawn. Barbara Cathpert was shutting out the world. She had said her piece. Perhaps, she had said *too much.*

Chapter 37

J acob Blake nestled into his Adirondack chair on the back lawn of the Ocean Course Clubhouse. *Stay calm, and act natural*, Jacob internally repeated to himself.

"How do you like the island so far, Dave?"

"It's great! The Inn is fantastic. Thanks again for helping us with that."

"Don't mention it." Jacob looked up in the sky as the dark clouds continued to roll in.

"Looks like Hurricane Mary is *gonna* nail us!"

"Yeah, Sarah mentioned something about that this morning. The Inn has storm protocols, right? I can't imagine a place like that not having a good weather plan."

"Oh, absolutely. You ever been on an island in a hurricane?"

"Thankfully, no." David responded.

"It's about as scary as it sounds. There's flooding, rip currents, power outages, debris flying everywhere. Shoot, the entire island can just, sort of, *sink*."

"Crazy." David said as he studied the darker clouds in the distance. Jacob continued.

"The roads become completely impassable, except by boat. I've even heard stories of people who saw alligators swimming down the middle of the freaking street after it floods." Jacob said as he shook his head and crossed one leg over the other.

For the next twenty minutes Jacob regaled David with fabricated stories of Lowcountry hurricanes past. Specifically, about how determined homeowners hunkered down and suffered the dire consequences of their stubbornness.

David was being polite, but waiting on an opportunity to excuse himself and head back to the beach to find Sarah. After Jacob paused long enough to take a breath, he offered a simple directive.

"Basically, if the Inn says *leave*, you should go. Make sense?"

"Thanks for the heads up." David responded as he felt a raindrop hit the top of his head. And then another one on his arm.

"Speaking of the Inn, you should have gotten an email this morning. Assuming the weather is decent, the Inn is hosting a dinner tonight for members and guests. It's included in your room fee." Jacob informed.

"Great, we'll check it out. Thanks!" David glanced at the large standing clock near the putting green and realized he had been sitting there for a while.

"They do special events like this from time-to-time as a way to express their gratitude for all of the money you're paying to stay there." Jacob smirked at his own sarcasm.

Jacob kept talking and David's heart skipped a beat when he saw Sarah trudging up the sand toward the clubhouse with her hands full. She did not look happy and David knew he was in trouble. He interrupted Jacob, quickly excused himself, and jogged across the putting green to meet Sarah before she made it to the clubhouse. He reached her halfway up the walkway.

"Were you ever going to come back, or just leave me by myself all day?!" Sarah complained.

"I was coming back, babe, but I ran into Jacob Blake, and you know how chatty he is."

With Sarah's arms full of bags and beach towels, it was clear she was not interested in excuses. She handed David the sandy towels as penance for his abandonment.

"Jacob was telling me about the island's hurricane protocols."

"Yeah, well that's why I came up here carrying all of our stuff. I got a weather alert on my phone. We should catch the next shuttle back to the hotel before it gets bad."

"Okay. I'll see if the shuttle can pick us up here."

From his cell phone, David called the number the Inn had provided for the shuttle. As they walked into the Ocean Course Clubhouse's large, heavy side doors, he and Sarah wandered past the sitting area with the large fireplace and out to the front porch. They found two vacant rocking chairs where they would wait for the shuttle.

Sarah took a moment to call her son, Mark. She wanted to update him on their revised travel schedule.

While Sarah was on the phone, David set down the towels and casually wandered further down the front walkway. He overheard Jacob's unmistakable voice – he was sternly reprimanding someone. David couldn't help but eavesdrop.

"Like I told you before, the best way to get in undetected is through the *back porch*. Just keep an extra golf ball in your pocket and drop it in the backyard. That way, if you get caught, you can say you were just looking for the ball."

"We get that, Jake, but what if someone is *in the house*? We can't say we're looking for the ball *in the house!*" An unfamiliar, younger voice responded.

David was intrigued by the suspicious banter. He crouched and peered over a tall shrub's hedge. Jacob was huddled next to two young men wearing caddy uniforms.

"Worst case, just tell them you have a bathroom emergency. Maybe they'll buy that. And, remember, you shouldn't be in there for more than five minutes. You know what we're looking for. Just get in, and get out." Jacob instructed.

David heard the Inn's shuttle loudly pull into the clubhouse's circular driveway behind him.

Hey, Dave? The shuttle's here!" Sarah beckoned with her voice carrying.

David scurried back to Sarah and scooped up the sandy beach towels hoping Jacob had not heard Sarah's call. However, as they boarded the shuttle, David's heart sank when he glanced over his shoulder to find Jacob standing in the nearby walkway staring at him – his usual smile, gone.

David turned toward Sarah trying to avoid eye contact with Jacob.

After several seconds, David turned to look out the shuttle's window a second time. Jacob was now nowhere in sight. Then the rain showers started.

David decided not to tell Sarah what he had overheard. However, one thing was for certain: Jacob Blake was no ordinary golf pro.

Chapter 38

Bailey was sitting alone on a small sofa in the living room of Damian's cottage on Captain Maynard's Island. The remote, eleven-acre plot on the far side of Rhett's Bluff seemed like another world altogether. Hard to believe it was only a short two-minute drive from the luxurious Rhett's Bluff Inn.

Captain Maynard's Island was a naturally-fortified bunker – a security detail's dream. Isolated and largely hidden from unsuspecting boats passing by on the Kiawah River. Mediterranean fan palms, dwarf yaupon holly bushes, and saw palmetto plants filled the ground space between the abodes and provided further camouflage.

Just out the window and by a quick tally, Bailey counted four cottages on the plot, including the one she was staying in. Bailey's cottage appeared to be the smallest of the four. Damian's cottage was much larger, complete with three spacious bedrooms and a full kitchen with stainless steel appliances. The living room was brightly colored with vaulted ceilings which opened to a screened-in porch with panoramic views of the Kiawah River. This wasn't a *cottage*; it was a home.

However, Damian's place wasn't the largest of the group. The cottage next door was even bigger and the only one with its own boat dock. Earlier, Bailey noticed security guards with ear pieces going in and out of that space but never caught a glimpse of the VIP staying there.

While Bailey wanted to relax and enjoy her picturesque surroundings, she could not shake the red flags from the night before when they had arrived. She wasn't used to being out of the loop, but that's exactly where she found herself.

Bailey glanced out at the Kiawah River. A couple boats and kayaks buoyed in the choppy water. She even saw dolphin fins cresting as birds of various shapes and sizes skimmed the water's surface searching for their next meal. Even with the dark purple storm clouds overhead, it was a breathtaking sight which *almost* made up for the growing sense of impending danger developing in the pit of Bailey's stomach.

Chapter 39

Nearly a half hour later, Tara, the consultant, meandered into the living room of Damian's cottage wearing a low-cut blouse, short skirt, and high heels. She pulled a tube of lipstick from her handbag and reapplied a distinctive shade of red to her full lips.

Did she just come from Damian's bedroom? Bailey wondered, trying not to stare.

"We were just talking." Tara said, as if she had read Bailey's mind.

Bailey didn't respond. She wanted Tara to feel her judgment.

Tara then fixed herself a vodka martini with a twist and walked out to the screened-in porch.

It was unclear if Tara was staying with Damian in his cottage. In truth, Bailey didn't want to know. It would just complicate an already bizarre situation. Frankly, Tara being Damian's mistress would be one of the more logical explanations for the curious activity she had witnessed over the last two days.

Damian had instructed the group to dress for dinner that evening at the Rhett's Bluff Inn. The meal would be preceded by a short business meeting in one of the Inn's most private meeting rooms, *the Lagoon Room.* Bailey peeked at the time on her phone – it was 4:55 p.m. *Time to go.*

Rain was methodically tapping on the cottage's roof as Bailey scrolled through her phone to pass the time.

She had made a few calls to her husband, Hunter, earlier in the day, all of which went unanswered. It wasn't unusual he hadn't called her back. Bailey suspected he was likely in a billing frenzy at the firm, or his phone had died. It certainly wasn't uncommon for Hunter to engage in marathon work sessions where he didn't even take the time to use the bathroom, much less charge his cell phone. She planned to try him again after dinner.

Damian emerged from his bedroom fastening a silver cufflink on his shirt's left cuff. His royal blue suit, crisp white shirt, and striped navy tie, signified he was dressed for an evening of business and pleasure.

"We about ready, ladies?" Damian asked as he pulled his shirt sleeve down so it would extend past his jacket. Tara walked in from the porch.

"Yes, we're already late," she announced as if she had been waiting on him for hours.

Damian grabbed three keycards off of the kitchen table.

"Here are spare keys to my place in case you need to get in here for anything later tonight." Damian said as he walked out into the rain and flew down the cottage's wooden stairs to the waiting shuttle bus below.

Bailey smiled. Damian's gesture of publicly democratizing his room keys was, no doubt, made so as not to raise any suspicion about a potential midnight rendezvous with him and Tara. Still, despite his failed attempt at concealment, Bailey preferred to remain blissfully ignorant. Bailey slipped the spare key into an internal zippered-pocket in her dress, along with the keycard to her own room, and ventured out to the shuttle.

The rain was coming down harder and puddles were forming on the side of the half-mile private driveway from Captain Maynard's Island leading to Rhett's Bluff Road as the shuttle puttered along. Until then, Bailey had not considered what would happen if the driveway flooded completely. It certainly wouldn't be good.

Even through the rain, Bailey noticed something odd on the right side of the road. It was an old grave site, which piqued her curiosity.

"Excuse me, sir" Bailey called to the shuttle's driver. "Yes ma'am?" He responded in a Jamaican accent.

"Was that a cemetery back there?"

"Yes, it was," the driver responded. "*Dat* was *Mistah* and *Misses* Shoolbred. *Mistah* Shoolbred was *da* first British consul to *dah* U.S. *Dey* owned half of *dah* island in *dah* early eighteen hundreds."

"Hmm. Interesting, thank you." *Wow, this place really goes back a long way*, Bailey thought as the shuttle continued down Rhett's Bluff Road. She changed the subject.

"Damian, who are we meeting before dinner?" Bailey asked as they approached the Inn's wraparound driveway.

Damian looked at Tara, who shook her head indicating he wasn't to answer the question. Bailey witnessed the non-verbal exchange and rolled her eyes.

Perfect, she thought, *I have a boss who's wrapped around the finger of the ice queen*. Despite her usual poise, Bailey had a slight temper which occasionally reared its ugly head. Today was one of those days. She had had enough.

"You know what, Damian? This is getting ridiculous!" She shouted, commanding his attention and startling the driver.

"Who is this person and why am I being kept in the dark about *everything*? It's unacceptable and I deserve answers!" Bailey exclaimed as she pointed at Tara.

"Relax, Bailey, it's just a business meeting. It'll take too long to explain. Just go with it, okay? And as I said before, Tara is my personal consultant. That's it."

Bailey crossed her arms and huffed a sigh of frustration – she wasn't going to get answers from Damian. Consequently, she was done. That final blow-off had put her over the edge. When she returned to Atlanta, she would put in her two weeks' notice and beg Townsend & Moore to take her back. She just needed to get through the next two days, then she would be home free.

Chapter 40

Rain trickled down Special Agent Joseph Manheim's tinted car windows as his wiper blades flapped methodically back and forth.

Joseph suspected he could be onto the case of the century. He could see the headlines now: LOCAL FBI AGENT TAKES DOWN CATHPERT FAMILY. Joseph smiled just thinking about the fanfare.

Moments earlier, on the drive from downtown Charleston, Joseph had checked-in with his local FBI office's Special Agent in Charge (SAC). The conversation was brief, as usual.

Joseph reported he was following up on several leads related to Tommy Felton's death, which may also be connected to the missing SURC. He conveniently left out that he had visited the Cathpert residence. That minor detail would not have resonated well with his social-climbing boss. Joseph would have immediately been pulled off the case and relegated to a desk job until Christmas.

Although Joseph was known for his 'don't ask permission, ask for forgiveness' approach to investigations, if he went *too far*, his head would roll. It was a delicate balance, but a risk he was willing to take. Especially for the opportunity to bag a whale like Holton Cathpert.

The SAC concluded his obligatory CYA monologue, reminding Joseph about the disciplinary ramifications of violating the FBI's witness harassment policy. Joseph half-heartedly acknowledged the warning and rushed off the phone. He had things to do.

Joseph entered a roundabout near the entrance to Kiawah Island and pulled into Freshfields Village, the local market. He wanted to take a few moments to review the Cathpert family history book, in private, before speaking to Judge Cathpert. Perhaps it included details relevant to the investigation. However, Joseph was more curious than anything.

As he grabbed the book from his passenger seat, a small dust cloud shot into the air and settled on his car's dashboard. Joseph skimmed the book's fragile pages. He stopped on a chapter that detailed the Cathperts' connection to the 'Barrier Islands,' as they called them. The pages contained old maps of Kiawah when it was an Indian settlement. Back then it was spelled *Kayawah* and small stars were included on one of the maps. Joseph turned the page.

The brittle page was dog-eared and contained hand-written notations scribbled in the margin. The notes were written in old cursive and were barely legible. Joseph squinted and held the book close to his face. The only word he could clearly read was the word *gold*.

Coincidentally, Joseph had been a history buff since he was a teenager. In his youth, he had spent much of his free time either cleaning up at YMCA pick-up basketball games, or reading books about South Carolina's history.

To his closest friends he was a walking paradox; a nerdy jock. However, stereotypes aside, Joseph salivated at the opportunity to examine the archives of one of the most long-tenured families in the Southeast. Barbara Cathpert's suggestion that the family was involved in nefarious maritime activity only added to the intrigue as he moved from chapter to chapter.

The book was laid out chronologically and Joseph turned to the section describing Kiawah in the eighteenth century. He read how the Lords Proprietors granted Kiawah to Captain George Raynor in 1699.

Joseph recalled that Raynor was suspected, by some, to have been a pirate and sailed his ship, *the Loyal Jamaica*, into Charleston Harbor in 1692. Thereafter, rumor was that he successfully integrated into Charleston's polite society and the rest was history.

Joseph's eyes were glued to the pages as the cursive paragraphs described, in detail, multiple events in which the Cathperts conducted business and socialized with Raynor and other prominent members of Charleston society. But, unlike the history books, this account was written in *first person* by the Cathpert patriarchs.

The account detailed personality traits, family squabbles, financial information, and even drinking habits of some of the most celebrated names in Charleston's rich history. However, that information paled in comparison to what was waiting in the next chapter. Joseph's fingers turned the page and he read the first two sentences. His jaw dropped. *No way!*

Chapter 41

For ages, Lowcountry historians have studied the Golden Age of piracy and its connection to South Carolina. In the early eighteenth century, the epicenter of the pirate's stronghold was the Pirate Republic of Nassau in the Caribbean. Eventually, pirates crept up the coast and landed in the Southern coastal cities.

Charleston's most notable pirate event took place in May of 1718, when Charleston Harbor was blockaded by South Carolina's own "gentleman pirate," Stede Bonnet, and Edward Teach, more famously known as "Blackbeard."

As a history aficionado, Joseph possessed a nearly encyclopedic knowledge of Charleston's history leading up to the Civil War. Consequently, he was well-aware of Blackbeard's Charleston blockade.

While there are multiple accounts, Joseph recalled that the blockade lasted only for a few tense days as Blackbeard's ship, *the Queen Anne's Revenge*, anchored near the city. Charlestonians were understandably unnerved, but little did they know that Blackbeard did not desire riches or rum – he wanted medicine.

When Blackbeard received the medical supplies, he left Charleston and he and Stede Bonnet parted ways. Soon thereafter, Bonnet was captured by a Charlestonian named Colonel William Rhett, whose home still stands today near Market Street. Eventually, Blackbeard was captured and killed off the coast of North Carolina by British lieutenant, turned captain, Robert Maynard.

Joseph turned his attention back to the cursive text in the book. He squinted to see the words.

Of Charles Towne blockade, Stede Bonnet alerted Capt. Teach that my father, Dr. Cathpert, would provide medical assistance for a price. Capt. Teach requested Dr. Cathpert come aboard the Queen Anne's Revenge and treat the crew. Payment for services rendered was made at secret island location. Gold is safe, maps destroyed, and witnesses silenced.

—Montgomery Cathpert, 1718

Joseph looked up. *Does this say what I think it says?* He raised his eyebrows as reality sunk in. He was almost giddy.

The Cathperts gave medical care to Blackbeard during the Charleston blockade! He couldn't help but chuckle. Barbara Cathpert wasn't kidding. The Cathpert family did build their fortune colluding with pirates. That headline alone would be the leading story on every major news outlet in the state.

Joseph read on; his eyes glued to each word. The words *Kiawah* and *gold* were, again, mentioned several times in subsequent pages, along with thorough accounts of other commercial engagements between the Cathperts and notorious pirates. *This was too good to be true!*

The car's air conditioning system continued to blast cool air in Joseph's face causing his contacts to dry out. He was barely taking time to blink – this was all too intriguing. He stopped on a page titled *War of Northern Aggression*, a phrase used to describe the American Civil War.

Under the heading the page was blank, save for an unusual notation scribbled in all capital letters at the bottom.

VERITAS VINCIT SILENCED

Joseph was perplexed. Curious, he pulled his cell phone from his pocket and performed a quick internet search for the Latin phrase.

Apparently, during the Civil War, the phrase *Veritas Vincit*, meaning "truth triumphs," was written on the wall of one of the abandoned Kiawah mansions.

Veritas Vincit seemed to have some connection to the Cathpert family. *But what? What truth had been silenced?*

Joseph turned to the back of the book. The chapter entries stopped in 1921. The final entry contained no words, just a symbol: *a lightning bolt.*

It's the same symbol that was embedded in the stained glass at the Cathpert home.

The rain picked up and Joseph observed vacationers running for cover in the boutiques that lined the streets of Freshfields Village. Joseph set the book on his passenger seat and put the car into drive. It was time to pay Judge Cathpert a visit.

Chapter 42

The Rhett's Bluff Inn's Lagoon Room was truly one-of-a-kind, especially in the Lowcountry. The space was five-hundred square feet and could comfortably seat twenty. Unbeknownst to most Inn members was the fact the lobby level was clandestinely raised more than two-dozen feet above sea level, allowing the Inn's proprietors to build out the secret meeting space below the lobby without fear of flooding. Still, during the Inn's construction, no expense was spared utilizing costly, thick limestone walls at the foundation to ensure the lower level remained dry during storms and hurricanes.

The Lagoon Room featured a luxurious chandelier which hung regally from the middle of the twelve-foot-tall ceiling. The cream walls complemented the patterned carpet, upon which sat a number of hand carved wooden chairs with silk cushions that lined the walls, waiting to be placed.

The Lagoon Room's crowning feature, however, was the floor-to-ceiling *windowed wall* which abutted a manmade lagoon, giving the room an aquarium-like ambiance. The lagoon itself was deep and the windowed wall allowed only two feet of sunlight to shine through near the ceiling during the daytime.

Oftentimes during meetings, attendees would see alligators swim right up to the glass wall. The gators taunted the guests and flashed their razor-sharp teeth, as if playing a game of cat and mouse. The reptiles would then disappear in the cloudy water.

With one-hundred twenty-five ponds throughout Kiawah Island's thirteen square miles, and with between five and seven-hundred alligators running loose on the island, it was unclear how many alligators made *this* lagoon their home. Still, one thing was certain, with the alligators' ability to swim up to 20 mph, any living thing that fell into the lagoon didn't stand a chance.

At night, the Lagoon Room's chandelier was the only source of light. It was eerily cavernous and guests were left feeling vulnerable, wondering what predators lurked in the dark waters, watching them…ready to strike.

Damian, Bailey, and Tara sat quietly around a circular table in the middle of the Lagoon Room waiting for a VIP to arrive. The sun was sinking over the salt marsh and the red and orange colors of the sky made the lagoon's surface appear as if it were on fire.

Damian stared at the water's surface, almost in a trance. Bailey could tell he was burdened by *something*, but didn't want to address it in front of Tara who was preoccupied scrolling through her phone.

Suddenly, the door swung open. A tall older gentleman with a military-style haircut, bulging biceps, and no-nonsense disposition entered. Bailey recognized him as the same person who met them on the tarmac at JZI airport and who transported them to the Inn by SURC the night before.

The military man was followed by an individual who Bailey immediately recognized. It was Marcos Roberts, the White House chief of staff.

Marcos was middle-aged with short salt-and-pepper hair. He was of average height, athletically built, and looked great in a suit. His tanned skin and deep brown eyes handsomely accented his bleached white teeth. He was attractive, confident, and immediately commanded any room – a true politician.

Marcos strode toward them with his shoulders back and head up. The subtle orange pinstripes in his charcoal gray suit accented his rust-colored tie. Marcos fully embodied the appearance and swagger of a typical Washington insider.

Damian snapped out of his daze and Tara set her phone on the table. Both rose to greet Marcos. Bailey followed their lead.

"*Prometheus*, it's a pleasure to see you again." Damian extended his hand for a hearty handshake.

Prometheus? Why did Damian just call Marcos Roberts *Prometheus*? Bailey perished the thought and assumed it was a just nickname of which she was unaware.

"Likewise, Damian, it's great to be back at the Inn!" Marcos responded in his deep voice as he returned the shake with equal vigor. He then moved to Tara.

"Tara, good to see you, darling. I think the last time was late June, right?"

Tara nodded with an unexpected smirk.

"That's right. How have you been, Marcos?" She asked with an uncharacteristically energetic tone.

Bailey was thoroughly irritated that Tara was on a first-name basis with the White House chief of staff. *Does she have her claws in him too?* Bailey wondered, masking her annoyance. Marcos approached her and extended his hand.

"Hi there, I'm Marcos Roberts."

"Yes sir, I know who you are, Mr. Roberts. I'm Bailey Thompson, General Counsel for Menda Industrial Corporation. It's nice to meet you, sir."

Marcos turned back to Damian.

"Looks like you hired another shark to keep you out of trouble, huh, Damian?" Marcos winked at Bailey signaling he was joking before taking his seat.

The intimidating figure with the bulging biceps positioned himself at parade rest near the door.

"Oh, I'm terribly sorry, folks, do you know James Henderson?" Marcos pointed.

"He's head of my security this weekend. I told the secret service to take a hike for a few days."

"Yes, Sergeant Henderson transported us to the island last night." Damian responded.

Because time was of the essence, Marcos dove straight in.

"Well, as you know, Menda Industrial is the highest-earning company in our organization's private sector business portfolio. You've done a fantastic job, Damian."

That comment caused Damian to beam a smile. Marcos continued.

"Bailey, have these two filled you in on the details?" Marcos asked. Tara quickly interjected.

"No, Marcos, she doesn't know the *whole* story. Let's keep it high-level, shall we?" Tara glanced at Damian, confirming he agreed. Bailey was, again, offended by the blatant attempt to keep her uninformed. Still, she didn't dare respond unprofessionally in the presence of such a high-ranking political figure.

"Okay, I'll keep it at thirty-thousand feet. But she signed an NDA with the company, right?" Marcos questioned.

"Of course," Damian responded. Marcos continued.

"Sergeant Henderson tells me the bags arrived safely. Thanks for that. I assume it's the full amount we anticipated coming out of the Middle East channel this year?"

"Yes, sir, it's all there. Every dollar. And for our end, have the project commitments been finalized?" Damian asked with interest as he put his elbows on the table.

"We're still working on that. As you know, government contracts are tricky, especially overseas."

Never wanting to let disappointing news hang in the air, Marcos offered reassurance.

"The funds you delivered will certainly help, but we're still maneuvering our political contacts in the region to finalize. We suspect they'll cooperate, but it's taking longer than expected." Marcos pointed to Sergeant Henderson and continued.

"We have the muscle, and if all goes according to plan, Menda Industrial will be making boatloads of money over the next five years thanks to good ole' Uncle Sam. All completely legal, of course." Marcos lied as he smiled at Bailey.

Tara spoke up.

"Just keep us posted, Marcos. Also, I'm sure you've heard that we had an issue with another whistleblower this week."

"I know. It's not going to be a problem, is it, Damian?"

"Not at all, sir. This kid got all noble. I mean, we were willing to pay him off and then—" Tara interjected. Damian's oversharing annoyed her.

"I think he gets the point, Damian. No need for unnecessary commentary." Tara was stern. Bailey sat in silence, witnessing her type-A boss get reprimanded by a beautiful seductress in high heels. The puppet master continued.

"FARCO handled it for us, Marcos. The whistleblower met with members of our law firm in Atlanta before his death. They're *our* lawyers, so, the secrets are safe."

A cold chill flew down Bailey's back. *Oh, no – Hunter!* She prayed his name did not come up.

Marcos nodded, allowing his deeply analytical mind time to absorb the news.

Bailey could feel Marcos's stare. He was unsettled by her silence. However, Bailey simply didn't know what to say. The conversation was so cryptic that she had no clue what they were wanting her to do. Sensing Bailey's confusion,

Damian stepped in.

"Bailey used to work at the law firm, Townsend & Moore. Her husband, Hunter, is still a partner there. Isn't that right, Bailey?"

Bailey was between a rock and hard place. She was trapped in a room with one of the most powerful men in the country, and her boss was implying he wanted her to convince Marcos that her boy scout husband would cover up Menda's illegal activity. Bailey's only option was to go along with it until she was able to extract herself from the conversation, the Inn, and this job.

"I need a bit more information, but I can certainly address any legal concerns with Hunter right away...as long as what we're doing, or plan to do, is legal, of course." Bailey responded.

The room was uncomfortably silent. Marcos pursed his lips and looked at Damian, dissatisfied with Bailey's answer.

At that moment, there was a splash at the lagoon's surface. An enormous, scaly alligator crested the top of the water and then plunged down along the glass.

Marcos stood as he glanced at his expensive gold watch.

"I think it's time for cocktails. Will you all be joining us for dinner this evening?" Marcos asked as he pushed in his chair and buttoned his top jacket button.

"Absolutely. We'll see you up there." Damian assured.

"Is *everyone* here this weekend, Marcos?" Tara asked as she, Bailey, and Damian made their way to the door too.

"We had a few who couldn't make it due to the weather. But I'll brief them when I'm en route back to D.C. Everyone else is here." Marcos remarked as Sergeant Henderson opened the door for the group.

Bailey was full of anxiety. She had seen and heard too much and was coming dangerously close to being a co-conspirator in *something*. Whatever was happening this weekend, she wanted no part of it.

As the group made their way from the Lagoon Room and down the long hallway to the elevator, Marcos and Tara whispered to each other. Tara then turned and asked Bailey to accompany her down a side hallway which she claimed was a shortcut. Unbeknownst to Bailey, Marcos and Damian stayed back and took the elevator up to the Inn's lobby.

The further Bailey and Tara walked down the side hallway, the more the fancy décor diminished. Finally, they arrived at a door and Tara knocked three times. An armed FARCO operative let them in. Bailey gasped.

Her husband, Hunter, was tied to a chair with two other armed operatives on either side of him. She ran to him. He was barely conscious.

"What have you done?!" Bailey screamed.

One of the guards stuck a gun in Bailey's face.

"You gave Marcos Roberts the wrong answer in there, sweetheart. We don't know if we can trust you anymore. Now, you'll sit *here* until we figure out what to do with you and your husband." Tara coldly responded.

With that, an operative unfolded a metal chair and ordered her to sit. As her hands were being handcuffed to the chair, all she could think about was her children. She had to devise a plan to get her and Hunter off the island, and fast.

Chapter 43

As Joseph approached Kiawah Island's first security gate, he made sure the guest pass Barbara Cathpert had given him was prominently displayed on his car's dashboard. As a result, he sailed through the gate without issue.

He pulled his car over, rolled down the driver's-side window, and asked one of the guards if they had an extra island visitor's map he could reference.

The guard retrieved a map from his truck's glove compartment and handed it to Joseph. He thanked the guard and continued on Kiawah Island Parkway.

He drove for several minutes searching for an inconspicuous place to pull over. He had Judge Cathpert's island home address, but thought it prudent to better understand the *entire area* just in case he had to make a quick escape.

Joseph saw a sign for Night Heron Park and made a right turn onto Sea Forest Drive. He pulled into a vacant parking lot next to a soggy outdoor basketball court. Even though he was years removed from competitive basketball, Joseph always felt most comfortable near a court.

He unfolded the glossy paper map and was shocked by how many homes were on the island. *There was over a thousand.*

Joseph ran his fingers along the page until he located Rhett's Bluff. There were only a handful of structures reflected in that area, all of which had the word "PRIVATE" written in prominent, bold letters. *Nothing on Rhett's Bluff has identifiers…interesting.*

Joseph double-checked the address Barbara had given him and cross-referenced it with the GPS on his cell phone. He had plugged in the correct address.

According to the map there was only one road in or out of Rhett's Bluff. All other options of ingress or egress would have to be by boat on the Kiawah River.

Joseph also noticed a small plot called *Captain Maynard's Island* which sat on the backside of Rhett's Bluff – the name looked familiar to him. Then it clicked.

He typed the names *Rhett* and *Maynard* into his phone's internet search box, along with the word *Charleston*. When the results came up, he couldn't help but smile. *William Rhett* and *Robert Maynard* were famous for capturing notorious pirates, Stede Bonnet and Blackbeard. As such, it appeared that Rhett's Bluff and Captain Maynard's Island had been named after *pirate hunters*. Given what he had just read in the Cathpert family history book, the irony was almost comical.

Joseph folded the map, pulled out of Night Heron Park, and headed toward Rhett's Bluff. He breezed through the island's second security gate and then passed a bass pond.

The rain beat down more heavily. Joseph increased the speed on his windshield wipers as he saw the outline of an immaculate hotel in the distance. However, his car's navigation system instructed him to take a hard left turn away from the hotel's entrance and turn onto New Settlement Road, and then on to River Marsh Lane. Within minutes, his phone's GPS indicated he had arrived at the Cathpert beach house.

Joseph parked on the side of the desolate street. A single home was nestled back in the lot and away from the road. He grabbed the Cathpert family history book, the photograph he had confiscated from Dr. Lyons, and covered them both with his waterproof FBI jacket. He then exited the vehicle.

As Joseph ambled up the paved walkway, the home's front door opened. Judge Cathpert's sickly thin frame was easily recognizable, even at a distance.

The judge emerged on the front porch with a young, scantily-clad brunette woman who was not Mrs. Cathpert. They shared a passionate kiss as Joseph drew closer. He overheard Judge Cathpert instructing the woman to walk to the Inn in order to get a ride home.

"But, Holton, it's *rainin'. Aah'l* get my hair *whet*." The woman said in a whiney, childish voice.

"Take this, *darlin'*. This'll pay for a day at the salon." Judge Cathpert reassured as he handed her a large bill. Seemingly satisfied with the payoff, the young woman walked down the white front porch steps.

At that point, they noticed Joseph. The woman passed him with her head down, not wanting to be recognized. Judge Cathpert was staring, his bony arms crossed across his sunken chest.

"Excuse me, young man, but this is private property."

"Yes, sir, Judge Cathpert, I understand. I'm Special Agent Joseph Manheim with the FBI," Joseph held up his credentials.

"I have to ask you a few questions, sir." Joseph climbed the stairs and moved toward the retired judge. As he reached the door, lightning flashed, thunder rolled, and it began to downpour.

Chapter 44

Joseph was soaked as he walked into Judge Cathpert's elegant island home. As he crossed the door's threshold, water pooled on the checkered marble floor beneath him. Judge Cathpert didn't seem to mind. Muddied boots in the corner signaled to Joseph that the judge was used to the elements sneaking into his house. No doubt the Cathperts had a cleaning crew which kept the place tidy each week.

The large white foyer was grand with a red glass blown chandelier hanging from the tall ceiling. A dark wooden staircase ornamented with a distressed banister spiraled up to a second floor.

Judge Cathpert closed the large wooden door behind Joseph and led him into a narrow hallway leading to the back of the house. Hand painted pictures of island scenes hung on the walls as the hallway opened to a living room which also connected to a full kitchen. The home's layered features and coastal color schemes resembled something from a magazine.

Can *Aah* get you *somethin'*? The skinny jurist asked as he poured two fingers of bourbon into a small glass. Judge Cathpert leaned against the marble-topped island in the kitchen and eyeballed Joseph as he fixed his beverage.

"No, sir, Your Honor. I'll just ask my questions and be on my way. But I must say, my clothes are wet and I don't want to ruin your furniture. Do you mind if we sit on the back porch and chat?"

Judge Cathpert acquiesced. He moseyed onto the covered porch as the rain continued to pour. Judge Cathpert sunk down into a large, cushioned chair next to the porch's unlit stone fireplace and invited Joseph to sit across from him in a matching chair.

"No pool?" Joseph asked, half-kidding.

Judge Cathpert chuckled which caused his Gamecocks T-shirt to shake like a towel on a clothesline.

"What can *Aah* do for you? *Ya* know *Aah'm* being nice even *answerin'* questions." The judge reminded, encouraging Joseph to tread lightly.

"Well, sir, I've been visiting folks in town about the death of Mr. Tommy Felton, the local pastor who died earlier this week."

"Okay, *Aah'm* not really sure—" Joseph interrupted Judge Cathpert.

"...I believe there also may be a connection to a missing watercraft which was recently stolen from Joint Base. Frankly, sir, I think you may have information about both."

Joseph just went there and Judge Cathpert's smirk quickly turned into a scowl.

"Agent Manheim, *Aah'm* well-respected in these parts, and *Aah'm* sure my successor *sittin'* on the bench would not be happy to hear you *accusin'* me of—" Again, Joseph interrupted.

"Pardon me, sir, but when the SURC was stolen from Joint Base this became a matter of national security, and thus, a federal issue. I'm not sure your relationships with the local judiciary are relevant to my investigation."

Joseph regretted his knee-jerk jurisdictional tongue-lashing. *Too much*, he thought, *dial it back*.

Judge Cathpert turned bright red. He was fuming. Joseph had just given him the verbal middle finger. The slim jurist took a deep breath, composed himself, and responded.

"*Aah'm* a patient man, Agent Manheim, but *Aah* believe you're *comin'* dangerously close to *drawin'* conclusions you cannot substantiate with evidence. So, *Aah'l* ask you one more time – what proof do you have *connectin'* me to any of that?"

Judge Cathpert was now sitting on the edge of his seat, staring into Joseph's soul. His liquor glass rested on a side table. He was no longer interested in drinking. Joseph had sent a shot across the bow and Judge Cathpert wanted to send one right back.

"I spoke with your wife this morning, sir. She's a sweet lady, but awful chatty." Joseph retorted.

That sentence caused the judge's pitbull gaze to morph into a look of concern. Sensing the change in his demeanor, Joseph doubled-down.

"She gave me this book," he held up the Cathpert family history book which he had been hiding under his jacket.

When Judge Cathpert saw it, he looked as if he'd seen a ghost. His mouth opened and his eyes widened. The judge squirmed in his chair as the ruby red hue came back to his sunken cheeks. Joseph sensed he was onto something.

"I skimmed through it. Fascinating! The Cathperts had quite a colorful history with pirates, didn't they?" Joseph loved this game of cat and mouse. For him, the bigger the mouse, the better the catch. Judge Cathpert was the biggest mouse he had ever faced.

"In fact, one might even say the Cathpert family was involved in activities that were…morally questionable, at best."

Judge Cathpert's countenance transformed into defensiveness. His thick eyebrows drew down into a chilling frown.

"Just what are you *gettin'* at?" The judge was daring Joseph to verbalize his damning conclusion. Judge Cathpert wanted to hear Joseph's slanderous accusations against one of the most powerful families in South Carolina.

Joseph glanced out at the Kiawah River and paused. *Do I dare?* If he was wrong his career would vanish.

Unfortunately, for Judge Cathpert, Joseph did not cringe before power. He took a deep breath and went for it.

Chapter 45

Sarah and David were dressed to the nines as they entered the Inn's foyer. At David's insistence, they had both tossed business attire into their roll-aboard just in case a situation like this presented. Life at a large law firm had beaten the high-society rules into David's head and one of those rules was to always pack for a formal occasion.

As such, David wore a black suit with a crisp white shirt, monogrammed cuffs, and a sky-blue tie. Sarah sported a loose-fitting cream lace cocktail dress with a golden heart necklace David had given to her earlier that month.

Sarah didn't care much for stuffy dinner parties. She would rather be curled up on her couch with David and her son, Mark, binge watching re-runs of old sitcoms. However, these types of events were important to David, so, she pretended to enjoy herself.

The fire roared in the foyer's white stone fireplace and, even at a distance, David and Sarah could feel its heat. David was surprised to see a fire lit so early in the fall season. Perhaps South Carolinians were more sensitive to cooling weather, or maybe the warm fire simply drew more people into the lobby bar. Either way, it was a nice addition to the elegant ambiance.

The dark leather couches near the bar were filled with recognizable, celebrated people. David noticed several celebrity couples enjoying champagne in a circled cluster in the far corner. Past the celebrity table and outside, the Inn's illuminated swimming pool was being peppered with hard rain. The furniture on the pool deck was wobbling, evidencing the growing intensity of the wind.

According to the most recent weather report, Hurricane Mary was still barreling toward Charleston at breakneck speed, but you wouldn't know it by the crowd in the lobby. The well-dressed patrons were laughing and drinking like they didn't have a care in the world.

As Sarah and David walked under the foyer's crystal chandelier, they were greeted by the concierge, Simon Seifert. Simon's tortoise-shell glasses and gray suit coat, light blue button-down shirt and matching pocket handkerchief were drenched. His usually well-manicured hair lay flat and soggy on his tanned forehead and water dripped down his bronzed face.

"Good evening, Mr. Stoneman and Ms. Mercer. So glad you could join us tonight." Simon took Sarah's hand, performed a half-bow and kissed her knuckles. Sarah blushed.

"Please help yourself to a cocktail in the lobby bar and when you're ready, head into *Ballroom A* for dinner. Just as a reminder, food and beverages are gratis. Bon Appetit!"

"A little wet tonight, huh, Simon?" David asked with a grin.

Simon was embarrassed by his uncharacteristically disheveled appearance.

"Yes, sir. As I'm sure you noticed, the weather is giving us fits. I was only outside for a minute and I'm soaked."

"Any new updates on the hurricane? The news said it will be here within the next day or two." Sarah asked.

"Yes, ma'am, it looks like the Sea Islands and Charleston may get the brunt of it. But not to worry, our staff and island security team are closely monitoring the situation. If the Governor orders an evacuation, we'll notify you right away."

Sensing Sarah's anxiousness, Simon added a bit of reassurance.

"Who knows, it could blow right by us. That's happened before. You never quite know…excuse me." Simon hurried over to a young bellhop who was flagging him down near the front door. He then followed the bellhop back outside into the rain.

"Want to get a drink?" David asked as he extended his arm to escort Sarah to the bar. They weaved through the large leather chairs. David ordered a Manhattan cocktail and Sarah settled on a glass of house merlot. They sat near the toasty fire and basked in the luxury that surrounded them. They were blissfully ignorant as to what awaited them in *Ballroom A.*

Chapter 46

Judge Cathpert had all but dared Agent Manheim to accuse the Cathpert family of villainy. *He wants me to say it,* Joseph thought as he studied the unsettling gaze of the jurist. After a few silent seconds, Joseph bit.

"Well, Your Honor, for starters, I think your family got rich by helping pirates during the Charleston blockade, and many times after that. That's what it says in this book, anyway. Hard to refute what your ancestors wrote *themselves.*" Joseph exclaimed as he raised the Cathpert family history book in the air, yet again.

Agent Manheim waited for a staunch defense, but it never came. He continued.

"This book also mentions some pretty interesting names. George Raynor, Stede Bonnet, even Blackbeard, along with every Cathpert family patriarch over the last three-hundred years…"

Still no response. Joseph pushed harder, "…not to mention the fact that these barrier islands would be perfect for hiding stolen treasure. Doesn't take much imagination for a motivated socialite wanting to conceal the true source of their family's vast wealth. Huh, Judge?"

Joseph let his words sink in like sharp daggers. As the FBI had taught him to do, he studied his subject from head to toe. The way he was sitting, the wrinkles on his face, even the size of his black pupils were all instructive.

To Joseph's surprise, the judge just sat there, emotionless. After several awkward seconds, Judge Cathpert calmly responded.

"Agent Manheim, that is an awfully *interestin'* theory. You, of course, have actual proof of the Cathpert's illegal collusion with pirates, right?"

Joseph responded.

> All we need is *this book*. But, in addition, let's talk about your connections with modern-day pirates! I know about your friendship with James Henderson. And I'm going to bet that Henderson is the man who stole the SURC and killed Tommy Felton, both at your behest. It's only a matter of time before the FBI kicks down your door with a litany of charges, including conspiracy to commit murder. So…is there something you want to tell me, Judge?

Joseph had put himself out on a very thin limb. Now, it was time to see if the tactic worked, or if the limb broke.

"*Aah'm* afraid *Aah* don't know a Mr. Henderson," Judge Cathpert lied.

Prepared for his vehement denial, Joseph held up the picture he commandeered from Dr. Lyon's office. Judge Cathpert leaned forward in his chair and squinted at the photo. His nervousness returned.

"That's you in the photo, correct?" Joseph asked, knowing the answer but wanting the judge to acknowledge it. "Dr.

Lyons down at the Citadel told me all about you and Henderson. I'm confident he'll testify to that, too." Again, Joseph prayed his bluff would work. He had no other cards to play – only a hunch.

Judge Cathpert began breathing heavily. A ring of sweat formed at his T-shirt's collar.

"That's me a long *tahm* ago." Judge Cathpert finally replied as he pulled his navy-blue shorts up over his navel. He then took a sip of his drink and repositioned himself in his chair.

"*Lemme* see the photo again." Joseph reached his arm out, holding the picture. Judge Cathpert stared intently and nodded his head.

"*Aah* knew these boys, but *Aah* haven't seen any of them in a very long *tahm*."

Joseph's heart sank. Judge Cathpert was all too familiar with the practice of bluffing on cross-examination. He intended to stonewall Special Agent Manheim.

Having no option but to go deeper into the bluff, Joseph continued. "So, you see James Henderson in this picture, Your Honor?"

"Yes."

"When was the last time you saw him?"

Judge Cathpert puckered his lips and looked up at the sky before answering.

"*Aah* can't remember. It's been decades." The judge then looked out at the Kiawah River. The rain had temporarily slowed to a light drizzle, but the sky remained dark and ominous.

"Ken Lyons and *Aah* were cadets together, but Henderson wasn't *Citadul* material. Always resented it too. He had the brains, but he was a troubled soul. Last *Aah* heard, Henderson disappeared after Desert Storm and hasn't been seen since." Judge Cathpert looked at Joseph, stoic.

"And Paul Stoneman, also in the photo...how did you know *him*?"

Judge Cathpert grinned. "Didn't he die a while back? *Aah* hadn't seen him in ages either."

Again, the judge leaned forward and lowered his voice.

"Agent Manheim, it may not be wise to go *searchin'* for the boogie man – you might just find him."

Joseph was unphased by the not-so-veiled threat.

"I appreciate your concern but, to me, James Henderson is a person of interest in my murder investigation. So, if you know where he is, I need to know now!"

Judge Cathpert smirked a second time.

"You know, Agent Manheim, it'd be a *cryin'* shame if some evidence came to light that you were involved in *Tahmmy* Felton's death. Evidence can just pop up in these parts."

Is he threatening to plant evidence on me?

Judge Cathpert took a big gulp to finish his liquor drink.

"Aah need a refill. Excuse me." The judge slowly rose to his narrow, elongated feet, looming his tall, thin frame over Joseph.

The rain had paused for a moment and the sun was going down. The contrast of the dark clouds with the sunset created a deep purple, which silhouetted the outlines of the dense island greenery in the distance.

Joseph placed the confiscated photograph between the pages of the Cathpert family history book and laid the book on a side table. He needed to stretch his legs too.

He wandered into the judge's backyard which backed up to the Kiawah River. A wooden dock extended out into the water nearly a hundred feet. Joseph walked out on the rickety dock as the wind began blowing more heavily.

He glanced to his right and saw the back of the luxurious hotel he had seen coming in. He did an about-face and turned back toward the judge's house. The home was mostly dark, save for a couple lights on the first floor and a well-lit turret on second floor which was illuminated like a Christmas tree. Even from the boat dock Joseph could clearly see the turret room's large stained-glass window with an unmistakable image at the center – it was a lightning bolt.

It's the same symbol as on their home in Charleston.

Just then, Joseph heard a boat's engine coming from the water. As he turned, he caught a glimpse of a military boat passing the dock and heading toward the hotel. Even in the fading light, Joseph immediately recognized the distinctive boat – it was a SURC!

His adrenaline pumped as he sprinted up the dock and through the backyard. He had to intercept the SURC before it disappeared again, maybe forever.

As he hurried onto the back porch, mysteriously, the Cathpert family history book was missing from the table where he had left it. Joseph flung open the sliding back door and hurried into the living room, muddied shoes and all, to find Judge Cathpert and two other stern-faced, muscular men in military fatigues. One of the men pulled a taser from his utility belt and aimed it at Joseph's chest. The other man aimed his assault rifle at Joseph's head.

"Let me see your hands!" The man with the taser shouted. Joseph reluctantly raised his arms above his head. *I knew it! I just knew it!*

The men patted him down, located his sidearm on his ankle holster and confiscated it. Joseph glared at Judge Cathpert. Sensing Joseph's judgment, the old jurist spoke up.

"*Aah* warned you…you might just find the boogie man."

With those words the operative shot the sharp taser barbs into Joseph's chest causing him to collapse on the living room floor. The other operative raced over and stuck a needle into his right arm ensuring he would be unconscious long enough for them to move him. In seconds, Joseph's world went completely black.

Chapter 47

Nearly an hour had passed and David and Sarah's glasses were empty as they sat near the crackling fireplace in the Rhett's Bluff Inn. The generous pour of red wine was playing tricks on Sarah's usually mild-mannered personality. David gleefully observed his beautiful girlfriend stumble over basic words as she laughed for all to hear. David gazed lovingly at the woman who was now the longest romantic relationship of his life.

Sarah and David had exchanged the "L" word a few times, but David's resistance to romantic commitment prevented it from becoming a regular habit. Sarah claimed she understood and agreed to let David wade into the relationship at his pace. After all, he was worth the wait.

Many of the guests were now making their way into *Ballroom A*. David and Sarah followed suit, excited about their impending first-class dining experience.

Big band music playing Frank Sinatra's greatest hits could be heard throughout the lobby and lured in the guests. The ballroom was large with over two-thousand square feet adorned with light, floral patterned carpet. Three French doors led outside to a now-flooded courtyard, which was obviously closed. The brass band was nestled in the corner near the small, temporary wooden dancing floor.

There were nearly a dozen sizeable round tables each surrounded by six coral chairs neatly tucked under cream tablecloths. In front of each of the chairs was a formal place setting.

The room was crowded and most of the guests were already seated and chatting. David and Sarah found a spare table near the ballroom's entrance and parked themselves to skim the dinner menu. David's mouth watered – pan seared scallops, local catch bouillabaisse, and crab bisque all sounded delicious, and the smell of the exquisite cuisine wafted in the air.

"What are you thinking, babe?"

Sarah was intently studying the menu.

"Everything looks fantastic, but I'm leaning toward the shrimp and grits."

Just then, an attractive woman in her mid-forties with red hair and a very low-cut dress sat down in the unoccupied seat next to David. She didn't waste any time hitting on him.

"Hey there, sexy, I'm Callie. What's your name, green eyes?" The woman asked in a sensual tone. David could smell the vodka on her breath. Sarah leaned forward, marking her territory. David had to quickly diffuse the uncomfortable situation.

"Hello, ma'am. This is my *girlfriend*, Sarah." David hoped the introduction would quash the woman's obvious intentions. It did not. She barely acknowledged Sarah as she put her hand on David's shoulder.

"I saw you from across the room, honey, and just knew I had to meet you. Are you from Hollywood?"

David appreciated the compliment, but sensing Sarah's growing irritation with the drunk interloper, he parried the comment by asking a question of his own.

"No, I'm not from Hollywood. Sorry to disappoint. Who are you here with tonight?" David asked, searching for the woman's chaperone.

She rolled her eyes and pointed to the other side of the room.

"My husband, unfortunately."

David glanced in that direction. Sarah half-stood to get a clear look, fully expecting to see an angry gentleman staring back at her. But all she saw was a long dinner table with roughly forty guests seated around it. *Reserved* signs were placed in obvious locations at both ends of that table. It was clear the group was special. Sarah recognized several famous faces too. Now, more curious than mad, Sarah had her own questions for the drunk woman.

"It looks like your husband is at a table full of VIPs. Are *you* married to a movie star?" Sarah put her right elbow on the table and rested her chin on her fist.

By then, David was also studying the mystery table. He, too, recognized celebrities, politicians, and business tycoons. David thought he even caught a glimpse of Marcos Roberts, the White House's chief of staff, but couldn't be sure.

David's intrigue was compounded by the sheer number of security guards standing near the table. They looked bigger, tougher, and meaner than traditional hotel security. The drunk woman's response caused David to turn his attention back to her.

"My husband is just your run-of-the-mill billionaire." She said loudly.

"He runs a global tech company. But he's a nasty guy. Trust me on that." The woman tipped forward but caught herself and sat upright.

"He's been texting his mistress for the last hour with me sitting right next to him. What a jackass!" The woman crossed her arms and slumped back in her seat before remembering she was supposed to be hitting on David.

"That's why I came over here to talk to you, honey. Let's get back at him together. You have a place we can be alone?" She made a kissing gesture as her drunk eyes tried, but failed, to align with David's. He dismissed the woman's advances and winked at Sarah. They both had more questions.

"Apparently, your husband is at the only *Reserved* table in the room. How does someone get a seat at *that* table?" Sarah inquired.

The woman chuckled and leaned in toward David. She was just a few inches from his face. At one point, he even thought she might try to kiss him.

"*They* have to invite you."

She closed her eyes and smiled, "You see, it's a secret group."

"Secret?" David prodded. "How so?"

"For starters, they only meet once every five years. This hotel is *their* place. I can't say much else or they'll kill me." The woman put her index finger to her lips signaling that the information she had just shared was confidential.

"What does this special group do?" David asked with a smile.

The woman looked back at the table and then raised her voice as she threw her hands up in the air trying to make a scene in a desperate attempt to get her husband's long-lost attention.

"They rule the world!!" She shouted. Even with the band's music playing loudly, most of the people in the room turned to look at the woman. She immediately regretted her outburst.

Her husband waved over a member of the security team and pointed to his wife. Even from afar, David and Sarah could tell he was irate. Two security guards weaved through the tables, barreling toward them. The woman pleaded with David to save her from the men. David pulled away as she clung to his suit jacket, begging for help.

One of the security guards grabbed the woman's shoulder and yanked her out of the chair with brutish force. He had a firm grip on her arm as he whispered something into her ear. David could not hear what was said, but whatever it was, it caused the intoxicated woman's face to twist in fear. She was escorted from the room as tears rolled down her face. The other security guard turned to David with a no-nonsense look.

"I apologize for that, sir. What did she say to you?"

Sensing the truth would get the woman in deeper trouble, David downplayed the interaction.

"Not much, really. She just said that her husband was cheating on her." The security guard seemed satisfied with the answer. He nodded his bald head and he, too, left the ballroom.

"What just happened?" Sarah asked.

"I have no idea, but that was *bizarre*."

Before they had time to discuss the incident further, two other couples sat down at their table and introduced themselves. They seemed normal, semi-sober, and completely unaware of what had just happened.

During the meal, David kept glancing over his shoulder at the *Reserved* table. Generally, David would dismiss crazy conspiracy theories, but the prominence of that table caused him to wonder if the drunk woman's allegations were, in fact, true. As David pondered the question, Sergeant James Henderson watched him through a crack in the ballroom's hidden door.

"She talked to Stoneman," he blurted into his radio. "Of all the people in the room, she had to talk to *Stoneman*. You know what this means, boys. Give her the needle and dump her body in the marsh. Her husband will be thrilled."

Chapter 48

Special Agent Manheim gradually regained consciousness. He lifted his throbbing head and attempted to move his arms, but he couldn't. He was tied to a chair with a scratchy rope wrapped firmly around his torso. Joseph also felt cold metal on his wrists – he was handcuffed too.

The room swirled. *The drugs must still be in my system.* He closed his eyes, hoping his body would quickly pass the toxins and restore equilibrium.

Joseph's chest where he had been tasered was sore. He blinked his eyes several times to remove floaters in his vision. Again, he lifted his head and took two deep breaths trying to calm himself. Even drugged and disoriented, Joseph had mastered the art of mental toughness.

He had worked with a sports psychologist while playing ball at Clemson, and that experience, plus the FBI's agent training, had chiseled him into a mental juggernaut. However, all the mental coping strategies in the world would not free him from the chair.

He turned his head and realized he was not alone in the room. A man and a woman were sitting in a dark corner whispering to one another. They, too, were handcuffed and tied up.

"Hey, buddy, are you alright?" The man asked.

"You've been unconscious since they brought you in hours ago. They must have slipped you something strong."

Joseph tried to find the words to respond. His mind was cloudy, but he did his best to communicate with the strangers.

"I...uh, I'm FB...I. FBI. I..., uh. The judge..."

The couple was trying to make sense of Joseph's incoherent comments.

"FBI? If you're FBI, won't your people come looking for you?" The woman asked.

Joseph shook his head, "No...I, uh. I work alone. No one, uh...no one knows I'm here."

The couple looked disappointed and again, whispered to one another. Even with his foggy mental state, Joseph wanted to learn more about his fellow prisoners. Maybe they could work together to escape. *Be cautious*, his FBI training warned him, *you don't know if you can trust them.*

"Who...are you?" Joseph managed. His speech was sluggish, but improving with each sentence.

"I'm Hunter Thompson and this is my wife, Bailey. We're from Atlanta."

"Why are you here?" Joseph asked.

"It seems we work with the wrong company. Do you know Menda Industrial Corporation?"

Joseph shook his head. Bailey continued.

"Menda is caught up in something bad, and when I didn't go along with the plan, I was brought here. My husband was nearly beaten to death when he started asking questions." Bailey paused, as if she had just remembered something.

"Does the name *Tara* mean anything to you?" She asked.

Joseph shook his head, "No."

His mental faculties began to sharpen. The drugs were wearing off.

"We believe a lady named Tara is pulling the strings at Menda Industrial. You said you were with a *judge*. What judge?"

Joseph's nausea returned and he took a few more deep breaths, worried he was going to vomit. The feeling passed. As Joseph continued to breathe deeply his brain fog cleared. He finally felt like himself again.

"Judge Holton Cathpert. He's local. I was investigating a death and a stolen boat. The trail led to Cathpert. By the fact that I'm sitting here with you, I guess my hunch was correct."

Joseph couldn't feel his wallet in his back pocket, nor his cell phone. His assailants must have taken both. If they were smart, and they probably were, they would toss the phone in the back of a truck heading toward Charleston so its tracking feature would lead the FBI in the opposite direction if they came looking for him.

With wishful optimism, Joseph asked his fellow prisoners a question.

"Any chance they let you keep your phones?"

"Nope. Phones are gone." Hunter responded as he studied the agent.

"I don't think we caught your name, sir."

"Special Agent Joseph Manheim."

"Is Menda Industrial on your radar *at all*?"

"No…should they be?" Joseph inquired. Hunter ignored his question and continued his cross-examination.

"Are you sure you've never even heard of Menda?" Again, Joseph shook his head. Hunter turned to Bailey.

"I don't think this guy can help us, Bail. He doesn't know anything."

Hunter looked back at Joseph with one final question.

"Do you know who *Dominic Harkness* is?" Hunter thought maybe Dominic, the whistleblower, had contacted the FBI before speaking with the attorneys at Townsend & Moore. It was a long shot, but he had to try.

"Doesn't ring any bells. Unless those folks are members of the Cathpert family or have lightning bolts tattooed on their foreheads, I don't think we're in here for the same reason."

Hunter's face lit up.

"What do you mean, *lightning bolts*?"

"I'm sorry?"

"How do you know that Menda Industrial's whistleblower mentioned a lightning bolt when he came to speak with us?" Hunter asked.

"Are you some kind of crooked fed who's working for Menda?! How did you know that, you bastard?! Tell me!!" Hunter yelled. His tone caused the room's locked door to blow open. A gun-toting FARCO operative entered.

"What's going on in here?" The operative barked. Not wanting his wife to suffer for his short temper, Hunter blurted out a confession.

"It was me, jarhead!" Hunter said as he spit in the operative's direction. The man marched toward Hunter. The thud of his feet on the concrete floor sounded like a giant's footsteps.

"Worthless piece of sh—" The operative silenced Hunter's condescending statement with a hard right hook to the left side of Hunter's face. The hit nearly caused him to capsize in the chair. Bailey pleaded for the man to stop as her husband teetered on the verge of unconsciousness. The operative just smiled and continued the beating.

A combination of brutal jabs, crosses, and uppercuts silenced Hunter. Blood poured out of his mouth and onto the floor.

"Make another sound, and I'll make sure you eat out of a tube for the rest of your miserable life." The operative shook out his fist which was covered in Hunter's blood and left the room. Joseph heard the door's deadbolt lock behind him.

The dried blood on Hunter's face was now covered with fresh blood which had soaked his shirt.

Joseph finally answered Hunter's question, "No, man, I'm not crooked. I just think the lightning bolt symbol has something to do with all of this."

Through the red, Hunter smiled.

"Okay, Mr. FBI, I believe you…and did you get a good look at the key ring on the left side of the guard's utility belt?"

Joseph grinned, realizing Hunter was helping him gather intel on how they could escape.

"I sure did."

"Well, I already pissed him off and I'm happy to do it again. This time, when he walks by you, ram him with your chair and push him into me. From there, we'll knock him out, take his keys, and make a run for it. Bailey, you stay back until it's over."

Bailey acknowledged the instruction. Again, Hunter started screaming.

"HELP!! HELP US!! CAN ANYONE HEAR ME!?"

The operative quickly re-entered the room and Hunter yelled even louder.

"DOWN HERE!! HELP!!"

The operative raced toward Hunter with his fist drawn back, ready to strike. As he flew past, Joseph rose to the balls of his feet and thrust himself forward, putting his right shoulder into the man's back. The operative lost his balance and stumbled forward, face first. Simultaneously, Hunter whipped his chair's back legs toward the man's head, which was now waist-high. His head hit the chair with a loud crack.

The operative howled in pain and crumbled to the floor. For the next several seconds, Hunter and Joseph took turns ramming their chairs' metal legs into the man until he lay unconscious.

"Hurry, let's go! The door's open!"

They had to move fast.

Joseph crouched with his hands behind his back and retrieved the operative's ring of keys from his belt. His training kicked-in and he felt the size and shape of handcuff keys and was able to jostle the correct key into his handcuffs and free himself. Then, he shimmied out of the ropes.

Joseph glanced at the guard's military-grade watch wrapped around his wrist – it was 7:00 a.m.

As Joseph was freeing Hunter and Bailey from their bonds, he heard voices coming down the hall toward them. He worked as fast as he could and, once he had freed them, the three prisoners sprinted out the open door and ran the opposite way down the dark hallway.

Chapter 49

David awoke to the sound of hurried footsteps outside his room. He pressed his phone to check the time. It was 7:10 a.m. *What is going on this early?* He heard the rain pouring down outside the bedroom window followed by bright flashes of lightning and crackling thunder.

David desperately wanted to fall back asleep, but couldn't. He turned in bed to find Sarah still snoozing. She looked so peaceful. As he quietly rose to his feet he had a splitting headache, likely due to his overindulgence in bourbon the night before. He was now paying the price.

After the strange encounter with the drunk woman who bombarded their dinner table, David and Sarah made friends with two other couples at the event. Both couples were regular members of the Rhett's Bluff Inn thanks to their families' prominent names and ample trust funds. Still, David enjoyed hearing stories about their yachts and elaborate vacations in the French Riviera.

Hearing those stories, part of David still pined for the golden spoils of the corporate rat race. This time two years ago, David was chained to his desk at a D.C. law firm billing as many hours as he possibly could. Now that he and Sarah were financially secure, David gave himself permission to enjoy life a bit.

After dinner, David and Sarah danced the night away until well after midnight. Sarah seemed to enjoy herself, and she deserved it.

David wandered over to the bedroom's large window and opened the curtains just enough to peek outside. He was surprised to see that deep puddles had formed across much of the Inn's back lawn. Further in the distance, David noticed the waterline of the Kiawah River was dangerously high.

He heard more hurried footsteps and raised voices in the hallway. David walked over to the room's front door and saw a cream envelope that had been slid under the door. He peered through the door's peephole and saw a uniformed member of the hotel staff holding similar envelopes and placing them under the door of the room across the hall.

David leaned down and picked up the envelope and then stumbled in the dark to the bathroom. He flipped on the light and closed the door. His bladder felt like it was going to explode. He decided to multi-task and read the letter as he relieved himself.

The letter's subject line was concerning. He flushed the toilet and sat on the edge of the tub to read more intently. MANDATORY EVACUATION NOTICE was written in all caps. David read on:

Dear Valued Member/Guest:

As part of Rhett's Bluff's emergency management plan, the Rhett's Bluff Inn ("the Inn") would like to make you aware of a potentially dangerous weather situation currently developing. Early this morning, representatives from the local barrier islands conducted a teleconference with the Charleston County Emergency Management Department regarding Hurricane Mary. According to the National Hurricane Center, over the next twenty-four hours, Hurricane Mary's trajectory has Charleston, and the local barrier islands, in its cone of uncertainty. Consequently, Rhett's Bluff is expected to endure significant weather impacts including heavy rainfall, strong winds, and storm surge, which will likely cause severe flooding, starting today.

As such, Inn members and guests must make preparations to vacate immediately. Further, the South Carolina Governor is expected to issue an executive order declaring a state of emergency and will likely order a mandatory evacuation for all of Charleston County. Please note, for planning purposes, we are in Evacuation ZONE A, and the Evacuation Route is through Kiawah Island to Bohicket/Main Rd. to US 17. US 17 south to SC 64 where you will go to Walterboro, then to North Augusta. Note: weather permitting, the helipad on the Inn's roof can be made available for private helicopter transportation, upon request.

We implore all members and guests to remain calm as you gather your personal belongings and make your departure plans. Due to the emergent situation, we plan to formally close the Inn at noon today.

Sincerely,
The Rhett's Bluff Inn Management

David attempted to rouse Sarah and give her the urgent and unfortunate news, and he was still unsure what travel plans had to be made to get them safely back to Washington. At this point, the private charter jet which had brought them to Charleston was almost certainly booked.

However, the pilot, Randy, encouraged David to call him directly, so he did. The call went straight to voicemail with an auto-message indicating the voice mailbox was full. *Great.*

As suspected, they needed another travel option.

"Hey, Sarah?" David gently tapped Sarah's shoulder. She groaned and rolled over. David tried again.

"Babe, you have to get up. The hotel is evacuating due to the hurricane."

Sarah opened one bloodshot eye.

"You've got to be kidding." She responded with a sigh.

"Dead serious. It's getting pretty bad out there. Take a look at the back yard." David walked over to the window and opened the curtains.

"The river looks high too. And, I think there's only one road on and off the island, right? If that road floods, we could be in big trouble." David warned.

Sarah yawned and set her feet on the soft carpet as she sat up and stretched her arms over her head.

"Okay. I'll get cleaned up. Can you walk down to the front desk and see what's going on?" Sarah asked as she ambled into the bathroom. Seconds later, David heard the shower running. He threw on workout clothes consisting of black mesh shorts and a patterned athletic shirt, combed down his hair, and headed for the lobby.

Chapter 50

Bailey's black cocktail dress was drenched as she crouched behind her husband in the torrential rain. She and Hunter hid behind a tall line of shrubbery on the Inn's outer wall. Special Agent Manheim sprinted to an adjacent bush to gain a better vantage point.

They had to stay out of sight. Moments earlier, by sheer luck, the trio had followed a dark hallway until they discovered a service stairwell. They climbed the flight of stairs to emerge, undetected, from a hidden door at street level.

The rain continued and the wind hissed and howled causing the green trees to whip and bend on the once-immaculate grounds. The pooled water on the Inn's lawn was now ankle deep and rising by the minute. Hurricane Mary had arrived.

Joseph's mind was racing. He felt responsible for Bailey and Hunter. Although they seemed tough, Joseph suspected both could crack under the pressure of extensive physical torture if they were caught.

Joseph noticed cars filtering through the Inn's porte cochere. He ducked and ran back to Hunter and Bailey.

"Y'all stay here. I have to get close to the front doors to see what's happening." Joseph said as he caught his breath.

"I'm coming with you!" Hunter insisted.

"No, no. I need you to stay. You're safe here. Trust me!" Hunter acquiesced and Joseph took off around the corner.

After what seemed like a lifetime, Joseph returned dragging an old canoe behind him. Hunter left his hiding place and helped Joseph pull the boat to the side of the building just as a car pulled out of the Inn's entryway.

Joseph leaned against the wall and collapsed, exhausted. He sunk down into six inches of standing water.

"We can *float* out of here," Joseph said as he pointed to the canoe. He continued.

"There are too many people at the front. Stealing a car would draw attention and golf carts won't run in water this high. I found this canoe in an old equipment shed."

"It has a crack on the bottom, but it should still float."

"This water isn't deep enough," Hunter cautioned as he stomped his large foot, testing the water's depth.

Joseph pointed toward the Kiawah River. Hunter and Bailey followed his finger.

"You've got to be kidding me," Bailey protested, "we can't take a broken canoe out into a river in a storm. We'll be killed!"

"She's right, it's too dangerous. We'd have a better chance just making a run for it." Hunter protested.

Joseph was still seated and held his open hands in the air, asking for assistance. Hunter pulled him to his feet.

"Listen, when I was at Cathpert's beach house, I walked out on his dock. The banks of the river are slanted upward into the bank, almost like a beach."

"So…?"

"With the flooding, that elevated space at the river's edge will keep us out of sight and we'll know exactly what's just a few feet under us – river bank. It's like floating over a sandbar, we just need to stay near the shore and not drift too far out."

His explanation caused the two attorneys to think of possible counter-arguments, but they came up with none. It was a good idea.

"We follow the river *away* from the Inn and look for higher ground on the other side. Then we can regroup and reevaluate. I'm sure they've already realized we've escaped, so, we have to get away from this place now!" Joseph emphasized.

"Do you have paddles?" Hunter asked, still skeptical.

"There's *one* paddle in the boat. It's small, but it should do the trick. I can paddle for us."

Hunter shook his head, "I rowed crew in college. *I'll* paddle." Hunter glanced at the river and continued.

"Okay, this could work, but we have to stay close to the embankment."

Suddenly, Bailey had an idea.

"I've got it!" She pointed toward Rhett's Bluff Road. There are cottages on a plot of land just down this road. The cottages Damian and I are staying in."

"I'm sure those are flooded too. How does that help us?" Joseph asked. Bailey clarified.

"The cottages are raised up on pilasters. If we can make it back to my cottage, we can call for help on the room phone or send an SOS message from my computer. Maybe we can get help to *come to us*!"

Hunter smiled at his wife's brilliance. Joseph nodded and Hunter grabbed the paddle.

"Okay, let's get to the cottages. Joseph, help me carry the boat to the water." Hunter picked up the bow of the canoe and Joseph carried the stern. The water continued to rise – there was no time to lose. They said a silent prayer and made a beeline for the river.

Chapter 51

Simon Seifert's concierge desk remained empty and his desk's lamp was off. David thought it was strange the concierge was not present to facilitate the mandatory evacuation from *his* hotel. The lobby was mysteriously vacant. *Where is everybody?*

David turned and saw a familiar face scurrying through the lobby bar and into *Ballroom A* where they had dinner the night before – it was Jacob Blake. He was on a mission.

Suspecting Jacob was running some kind of illegal scam with his caddies, David didn't want to interact with him more than he had to. However, Jacob was probably the best source of information on how to get off the island in a pinch. So, David scurried after the golf pro.

When David entered *Ballroom A*, Jacob was already on the far side of the room. Just as he was about to call out to get his attention, Jacob opened what appeared to be a secret door hidden in one of the walls. In a flash, Jacob disappeared.

As the secret door began to close, David sprinted across the room and his fingers caught the door just in time. The secret passage led to a secret stairwell. The stairs went up and down.

David listened intently and heard Jacob's footsteps *above* him. He climbed the stairs quickly, but quietly.

At the top of the stairwell's landing, there was an unmarked door. Unsure where he was, David questioned whether he should turn back. However, his curiosity got the better of him and he opened the door to find a luxurious hallway with floor-to-ceiling windows on the outer wall.

Cautiously, David entered the hall. He looked out the large windows and realized he was on the backside of the hotel. He also recognized the seriousness of the weather outside. It was a scene out of a nightmare. The sky was black and the heavy rain beat down as far as his eye could see.

By the view, David could tell he was on the Inn's top floor. The Kiawah River had now completely consumed the back lawn. It was difficult to see through the rain, but he thought he saw people in a canoe paddling down the river. *Good luck*, he thought, as he continued down the hallway.

David stopped in his tracks when he heard voices around the corner. One of the voices was Jacob Blake. He listened intently.

"...that's what I'm telling you. Everyone is preparing for the meeting and Henderson is with the Executive Council in the Lagoon Room."

"Well, my orders are to stay here and guard the meeting space."

"Look, man, you want to tell Marcos Roberts you were up here doing nothing while the entire Exec Council is downstairs with minimal security?"

"Henderson said they may cancel because of the storm."

Jacob laughed, "After waiting five years, you think they're going to postpone because of the weather? No way! Now get down there!" Jacob barked.

David heard footsteps drawing closer, so, he ducked into a shadowy lavatory and pulled the door closed, leaving just a small crack. He saw a tall, stocky man wearing military fatigues walk briskly down the hallway toward the secret stairwell. No sign of Jacob.

After a few seconds, David carefully opened the door and, once again, crept into the empty hall. He tiptoed around the corner to find a shorter hallway which led to a large conference room set up for a meeting. There was a registration table near the room's entrance on which sat nearly fifty magnetic nametags. On the corner of the table was a biometric fingerprint scanner and a numeric keypad. *Interesting.*

The conference room's décor mirrored *Ballroom A*, just smaller. There were five rows of long tables covered in white table skirts with a center aisle in the middle, like a lecture hall. At each seat was a wireless tablet and a folder with a notepad and pen. There was a large screen in the front of the room which hung behind a black podium which carried a lightning bolt symbol. David recognized it as the same symbol Simon Seifert was wearing on his lapel pin when they first checked in.

David noticed Jacob in the back of the room rifling through boxes and putting sound equipment into a camouflage backpack. *He's stealing them.* Angered, David forgot why he was following Jacob in the first place and decided to call him out.

"Hey!" David hollered.

Jacob nearly jumped out of his shoes and spun around. Even though David was silhouetted, Jacob recognized him and tried to hide the camouflaged backpack behind him.

"Mr. Stoneman, what are you *doin'* up here, man?

"Drop the bag. I'm onto you!" David marched toward the golf pro.

"What are you talking about? There are—" David interrupted.

"Cut the crap! I know you're ripping people off. I overheard you talking about the operation with your caddies and I'm guessing that equipment behind your back doesn't belong to you either."

Jacob was speechless.

"So, drop the bag. I'm taking you down to the front desk and turning you in." David was stern in his directive. Jacob's once nice-guy demeanor instantly turned serious.

"I'm sorry, Dave, I can't do that. I'm leaving with this bag." Jacob held the backpack in the air.

"Not going to happen." David was also resolute and his muscles tensed.

"Stoneman, I'm going to tell you one more time. I need this bag. This is your last warning."

David stood stoically with his flexed arms at his side. David was no streetfighter, but he was sure he could out-muscle an aging golf professional. At that moment, Jacob raced toward David, backpack in hand. David wasn't going to let him pass without a fight but, to David's surprise, it wasn't much of a fight.

Jacob made a fast judo move and relocated himself behind David. In a flash, Jacob had David in a debilitating chokehold. Jacob was stronger than David expected.

David dropped to his knees and clawed ferociously at the golfer's forearm. He could feel himself beginning to blackout. David tapped twice on Jacob's forearm, signaling his surrender. Drool was dripping down his chin and onto the floor and his vision was growing hazy.

Jacob released his death grip. David crumbled to the floor and coughed air back into his lungs. He rolled over to find a handgun in his face. Even gasping for air, David managed a question.

"What kind of golf pro carries a gun?"

Jacob lowered the gun.

"Golfers don't carry guns…but CIA officers do. Follow me and I'll fill you in. We have to hurry."

Chapter 52

After canoeing undetected along the banks of the Kiawah River, Bailey, Hunter, and Joseph finally reached the flooded driveway leading to Captain Maynard's Island.

The fear of being discovered and captured caused Bailey's hands to shake as she climbed the steps to her cottage. Hunter and Joseph secured the canoe on the stair's landing, just in case they needed it again.

Bailey clung to the wooden spindles of the banister. Exhaustion was setting in and she was soaked to the bone. *Almost there*, she thought as she scaled the final step.

She pulled her cottage keycard from her cocktail dress's secret zipper pocket. She felt a second keycard and remembered that was the spare key Damian had given to her and Tara the night before. But neither Damian nor Tara were anywhere in sight.

Bailey swiped her card across the entry-pad. The green light illuminated and she heard a loud click. As she pushed open the door, a feeling of anxiety shot through her – her cottage had been ransacked and the computer bag she had left on the couch was missing.

Hunter put his arm on his wife's shoulder, "What happened?"

"See if the landline works," Joseph suggested. Bailey hustled to the phone hanging on the wall and picked up the hand receiver with bated breath. The phone was dead. Bailey sank down into one of the kitchen chairs and began to cry.

She and her husband were trapped on a flooded island in the middle of a hurricane with armed mercenaries chasing them and she had no way to call for help. Bailey couldn't help but think about her children. It was entirely possible that they would be orphans by the end of the weekend.

However, that thought actually emboldened Bailey. She was no longer upset, she was angry. Her protective maternal instinct took over. Then it hit her, *Damian's cottage!*

She reached into her secret zippered pocket and retrieved Damian's cottage key.

"Okay, boys, come on! We're going across the street!"

Chapter 53

Hunter and Joseph tried to keep up with Bailey as she sloshed through the knee-high flood water toward Damian's cottage. The cottages were roughly two-hundred feet apart, but Bailey made the treacherous trek in record time.

Damian had brought her to the island under false pretenses and left her to die in a luxurious prison. *Screw him*, Bailey thought as she approached his place, *I'll deal with him later*.

Bailey was several paces in front of her two male companions when she reached Damian's steps and climbed to the stair's landing and turned around to wait for them. The wind blew harder and the downpour continued as heavy branches fell around her – the scene was chaotic.

Hunter's and Joseph's athletic frames trudged through the flood waters. Then, Bailey saw it. Even through the rain, she recognized the methodical back-and-forth movement of an alligator tail gliding toward the men.

"Alligator!! Behind you!!" Bailey screamed. Hunter and Joseph turned to find the reptile closing in on them.

"Run!!" Hunter yelled as he and Joseph picked up their knees and wildly swung their arms.

Bailey raced down to the second to last step, just above the waterline. Joseph was in front of Hunter and flew past Bailey and up the stairs. Once he was safely on the front porch, he looked down in horror at the Thompsons.

Hunter reached out to his wife when his foot snagged on a large tree root. Then the worst happened.

His arms waved as he fell forward. Bailey held the nearest spindled banister with the tightest grip possible and extended her arm to her husband, but it wasn't enough. His fingertips touched hers as he plunged into the dark water. The monstrous alligator also disappeared under the water.

Knowing an attack was imminent, and still submerged, Hunter flipped on to his back underwater as the alligator opened its large jaws. The animal attempted to chomp down on Hunter's leg, but the heel of Hunter's shoe hit the alligator in its long snout as he feverishly kicked.

Hunter regained his footing and shot up. Bailey grabbed his arm and tried to pull him to safety. But, just then, the alligator bit down on Hunter's right calf. He let out a horrifying scream as the monster's massive teeth tore through his flesh. The alligator had its prey in its jaws.

Joseph watched helplessly as the scene unfolded. The reptile yanked Hunter away from the stairs and into deeper waters. Joseph knew that if the alligator pulled Hunter underwater, he would be dead.

Without thinking, Joseph jumped over the front porch railing and descended a dozen feet down, landing on the alligator's scaly back. The sudden impact caused the animal to release Hunter as it recoiled in surprise. Joseph bounced off the gator and rolled past its tail and into the water.

While the alligator was distracted, Hunter limped to safety on the steps. In seconds, realizing it had lost its prey, the alligator turned and hissed at Joseph whose eyes remained trained on the predator in front of him, like a courageous warrior facing an adversary.

For a moment, it seemed like the alligator was staring back, daring Joseph to make the first move. It was a standoff between man and beast. Joseph's only chance of survival was to get back to the stairs and climb to safety.

The water was still rising and each minute that went by the alligator gained a greater advantage as the muddy water deepened. The large reptile glided forward, like a cat creeping toward a mouse. Out of his peripheral vision, Joseph saw a palm tree branch floating on the water. He had an idea.

The FBI agent picked up the branch and, just as the alligator lunged forward with its jaws opened wide, Joseph threw the branch into its mouth and spun to his right. The animal ferociously chomped on the branch in confusion. Then, all in one motion, Joseph leaped over the reptile's swinging tail and looked up to find Bailey's outstretched arms reaching for him.

"Come on!!" She yelled as Joseph clutched her forearms. Bailey fell backward and pulled with all her might. Again, the alligator hissed as it catapulted toward them. Bailey screamed and kicked at the animal, keeping it at bay. Relief flooded over them as they saw the gator finally give up and swim away.

Bailey and Joseph joined Hunter on the cottage's front porch. Hunter had removed his belt and tied it tightly above the bite in his calf to stop the bleeding.

"Hey man…you saved my life. Thanks!" Hunter acknowledged as he winced in pain.

Joseph simply nodded and the three of them took a short minute to celebrate their victory.

"Was alligator wrestling a course at Quantico?" Bailey asked with a smile.

Joseph smirked.

"No, those moves came from playing basketball for twenty years."

They laughed as Bailey removed Damian's spare key from her dress's pocket. She pushed the cottage door open and let out a sigh of relief when she saw that Damian's cottage was still intact and undisturbed. This was their chance.

Chapter 54

D avid followed Jacob into the secret stairwell. They then descended until they reached the bottom floor, one level below the lobby. *Where is he taking me?* David wondered, growing more nervous with each step.

"Let's go, hurry!" Jacob leaned forward to glance up the concrete stairs to ensure no one was following.

David then tailed Jacob down a shady utility tunnel which became more remote, *more dangerous*, with each step. It occurred to David that if Jacob attacked him, no one could hear his cries for help.

They came to the end of the tunnel where the fluorescent light above them was intentionally burnt out. Jacob relocated a tall stack of cardboard boxes which were piled against the wall, and pushed aside an old bookshelf. It was another hidden door. This one, however, had a high-tech manual keypad built into it. Jacob plugged in several numbers and the door sprung inward to reveal a small room furnished like an office.

David noticed a Beretta 9mm handgun on the desk, along with two computer screens, a printer, and a sophisticated radio device with a built-in speaker.

"You say you're CIA, but I need to see some credentials," David demanded.

Jacob stacked manila folders on the corner of his desk. He opened one of his desk drawers and pulled out a government-issued ID card. It looked legitimate.

"That's all I've got down here, so that'll have to do. I've been undercover on this op for five years now."

David studied the card, searching for signs it was a fake, but he could find none. David had *a lot* of questions and wasted no time asking them.

"Let's cut to the chase – who are you? Why are you here? And why are you ripping off houses on the golf course?"

Jacob chuckled. A barrage of intense questions from a lawyer? It was so cliché it was comical. Jacob sat in his cheap desk chair. He invited David to sit in the metal folding chair in the corner of the room, but David declined.

"You really don't know what's going on, do you?" Jacob asked, genuinely surprised by David's ignorance.

"Not really. It'd be great if you could enlighten me."

"But you're *David Stoneman...*" Jacob said, implying that should mean something. He continued.

"You're the famous lawyer who blew the lid off the Division Act."

"So what?"

"We thought they had turned you," Jacob confessed as he leaned back in his chair and folded his arms, looking David up and down.

"Wait, who's *we*, and who's *they*?"

The faux-golfer leaned in and put his elbows on his knees to explain.

"If you are one of them, I'll figure it out by the end of our conversation. I'm trained to do that stuff, you know." Jacob looked David right in the eye, searching for signs of deception. His next comment sent chills down David's spine.

"If I think you're one of them, I'll bury you." Jacob's gaze was haunting. He was dead serious. After a few tense seconds, Jacob's demeanor softened and he began to answer David's questions.

"The '*we*' is the CIA. The pilot who flew you into Charleston on the private plane…Randy. Yeah, he's one of ours. Why do you think he was asking so many questions? He recorded the entire conversation and sent it to me before you arrived."

"Recorded our conversation, why?"

Jacob was silent, again looking David up and down, still skeptical of his ignorance.

Sensing the mistrust, David became frustrated, "Well, Jake, I bet you and Randy got a kick out of this little operation here. But if you're not going to tell me anything, I'm getting out of here. Coincidentally, a storm is bearing down on us, so, why don't you call your pal, Randy, and see if he can fly us out of here!"

David turned toward the door planning to make a dramatic exit. Just as his hand found the door's handle, Jacob responded.

"I haven't heard from Randy in days. In our business, that means you're dead. I'm sure they killed him."

"Again, who is *they*?!" David demanded, growing impatient with Jacob's half-answers.

"I'm going to assume you're trustworthy, Mr. Stoneman. Again, I reserve the right to change my mind and snap your neck at any time. But, until then, what I'm about to tell you is highly classified. You got it?"

David nodded.

"Are you aware that you're staying in a hotel owned by, arguably, the most powerful organization in the world?"

"What group are you talking about?"

"They call themselves *the Cohort*."

Chapter 55

The Cohort was a modern-day, radical faction of a dormant secret society known as *the Society of the Elect*. Founded in 1891 by English businessman and imperialist, Cecil Rhodes, for which the famous Rhodes Scholarship is named, *the Society of the Elect's* original purpose was to re-establish British rule throughout the world.

With that goal in mind, Rhodes established *the Society*, run by him and a small leadership team known as "the Junta of Three." The group's leadership hand-picked elite members of society who would support their cause – they were "the Elect." The Elect would then assume significant positions of power and influence, in both the public and private institutions, to promote the organization's global agenda.

Outside of the inner circle, the Society also engaged "Helpers." Helpers were deemed unworthy of *Elect* membership but carried enough influence to support the Society's goals at a tactical level.

The Cohort mirrored the Society's governance structure with a Cohort President, an Executive Council, hand-selected Members and District Leaders, and an outer circle of supporters called Associates. The Cohort also drew inspiration from the organizational structure of the

American Mafia and could be equally intimidating and lethal, if needed.

Threats of being blackballed from elite clubs, removed from positions of authority, blackmail, and even murder, were all tactics the Cohort employed to secure their ideal membership. The Cohort operated both in secret and in plain sight. Anyone who attempted to cast light on them disappeared without a trace.

The Cohort had a *multi-decade* strategic plan and nearly unlimited resources to execute those plans to perfection.

David sat, astonished, as Jacob downloaded him on the group's nefarious hidden history.

> The exact number of their membership remains a well-guarded secret, but we know it includes business leaders, politicians, global entrepreneurs, state and federal officials, media personalities, and even movie stars. Our intel says that the Cohort's mission since the 1920s has been to completely reframe global institutions to align with *their* ideology. Financial crimes, war crimes, murder – you name it, they've done it! The scary thing is, the Cohort's reach is *everywhere*! Whenever you tune-in to your favorite news network, you could be listening to one of their Members report *their version* of the news. Each time you purchase something at the store, you could be funding a company whose CEO is a Cohort Associate. They've entrenched *that deep, for that long in American society.* That's our challenge, Dave.

Jacob paused and looked up at the ceiling and then back to David. It was a lot to take in. Jacob recognized he had not yet fully connected the dots.

"A perfect example was under your nose just last year with the Division Act. That was the Cohort's handy work – it's standard tradecraft for this group. The Senator you took down was just one of their many government Associates, and that fiasco was a beta-test."

"Wait, does that mean—"

Jacob interrupted. "You *really* never knew?" Jacob was still shocked that David was completely clueless about the Cohort's existence. Jacob continued.

"As you saw, one of the Cohort's many global objectives is to wipe religious institutions from the face of the earth and replace them with a deity-free, one-world government where *they* call the shots. Religion threatens that agenda. That's what the Division Act was all about." Jacob flipped through folders on his desk until he found what he was looking for. He handed David photos of grainy secretly recorded footage of a roaring fire in a room full of people.

"This was taken at one of the Cohort meetings at the Senator's Club in D.C. It's one of their spots."

David was all too familiar with the Senator's Club.

"They *always* have a fire burning at their meetings. I assume it's related to the groups' symbol somehow."

"Symbol?" David asked.

"Yeah…the Cohort's symbol is a lightning bolt."

Chapter 56

The gravity of the situation was sinking in for David. *It all makes sense.* A question popped into his head.

"You said this was *their* hotel. What did you mean?"

Jacob shook his head realizing David was, in fact, clueless.

Dave…the Cohort owns the Inn. This is *their* meeting place. Many of the Inn's members are Cohort Members or Associates. Our intel says they will formally convene here every five years for a multi-day meeting. Before the Inn was here, they met every five years in Washington.

David's mind was racing. He rubbed his stubbled chin. Jacob remained in the chair with his arms crossed and recalled another important detail.

"And FARCO! FARCO is their muscle. Have you heard of FARCO?"

David couldn't help but smile – a year earlier he was sitting at a table surrounded by armed FARCO operatives with a gun to his head.

"Yes…I've heard of them."

"Their leader is a guy named James Henderson. He's a real ball-buster. A ruthless SOB. We have a *very* large file on him."

Henderson? That name sounded so familiar to David. *Where have I heard that name before?* David perished the thought as Jacob continued his debrief.

> Think about it…it's a members-only hotel on a private section of a secluded island. People don't think twice when they see celebrities or politicians walking around this place. To the casual observer, this is just another destination for the rich and famous. That's why Randy and I thought *you* may be the Cohort's newest recruit. We thought they had turned you or paid you off to keep you quiet, and then invited you here.

David resisted the temptation to take offense.

"Okay, so I understand the sting operation here in the hotel, but how in the world did you get the gig as a golf pro, and why do you have caddies stealing from houses?"

Jacob laughed.

"I played golf in college. When the CIA Director said he wanted me to go undercover for this operation, we decided I would come in as a golf pro. I mean, come on – who would suspect the golf pro of working for the CIA?"

David was genuinely impressed. The cover certainly had him duped.

"I put in nearly a thousand hours of extra practice to elevate my golf game to a semi-professional level to make the scam more convincing. The taxpayers funded my private golf lessons – how many people can say that?" Jacob leaned back in his chair and crossed his legs.

"To your question about the caddies, intel said that Cohort Members purchase large stained-glass windows, all of which carry the Cohort's lightning bolt symbol."

David scoured the recesses of his first-rate memory. He recalled the lightning bolt lapel pin on Simon Seifert's jacket and remembered seeing the same symbol displayed on the podium in the meeting space where he had confronted Jacob.

"I paid a couple caddies to sneak into houses that carried the stained-glass symbol to gather information from their home offices. The caddies thought they were working a blackmail operation, but that was just a cover. Oh, shoot!" Jacob looked at his watch and sprang to his feet.

"The meeting begins soon and we need to get you ready!"

"Ready? What do you mean, *get me ready?*"

"We only have one chance every five years to infiltrate this meeting. Before we had you, we only had hidden cameras and sound devices planted in the meeting space. But with you wired up, we can capture in-person interactions *in the room.*" Jacob grabbed David by the shoulders.

"We may only get one shot at this, so, we have to make it count. David, the CIA needs your help and we need it now! Are you in?"

Chapter 57

According to the United States Federal Reserve, the wealthiest ten percent of Americans own almost seventy percent of the country's wealth. That was by the Cohort's design and the result of a well-executed, century-long master plan.

The Cohort had manufactured income inequality with one goal in mind: to develop a minimal membership with the highest possible net worth, and then leverage that wealth and influence to bend global economic, social, religious, and political institutions to *their* will. It was simple, but certainly not easy.

The Cohort's President was arguably more powerful than the President of the United States. However, unlike POTUS, the Cohort President operated from the shadows in order to maximize their effectiveness. Past Cohort presidents included *Fortune 100* CEOs, Governors, and even a movie star.

White House chief of staff, Marcos Roberts, was two years into his ten-year Cohort presidential term. He was the first Cohort leader to work directly for an American President, which had massive benefits and undeniable risks. Marcos's presence in the Oval Office was a giant leap forward for the organization. That's why he was chosen.

Marcos took a sip of his steaming coffee as he sat quietly in the Lagoon Room. The glass mug carried the group's lightning bolt crest. He looked across the circular table at his partners-in-crime. The seven members of the Cohort's Executive Council were socializing and comparing personal triumphs. All the men were internationally famous, aside from Judge Cathpert, who was content simply being a celebrity in South Carolina.

Although it was not widely advertised, Marcos was Judge Cathpert's son-in-law. He had married the judge's only child, Margaret. While Margaret wanted nothing to do with the Cathpert family or the Cohort, it was Judge Cathpert's influence and dark money campaign contributions that catapulted Marcos into his chief of staff position.

The combined net worth of the men at that table was hundreds of billions of dollars, and their collective global influence was off-the-charts. As a lowly millionaire with an Ivy League education, Marcos was just a pauper compared to present company. But what he lacked in wealth, he made up for in power.

As chief of staff, his phone's contact list was second to none. With a simple call, Marcos could influence federal policies that could tank the fortunes and freedoms of every person at that table. That was *real* power.

Marcos was energized by the fact that, after decades of planning and positioning, the organization was finally poised to enact the change it desperately desired. Finally, America's progress would not be stalled by archaic dogmatic practices and backward policies. It was time to solidify a new path forward – the Cohort's path.

Ironically, at its core, the Cohort was a *capitalist* enterprise. However, the dimming façade of the American dream had given way to a web of puppet masters steering their fiefdoms in the direction the Cohort's leadership determined they should go. And the plan was working.

A Cohort-led United States would reverse misguided ideologies which had crippled the country's progress made throughout the twentieth century. That goal was now attainable in mere *years*, not decades. All the pieces were moving into place.

Each global geographical region with a significant Cohort presence was assigned a district number, and the Executive Council selected a District Leader, usually the most long-tenured or influential Member in that region. District Leaders then served as that district's representative at Cohort meetings, which took place every five years.

However, the real genius of the Cohort's operation was its "Associate model" which mirrored *the Society of the Elect's* "Helpers" system. Becoming a Cohort Member was virtually impossible for the average person. However, Cohort Members were encouraged to nominate local contacts within their personal and professional networks to become Cohort "Associates."

Associates were accomplished, usually upper-middle class professionals, such as doctors, lawyers, accountants, engineers, academics, local elected officials, and business leaders. All of whom enjoyed positions of influence within their communities.

Associates needed to have a demonstrated track record of both being sympathetic to the Cohort's causes, and/or easily lured by the prospect of becoming rich in doing so.

District Leaders would pass down orders to Associates in their district and the Associates carried out those orders at a tactical level. For their effort, they were amply rewarded.

In the past, Associates who were doctors were instructed to embellish, or tank, a professional athlete's medical charts to affect a big game. City council Associates were forced to pass zoning laws that aligned with the Cohort's redistricting agenda in that city; and accountant Associates would be asked to cook the books of a Cohort-owned company, just to name a few. The Associate model had been in place since the mid-twentieth century and the number of Associates was exponentially increasing each year.

If, God forbid, an Associate was arrested and indicted for the crimes they were ordered to commit, it was understood that if they kept quiet, the Cohort would take care of their families. If they ratted, it was the opposite.

"Hey, *Prometheus*. You okay?"

One of the Council members asked Marcos as he took a drink of his orange juice. The others paused their conversations and glanced at their leader.

Per tradition, *Prometheus* was the name bestowed on the current Cohort president. In Greek mythology, *Prometheus* was the crafty Titan god of fire who stole fire from the gods and gave it to mankind in the form of knowledge. The Cohort did just that, and their lightning bolt symbol represented the natural fire that fueled their global agenda. Other Cohort Members and Associates were also occasionally assigned pseudonyms to conceal their true identities if it was suspected the feds were monitoring their communications.

"Yeah, I'm fine. Just thinking about the meeting." Marcos responded, followed by a politician's reassuring smile. He raised his coffee mug to offer a toast.

"Gentlemen, we have an opportunity here. A very *rare* opportunity. Frankly, I think the next two years are going to be a game changer for us."

"Here, here," the Council roared as they guzzled their breakfast beverages. A portly CEO took a large bite of a blueberry muffin, "What, *specifically*, excites you about the next twenty-four months, Marcos?" The man asked with his mouth full and crumbs in his white beard.

"Mainly, activating more Associates at the local level. And with me in POTUS's ear every day we've got the national issues covered as well. So, don't forget to donate to the President's re-election campaign and our Super PACs. If he stays, I stay; and if I stay in the White House, the Cohort does too."

Judge Cathpert sat to Marcos's right and nodded in agreement.

"Well, when the time comes, just tell me where to send my obnoxiously large check," the wealthiest member of the Executive Council announced. The group roared with laughter as the other leaders also committed their financial support.

Marcos took another sip of his coffee. His political fundraising was done for the day – actually, it was done for the year. He had just raised more money for the President's re-election campaign in five minutes than could be raised in months on the campaign trail.

The Council returned to their breakfast and private conversations and Marcos continued to strategize. He was confident the Cohort's quinquennial meeting was going to be the best in the group's history. The financial report was fantastic and the organization had successfully entrenched Members in twice as many government seats, media outlets, and C-suites, as had been projected.

Decades of buying influence, curbing elections, facilitating corporate hostile takeovers, tampering with juries, military coups, and other power-grabs, had all led to this point. Like a twisted chess match, the Cohort would take two steps forward and one step back. But they gained ground, year-after-year, and were very near checkmate.

A FARCO operative quietly entered the room and whispered into Marcos's ear.

"Eight minutes until we have to head upstairs, sir."

Chapter 58

D amian's cottage was eerily quiet. Bailey, Joseph, and Hunter cautiously crept over the door's threshold. Bailey methodically flipped on the lights. One by one, the sections of the large living room illuminated.

"Psst!" Hunter beckoned as he pointed toward the master bedroom.

Hunter put his index finger up to his lips signaling they may not be alone. Hunter waved to Bailey to get by the front door. A tapping noise was coming from Damian's bedroom. It grew louder and louder as Hunter and Joseph approached.

"I'll go first," Joseph offered. The door was slightly ajar. Hunter clenched his fists. Everyone held their breath as Joseph flung the door open.

Relief flooded over him as he saw a pesky tree branch banging against one of the bedroom's windows.

"It's okay. No one's here."

Hunter relaxed his clenched, white knuckles.

"Alright, Hunter, you and I are looking for any information the FBI can use to nail these lunatics."

Bailey emerged from the kitchen, "Damian's laptop is gone."

Joseph lifted the landline phone which sat on the bedside table.

"Phone's dead." He announced as he hung up the receiver.

"I got it!" Bailey blurted. The two men looked at her.

"I made sure the Menda IT department gave Damian a back-up iPad in case something happened to his laptop while traveling. It has a built-in hotspot and access to email already pre-loaded. I bet he left that here."

Bailey walked over to her boss's suitcase which was on a luggage rack in the corner of the room. After several seconds of rifling through his expensive clothes, she felt something cold and metallic near the bottom of the suitcase. She hoped it wasn't what she thought, but as she gripped the handle, she knew it wasn't an iPad. It was a gun.

Bailey pulled the weapon from the suitcase and held it in the air, "Look what I found!"

"What is Damian doing with a gun? He's just a suit, isn't he?" Hunter asked as he took the sidearm from his wife and studied it carefully.

"Here's a walkie-talkie too. Looks military-grade." Joseph said as he pulled the device from the top drawer of the bedside table.

"Even *corrupt* businessmen shouldn't have this equipment in their bedroom," Hunter said as he set the handgun on the bed and asked to see the walkie-talkie. He turned it on and heard only static. Then a voice rang out.

"Alpha Team, this is Henderson, Cohort Exec Council is preparing to move to primary meeting location. ETA, five minutes." Hunter looked up at Joseph.

"What's the *Cohort Exec Council?*"

"No clue," Joseph responded as the static returned.

Bailey searched for Damian's iPad with heightened urgency. She finally found it in a protective case in a side section of Damian's suitcase.

"Got it!" She announced as she carried the device into the kitchen and set it on the table. Joseph followed her, prepared to give detailed instructions on how they could contact the local FBI office via a secure online portal.

The iPad's login screen requested a password. Luckily, Bailey had convinced Menda's IT director to share Damian's username and password with her just in case Damian forgot it in a pinch. Not wanting to get in trouble with the company's new General Counsel, the IT director begrudgingly obliged.

Joseph was leaning over Bailey's shoulder.

"The password is *lightning bolt*," she said as she typed. A chill flew down Joseph's spine. *Of course – the symbol.*

The iPad's home screen had a handful of standard icons. Bailey clicked on the internet icon and Joseph gave her the web address for the FBI online employee portal. Once he sent out the distress message, help would be on the way in a matter of minutes.

Still in pain from the alligator's bite, Hunter entered the kitchen and limped toward them with the walkie-talkie in hand. Then, a fateful message rang out loudly over the radio.

"10-4, Hunter. Targets have been located on Captain Maynard's Island and Bravo Team is en route."

Bailey froze and looked up just in time to see her husband aim Damian's gun at Joseph's head and pull the trigger.

The sound of the gunshot was deafening.

Bright red blood spattered on Bailey's face and across the kitchen table. Joseph Manheim fell to the floor, lifeless.

Hunter then pointed the gun at his wife.

"Sorry, Bail. I didn't mean for you to get caught up in this. You weren't supposed to be here. Damian promised you wouldn't be here! That bastard promised!"

Bailey was stunned. The man she had married, the father of her children, had just murdered an FBI agent in cold blood. Tears of terror welled in her wide, brown eyes.

"Why?!" was all she could manage. Hunter's response was unfeeling.

"Pretty simple. The Cohort promised they would make me managing partner of Townsend & Moore."

"The Cohort?" Bailey was trying to make sense of everything. "What's *the Cohort*?"

Hunter looked at her, puzzled.

"You're kidding, right?"

Bailey had no idea what he was talking about.

"Come on…the organization Damian works for. Do you really think Menda Industrial skyrocketed because of Damian's business acumen? Please…" Hunter chuckled as he kept the handgun trained on his wife. He continued.

"Menda is a cash-cow for the Cohort's money laundering activity abroad. You all filter hundreds of millions into the U.S. for them each year. Why do you think Menda's project backlog is so deep in the Middle East?"

Bailey's shock turned to anger. Her boss and her husband had both lied to her. Her entire life felt like a lie.

"How did they get to you, Hunter?!" Bailey shrieked.

"I always knew you were a self-righteous prick, but I never thought you were a heartless murderer."

Hunter smirked at the comment.

"Sweetheart, the Cohort needed a big law firm to cover their tracks. And they needed an ambitious insider, like me, to help them do it. I'm one of their best Associates. That's why I'm here this weekend. They're honoring me for my recent contributions." He lowered the gun.

"The whole kidnapping thing was just a sham to protect you and the kids. If you guys saw me get kidnapped, then you could claim ignorance if everything came out later. Although some of the punches were *definitely* real and unnecessary. I'm still pissed about that." Hunter continued.

"You know, Bailey, I'm kind of disappointed you didn't pick up on what was going on. I thought you were smarter than that."

Bailey's mind turned to recent Menda meetings with Townsend & Moore attorneys. Now it all made sense. Cryptic emails, closed-door conversations, and hushed hallway discussions dominated her recollection. She snapped back to reality.

Hunter sat down next to her at the table. He was calm and composed. *What a psychopath*, she thought as she glanced at Joseph's body which was sprawled on the hardwood floor surrounded by a growing pool of blood.

"So, what happens now, Hunter? Are you going to kill me too?" She scowled at her husband, sickened by the sight of him.

"I'm not sure. Like I said, you weren't supposed to be here. It's up to the Cohort now."

At that moment, the front door blasted open and FARCO operatives barreled in, ready for battle.

"It's okay, boys. I handled the FBI agent." Hunter pointed to the dead body.

"This is my wife, Bailey. She won't give us any trouble, right, Bail?" Bailey shook her head and rose to her feet.

"Give me something to clean and dress this bite wound." Hunter ordered the operatives, as Bailey was escorted down the cottage steps in the torrential rain and ushered into a small transport motorboat. They were headed back to the Inn.

Chapter 59

S ergeant Henderson was standing outside the door of the Lagoon Room squinting at his phone's tiny screen. He never liked the newest technology. He preferred to handle things the old way with his bare hands.

He had received an alert that Hurricane Mary was now in full force. *Good*, Henderson thought, *Mother Nature will cover our tracks.*

Throughout his career, Sergeant Henderson had encountered many natural disaster scenarios while on assignment. He had even developed the weather exfiltration plan for Cohort Members, if needed. But he wasn't concerned. The Rhett's Bluff Inn was specifically constructed to withstand powerful coastal storms and as long as the Members stayed inside the hotel, they would be safe.

Sergeant Henderson glanced at the face of his military watch. It was almost time. He heard the Lagoon Room's door open and looked up to find a feeble figure moving toward him. It was Judge Cathpert.

"Well, good *mornin'*, *Sawgent*. The thin jurist said as he stopped for a brief word on his way to the lavatory.

"Your Honor..." Sergeant Henderson replied as he stood at attention. Judge Cathpert looked around to confirm they were alone. He then pulled out a folded picture from his jacket's pocket.

"We may have a small issue, *Sawgent*." The judge said through raspy breaths as he handed Sergeant Henderson the photograph he had confiscated from Special Agent Manheim the day before. Judge Cathpert's thin face carried a concerned look.

"Does Stoneman know?" Sergeant Henderson asked as he studied the picture.

"No, *Aah* don't think he does. Are you *gonna* tell him?"

"He'll learn soon enough, won't he?"

"Well, shoot, James, if the FBI knows, don't you think it's just a matter of *tahm* before Stoneman connects those dots too?"

"But the FBI doesn't know. Associate, Hunter Thompson, terminated the FBI agent a few minutes ago. The message never got to Stoneman. We're in the clear on that front." Sergeant Henderson reassured and returned his gaze to the photo which portrayed himself, Judge Cathpert, Dr. Kenneth Lyons, and Paul Stoneman, David's father.

"It's not the right time. Soon." Sergeant Henderson said as he folded the picture and stuffed it into his camouflaged pocket.

"Very soon…"

Chapter 60

The Central Intelligence Agency's *Technical Services Division* had trained Jacob to change his identity in less than a minute. In fact, he had trained directly under the agency's Chief of Disguise and was able to become a completely different person in a matter of seconds.

David's unexpected presence in Jacob's utility tunnel office represented a golden opportunity for Jacob to utilize his unique disguise skills to infiltrate the Cohort's quinquennial meeting by having an asset mic'd up *in the room*. But they had to move fast – the meeting was set to begin in less than thirty minutes.

However, Jacob's plan was not without significant risk. Sending an untrained asset, like David, into the heart of a multi-year, undercover operation could be a recipe for disaster. Still, if he could pull it off, the intelligence gathered would be priceless. The alternative was to rely on hidden audio bugs and tiny cameras Jacob had carefully placed throughout the conference room earlier that week.

In his experience, well-positioned audio bugs, alone, *could* do the trick. After all, they had been used by intelligence agencies for years. Notably, in the *Gunman Project*, bugs were placed within typewriters in the U.S. Embassy in

Russia during the Cold War. The U.S. returned the favor with *Operation Octopus*, which sought to surveil the Russian Embassy in Washington. While the audio quality of the bugs had increased exponentially since the Cold War, an audio-video strategy still paled in comparison to a wired asset in the room.

Jacob had also considered aerial surveillance but to no avail. A local friendly offered to supply him with drones which carried a forty-hour fly life. Jacob had even tested the fly time on the golf courses, claiming he was creating aerial content for the courses' social media pages. But with the hurricane, any drone would either be blatantly obvious or be destroyed in minutes by the weather.

The main limitation, however, was the top-secret nature of the operation. Only a handful of people even knew about it. One leak to the wrong person and the op would be dead, along with Jacob. A computer server in a hidden room at CIA headquarters at Langley was the sole intelligence repository for gathered intel. And that server was completely 'off-the-books.'

Jacob's computer in his secret office was connected directly to that server at Langley. After all, this was, arguably, the most important, clandestine CIA operation within the last half-century, but it was barely-funded and egregiously under-resourced. That was until David showed up.

The quinquennial meeting was the best chance to collect enough information to begin handing down indictments to Cohort Members after more than half a decade of building cases against them. It could be the silver bullet Jacob had been waiting for.

"Dave, the CIA needs you to attend the Cohort meeting that starts in twenty-five minutes...*in disguise.*"

"What!? No!" David emphatically responded.

"It has to be you." Jacob said as he pulled out his disguise bag from under the desk.

"Don't worry, I've been trained on this. We'll transform you into a member of the Inn's wait staff. Meanwhile, I'll be in the lobby building an airtight alibi for us."

David racked his brain for viable alternatives but came up with none.

"Why can't *you* go in disguise in the meeting?"

"Like I said...only I can create an alibi for both of us. Plus, someone could recognize me, even in disguise. Remember, I've known many of these folks for years now."

Again, David attempted to lobby for alternatives with well-reasoned objections.

"But why can't you just go in as yourself?"

A fair question, but Jacob had a good answer.

"This meeting is invitation-only, except for the Inn's wait staff. It would raise serious red flags if the golf pro just wandered in, unexpectedly. No can do."

Jacob pulled out a variety of masks and facial accessories from his bag and spread them across his desk.

"Okay, let's make you invisible!"

Chapter 61

S arah was glued to the television. The South Carolina Governor was conducting a press conference discussing his mandatory evacuation order. The words *Emergency Operations Center* were etched into his podium along with the seal of the SOUTH CAROLINA EMERGENCY MANAGEMENT DIVISION on the back wall behind him.

The Governor began the broadcast by asking a military chaplain to offer a word of prayer. The chaplain obliged and, thereafter, the Governor read his statement.

Hurricane Mary is now a Category 4 hurricane with wind speeds of one-hundred fifty miles-per-hour. According to the most recent hurricane advisory report, the brunt of Mary is hitting the South Carolina coast today. Rainfall amounts of six to ten inches could cause dangerous flash flooding, especially in the marshlands. If you are still in the Lowcountry, we recommend you move to higher ground immediately. If you are in one of the evacuation zones, you should already be gone. If, for some reason, you haven't evacuated, please do so now, before it's too late. We apologize for any inconvenience this may cause, but the most important thing is to ensure the safety of all South Carolinians. The South Carolina National Guard

> has deployed one-thousand service members to support the orderly evacuation process…

Sarah couldn't listen to the rest. Her anxiety level was through the roof. She picked up her cell and called David, *again*. No answer. She had called and texted him several times in the last half hour, but no response – which was unusual.

Through the hotel window Sarah could no longer see the pristine lawn that had looked so pleasant the day before. The Kiawah River had completely enveloped the backyard. And with the constant downpour, the waters continued to rise. A bright flash of lightning, immediately followed by the deafening crackle of thunder, caused Sarah to nearly jump out of her skin.

She had crammed all her clothes into her suitcase and even packed most of David's clothes too. Sarah picked up the room's phone and called the front desk. She was surprised when she heard Simon's voice and not a front desk clerk.

"Concierge, how may I help you?"

"Mr. Seifert, this is Sarah Mercer in Room Six—" Simon interrupted.

"Uh, Ms. Mercer, I was under the impression you and Mr. Stoneman had already departed. It's really not safe—"

Sarah interrupted back, "That's just it, I don't know where David is. Have you seen him in the lobby?"

"No, ma'am, I'm afraid I haven't seen Mr. Stoneman at all today. Did he tell you where he was going?" Simon's tone grew more concerned.

"No, but if you see him, please send him back to our room right away."

Simon agreed and Sarah hung up.

She couldn't have been angrier. Really, she was scared, but being angry was more satisfying.

Sarah would scour the entire hotel until she found David. She put on her shoes and headed for the door, and then the room phone rang. She quickly snatched the receiver from its resting place.

"Hello?"

"Hi, Sarah, it's Jacob Blake, the golf pro."

"Hey, Jacob. Look, I can't talk now. I have to find David."

"That's why I'm calling. I just saw David and he asked me to call you. He's taking an important business call in one of the Inn's private conference rooms and can't break away. It sounded serious."

Sarah was red, "He's doing what?!" She yelled into the receiver.

"He left me in this hotel room with a Category 4 hurricane coming and he's taking a freaking business call?!" Sarah realized she was shooting the messenger. She took a moment to compose herself and, in a calmer tone, asked a follow-up question.

"Which conference room is he in? I'm going to find him."

"No, no, don't do that. It sounded very important. I'll tell you what, let *me* arrange your transportation off the island myself. I'll even send a member of the staff to your room to collect your luggage. Shouldn't be more than thirty minutes. Just hang tight, okay?"

The phone was silent while Sarah contemplated Jacob's suggestion. She suspected Jacob could expedite their departure, so she acquiesced.

"Alright, fine. But tell David to hurry."

"Will do."

The line went dead and Sarah walked back into the bedroom and sat nervously on the edge of the bed. The Governor's press conference concluded and the news was now showing live coverage of the Charleston Battery. It was a disaster zone.

The reporter on location was wearing a bright yellow poncho and could barely stand on her feet. The feed cut back to the meteorologist in the studio who continued commenting on the severity of the storm.

Sarah looked out the bedroom window a second time. The gale-force wind caused foliage and pool chair cushions to fly past the window as if they were weightless. *If we don't leave soon, we may not be able to,* Sarah worried as she bit her lower lip and eagerly waited for her boyfriend to return.

Chapter 62

Jacob hung up.

"She's mad, but she bought it," he warned David as he pulled a neatly pressed waiter's uniform from a metal locker in the corner of the office and carefully draped it over his desk chair. Jacob returned his focus to the task at hand.

David had a lingering question.

"Besides yourself, do you have other people embedded in the Cohort? Do you have other moles at this meeting?"

"I always have a couple surprises up my sleeve. But just worry about what *you* need to do in the room." Jacob said as he pulled a mouthpiece out of a box.

"Here, try on this dental façade." He said as he handed David the gum-colored mouth apparatus.

"What is it?" David asked as he studied the mouthpiece.

"We don't have the time or equipment to develop a full-face mask for you, so we have to use simple items that will change your facial features enough so even your mother wouldn't recognize you. This is called a *plumper* – it pushes your lips and cheeks out a bit and creates a new jaw line."

David bit down on the plumper. He tried not to think about who had used it before him as it slid into place.

Jacob dug deeper into his disguise bag and pulled out two wigs, one with short brown hair and the other with wavy black hair with hints of gray at the temples. He held both up to David's head and quickly selected the black-haired wig. Jacob tossed the wig to David.

"Push your hair back and try that on." David placed the fake hair on his head while Jacob retrieved the disguise's final accessory, a pair of non-prescription eyeglasses.

"Put these on and button up your uniform. I'll brief you on your cover story as you change. We need to hurry!"

Chapter 63

Marcos Roberts arrived early at the conference room where the Cohort's quinquennial meeting would be held. Most of the Cohort's District Leaders had already checked-in at the registration table and were enjoying casual conversation over coffee and breakfast hors d'oeuvres.

For an organization so layered and complex, the Cohort's quinquennial meetings and communication structure was surprisingly simple. That was by design – hide in plain sight and make things so obvious that they're overlooked. That's the way the Cohort had operated for decades.

There were no hooded robes or ritualistic sacrifices. That would draw too much attention. The Cohort was well beyond that – they were everywhere and could be anyone. They had achieved an elite level of anonymity.

Still, the quinquennial meeting demanded heightened security. As such, each attendee was assigned a unique eight-digit passcode which was sent in an encrypted email just hours before the event. The passcode, along with a fingerprint scan, was required for entry. At their seats, each District Leader was asked to re-enter their eight-digit passcode to access the presentation materials on a tablet.

FARCO operatives were just aching to nab an intruder. If that happened, they were ordered to shoot to kill.

The wait staff, however, was not required to adhere to the same rigorous registration process. Rather, they were only required to digitally clock-in, via fingerprint scan, at the concierge's desk upon arriving at work.

Jacob Blake was well-aware of this security loophole and was thrilled to have an opportunity to exploit it using David as the test dummy.

Marcos laid his thumb on the registration device and then typed in his eight-digit pin. When the device's green light illuminated, he made his way to the podium in the front of the room and set down his presentation notes.

Upon seeing Marcos, the nearly four dozen District Leaders in attendance quieted and settled into their seats. Sergeant Henderson and his FARCO team tactically placed themselves around the room, covering all the exits. They closed the conference room doors, leaving the wait staff outside until they were beckoned to serve.

Marcos shook the hands of a few long-tenured District Leaders in the front row and then returned to the podium to study his talking points.

On top of the podium, a brown, wooden gavel was waiting for its handler. Marcos clasped the wooden handle and with a quick flick of the wrist and robust enthusiasm, the meeting was underway.

"Let us rise and with one voice, loudly proclaim the Cohort's mission." Marcos ritualistically stated as the

District Leaders stood and put their hands over their hearts. The group then recited the Cohort's creed.

We are the light in a dark world. One spark can ignite the flames of progress, liberty, and justice for all. The Cohort is the future and, together, we will prevail.

The words echoed throughout the room. The Cohort was not a religion, club, or cult – it was a *mindset*. And its philosophy was to be protected at all costs and by *any* means necessary.

Chapter 64

David finished changing into the Rhett's Bluff Inn waiter uniform. He never thought his summer in college waiting tables at the local steakhouse would come in handy, but it would certainly help today.

What choice do I have? He wondered as he buttoned the crisp white shirt. David's self-reflection was interrupted by Jacob.

"This uniform was sent directly from Langley. It's an exact replica."

David nodded. Jacob continued.

"Typically, there are a dozen waiters who are selected to serve at these Cohort events. Simon Siefert manages them all. Each staff member is given one of these access badges – so, keep this with you at all times, even though it's not scannable." Jacob raised the fake ID badge. Another gift from CIA headquarters.

"Trust me, becoming a waiter here is about as difficult as flying on Air Force One."

"If it's that exclusive, won't the other waiters know I'm a phony?" David asked as Jacob handed him the laminated badge.

Maybe. It's hard to say. If someone asks who you are, just show them your badge and tell them you're a new hire brought on for the fall and winter seasons. Your cover name is Tony Weber. You're forty-two and grew up in Greenville, South Carolina. You live on James Island with your wife, Janet, and two sons, Matt and Peter. Now, repeat that information back to me, verbatim.

"That's going to be enough?" David asked, concerned the thinly-veiled story may not hold up under intense scrutiny.

"Likely, yes. The other staff members will be too busy to pry too much, and the Cohort Members will completely ignore you. All I need is ten minutes of in-room footage, then you're done." Jacob said as he handed David the waiter's jacket and white gloves.

"There's a clock on the wall in the meeting room. After ten minutes, come straight down here. Got it?"

David agreed. Jacob retrieved a South Carolina flag lapel pin from his desk and pinned it to David's jacket.

"This pin has a camera in the flag's crescent moon, along with audio." Jacob looked down at one of his computers' monitors to ensure the device was working correctly.

"This little guy was a gift from OTS!" Jacob said with a grin.

"OTS?"

"Yeah, CIA's *Office of Technical Services* – they send us the fun spy gadgets. It's the closest we get to being James Bond." Jacob continued his instructions.

"As you move through the room, make sure you angle your torso toward any presentations being given, or at the attendees' tablets. We need to collect as much info as possible in the limited time you're in there, and we'll only have one chance to do it."

"Tablets? What's on the tablets?"

"Our intel says that each attendee is assigned a tablet with the presentations pre-loaded just hours before the meeting. No way to get past the devices' security settings to remotely hack it, and the tablets are then wiped clean immediately after the meeting. Our best chance to view that information is for you to capture the data in real-time on this camera."

David gulped, becoming increasingly aware that the success of this multi-year covert operation rested on *him*. A bead of sweat dripped down his forehead.

"Shouldn't we go over my backstory again?"

"No. If you have to go into more detail than that, you're screwed anyway. Oh, and if your cover is blown, *run*! FARCO will shoot you."

David waited for a sarcastic grin from Jacob, implying he was kidding, but it never came. He was serious. David's mind was racing. He didn't understand why he was even doing this. He was just a lawyer from D.C., not a trained CIA spy.

Jacob put the finishing touches on David's disguise. He stood up straight and looked David in the eye.

"Whatever you do, Dave, avoid Simon Seifert. He's the only one who will immediately know you're a fraud. If he notices you—"

"*Run*...I got it."

Jacob looked David up and down, "You've been in fancy places before, Dave. You know what to do. Just be polite and attentive, and try to capture as much as you can. All I need is ten good minutes. The CIA is counting on you."

David's emotions began to bubble. Fear rose inside him.

"Jacob, I don't think I can do this. This has nothing to do with me or Sarah. I—"

Jacob raised his index finger, silencing David.

"Wait...you don't know, do you?" Jacob asked as he cocked his head to the side, confused.

"Know what?"

"This absolutely involves you, Dave. Especially *you*. I can't believe you don't know."

Sensing David's ignorance was sincere, Jacob continued.

"David, you have a *direct* connection to all of this. Someone very close to you was—" Jacob caught himself, mid-sentence, "just forget about it for now, we're out of time and you need to get up there...we'll talk when you get back."

Chapter 65

M arcos studied his audience – it was his first time running the quinquennial meeting as Cohort President. He couldn't help but see the pride on the District Leaders' faces as they stood, chests out and shoulders back, reciting the Cohort creed. Marcos thought it best to begin with inspirational commentary to set the tone for the day.

"Friends…" He paused and canvassed the room. "A fire has been burning in the Inn's lobby this entire week. As you know, this is tradition. The flames serve as a reminder that the Cohort's mission should always be burning inside each of us. May it never be extinguished." Robust nods of approval gave Marcos confidence to escalate his oration.

"As was discussed at the last quinquennial meeting, the Executive Council encourages all Cohort Members to proudly display our symbol, the lightning bolt, in stained glass in your homes." He paused.

"This signals to the other Members, and our Associates, that we are united behind our global cause." Marcos glanced at Judge Cathpert seated in the front row. To his right were Damian and Tara.

Another pregnant pause had the District Leaders on the edge of their seats. Like a symphony, Marcos's tone grew louder and his hands, more energetic. He could sense the enthusiasm in the room was building. It was time for the crescendo.

"After decades of strategic planning, we are finally ready for *Phase Two* of our organization's global initiative, which is set to commence in the coming weeks. Like a chess board, we have positioned Cohort Members in the highest ranks of American society and now it's time to activate them. The time for action has arrived!" Marcos's fists were clenched and raised victoriously over his head.

"We finally have the chance to free America, and the rest of the world, from the strictures of archaic, vapid, and backward societal ideologies and institutions which have hindered us for a century. We can replace them with a new system based on the tenets of science and reason. The power will soon be consolidated in the hands of the worthy few…in *our* hands! And, together, WE WILL PREVAIL!"

His audience erupted in thunderous applause.

Now their blood was pumping, it was time to get down to business. After several seconds of soaking in the adoration, Marcos waved the crowd back into their seats.

"To get started, I want to, first, thank everyone for attending. As District Leaders you have an awesome responsibility to our Members and Associates in your respective regions who look to you for guidance. You'll have a lot to share with them coming out of this meeting."

Marcos reviewed his notes and continued.

> Regarding the weather, Mr. Seifert tells me this hotel was built to withstand Category 5 hurricanes.

So, I assure you, even though the non-Cohort guests are being asked to evacuate ASAP, we are perfectly safe within these walls. However, in the event of an emergency, Sergeant Henderson and the FARCO team have secured two decommissioned Coast Guard helicopters which will run in shifts to fly us out of here, if needed. But just to reassure, you, your spouses, or any of your invited guests who are still at the Inn are completely safe.

Marcos scrolled through his notes on his tablet. He glanced up. Staring back at him were global business leaders, celebrities, social media influencers, media personalities, and politicians. He would have been intimidated if he didn't already work for the most powerful man in the world.

"Second, I am happy to report that, this year, we have vetted and elected *hundreds* of new Cohort Members, and engaged *thousands* of new Associates around the globe. Our mission truly is a movement and we couldn't pursue *Phase Two* without building that strong support network to carry out our goals at the local level." Again, the audience applauded.

"Moreover, the financial health of our organization is stronger than ever. Cohort-led businesses are posting billions of dollars in top-line revenues, with Menda Industrial Corporation out of Atlanta leading the way as the most profitable entity in the Cohort's private sector portfolio." More robust cheers.

"We will discuss the financial breakdowns by region and industry this afternoon. So, stay tuned for more information on that." Marcos scrolled his index finger down the digital page to stay on track.

"On the political front, as you know, we experienced a setback last year in Washington with the failure of the Division Act. As a result, we temporarily pulled back on our federal legislative agenda until the dust settles." Rumblings swept through the crowd. It was an unpopular topic and Marcos quickly moved on.

"However, thanks to our enthusiastic Associates, a few of whom have been invited to be with us today, our state and local political agenda is posting more wins than losses in key battleground areas." Marcos noticed a hand raised by a silver-tongued Governor seated in the middle of the room. Marcos invited him to speak.

"Thank you, *Prometheus*. Just so everyone's aware, in my state, our plans are moving along nicely and without significant opposition. Fingers crossed that trend continues. My question is regarding efforts abroad. How are we doing internationally?" The politician smiled and nodded at a handful of fellow politicos in the room.

Marcos was prepared for the question.

Thank you, Governor. And, just to clarify, I'm confident our *national* agenda will be back on track very soon. But to answer your question, our international growth remains strong. As you may recall, Governor, we had a notable win in 2021 in the Jhabua District in the Madhya Pradesh State of India. There, Cohort Members successfully influenced officials into instituting a ban on certain religious gatherings which were an impediment to our initiatives in the region. Even though that was years ago, our Indian District Leaders tell me these restrictions are still in place today, and even likely to expand, which allows our local agenda to develop. That's just one example that comes to mind.

Marcos's comments were met with affirming head nods from the crowd. He continued.

On a related note, because international Member numbers have increased, we have updated the Cohort's international non-disclosure agreement. Each Member, and all Associates, will be required to sign the updated version of this document before the end of the year. The Executive Council strongly recommends that the business leaders in the room also update the NDAs of your respective organizations to reflect the new changes in the Cohort NDA. Unfortunately, we recently had a situation with a whistleblower in Atlanta and want to limit those incidents moving forward. Copies of that NDA will be sent to each of you in an encrypted email file early next week to distribute within your district.

Another hand shot up from the back of the room. It was a young tech-billionaire wearing a wrinkled T-shirt, faded skinny jeans, and modeling a handlebar mustache. Marcos pointed to him.

"Quick question about crypto. Has the Council discussed the Cohort's long-term investment strategy concerning cryptocurrency and blockchain technology? My company has gone all-in on both." The young man sat down.

"Great question. The Council believes crypto will continue to be great for Cohort business due to its lack of regulation and the ease with which it can be utilized for cross-continental business. So, yes, we anticipate leaning into those technologies moving forward."

Judge Cathpert chimed-in from the front row.

"My *North'n* judicial contacts tell me that Ohio allows attorneys to hold crypto in escrow for clients. We have plenty of Associates who can help our Cohort businesses with that."

Before Marcos could return to his notes, a female CEO in the second row raised her hand with another question.

"*Prometheus*, I'm going to ask the question that everyone is wondering – when can we invite POTUS to join our ranks?" The room grew deathly silent. That was the question Marcos dreaded. Still, his answer was resolute and short.

"Never." The room stood still, disappointed by the clear message.

"As I've mentioned previously, the President can *never* know about us. As we saw with the Division Act last year, too much exposure in Washington could derail everything we've worked so hard to build. I can continue to promote our agenda in the White House without risking our anonymity, but he can never know about our organization."

No one said a word. Marcos welcomed the next item on the agenda which was a brief ten-minute refreshment break before the longer morning session began.

"Hearing no further discussion, I would like to welcome everyone, again, to the Cohort's quinquennial meeting – it's time to warm up your coffee. Sergeant Henderson, please allow the wait staff to join us with the morning refreshments.

Chapter 66

FARCO's Bravo Team took Bailey by boat to the service entrance on the far side of the Rhett's Bluff Inn. Her world had been turned upside down in less than twenty-four hours. Her seemingly perfect husband was a turncoat, cold-blooded killer and her boss was a corporate criminal. She was now being held at gunpoint by special military operators in the middle of a hurricane. It was not her finest hour.

The side service entrance was elevated above the rising waterline and rested at the top of an exterior metal stairwell. The flood waters continued to creep up the bottom steps.

Tears dripped down Bailey's wet face as the boat rocked back and forth, anchored in the choppy water. She glared at Hunter who was perched on the side of the boat. She was disgusted by the sight of him. Bailey had just been a pawn in Hunter's elaborate, murderous, social-climbing game. He used her to collude with psychopaths under the guise that, one day, he would run one of the largest law firms in the Southeast. He was dead to her.

The boat continued rocking as FARCO operatives roughly grabbed Bailey's arm and forced her onto the steps. Unfortunately, Bailey's only escape option would be to dive into alligator-infested waters. That would not improve her chances of survival. She had to wait and hope a better opportunity presented itself.

The FARCO operatives led her through the service door and down a back stairway. They walked through the hallway that Bailey recognized as the Inn's bottom level where she had been previously imprisoned. A burly operative opened the door to the room with which Bailey was all too familiar – the space where she and Hunter were previously locked up.

Another FARCO operative placed a chair in front of Bailey and tugged several feet of coarse rope out of his camouflage backpack. Bailey sat in the chair as one of the operatives began meticulously tying the rope tightly across her chest and legs in a zig-zag pattern. She scowled at Hunter as he stood casually scrolling through his phone without a care in the world. He eventually locked eyes with Bailey.

"Come on, Bail. I know you're pissed, but you have to understand why I'm doing this." He walked over and crouched down to look his wife in the eye.

"Join us." His words lingered in the air.

"The reason for my elaborate fake kidnapping was so you could remain blissfully ignorant regarding my involvement with this group. But your rescue plan at Damian's cottage ruined everything, didn't it? If you were one of us, none of this would be necessary." Hunter pointed to the ropes which were becoming increasingly more constricting. Bailey huffed and stared past Hunter.

"Join what? Did they finally let you into a fraternity, Hunter?"

Hunter laughed, "No. Not a fraternity…the Cohort. I help them avoid sticky legal situations and they help me rise to the top of the legal mountain. Whether you like it or not, the Cohort has been funding our lifestyle for years." Hunter shook his head as if that information were public.

"You thought your meteoric rise at Townsend & Moore and your being named Menda Industrial's General Counsel was because you're *that* talented? Please…" Hunter drew his eyebrows into a frown and shook his head.

"You're just their little errand boy, aren't you, Hunter? A pissant wannabe." Bailey could tell she was getting under Hunter's skin. Wanting to twist the proverbial knife, Bailey added a second ego slight.

"Actually, *errand boy* is too generous. You're not even good enough to run their errands, you're just—" before she could finish her insult, Hunter slapped her hard across the face.

"SHUT UP!!!" He screamed at the top of his lungs; his eyes wild with rage. "You don't know anything about it!!" He wagged his finger in Bailey's reddened face. She responded by spitting on him.

He wiped the saliva off his cheek and drew his hand back for another blow. She braced for impact, but the hit never came.

Bailey opened her eyes and saw one of the FARCO operatives holding Hunter's arm back and whispering in his ear. All Bailey could hear were the words, "He still needs her," as the operative shot a reproving look her way. Hunter tore his arm free from the operative's brutish grasp.

"Fine! Then I'm headed upstairs to change clothes – I'm already late to the meeting!" Hunter yelled in frustration. He limped hurriedly toward the door, but not without admonishing the operatives in the process.

"You guys didn't have to be so rough with me this week either. You better believe I'm going to report that activity to Marcos Roberts when we get out of here."

The FARCO operatives grinned at each other. To them he was just a pretty boy puppet and it was their pleasure to take him down a notch or two.

As Hunter stormed out, he issued a final warning to Bailey.

"They'll give you *one chance* to join us, Bailey. That's it! You better think long and hard about what you're going to do. I'd hate to tell the kids that mommy died in a hurricane in South Carolina." He said as the door closed behind him.

Chapter 67

The wait staff moved surgically from table to table as they had been instructed to do, serving the District Leaders coffee and juice.

Marcos circulated the room. He always made it a point to shake hands with the most influential District Leaders – an old political habit he had mastered.

However, as he glad-handed, Marcos noticed one staff member awkwardly lingering near one of the District Leaders who was still seated and scrolling through his tablet. *That's odd*, he thought.

The staff member had salt-and-pepper hair and wore ill-fitting glasses. But it wasn't his appearance that bothered Marcos; it was his curiosity regarding the information on the District Leader's tablet that bothered Marcos the most.

David was shocked at the non-secretive nature of the Cohort's meeting. He had expected an elaborate ceremony with scary robed figures carrying out ritualistic blood sacrifices. There was none of that.

It was brilliant. To any normal person, the Cohort meeting would appear to be a simple business conference. That's likely how they managed to operate under the radar for decades – *they hid in plain sight.*

David had positioned himself behind an oblivious attendee who was scrolling through presentation slides on his tablet. David leaned in to ensure his lapel pin camera was capturing all of it. Jacob was going to be thrilled with what he was getting.

However, a cold chill flew down David's spine when he glanced up and noticed Marcos Roberts staring directly at him. *Just remain calm and pour the coffee,* David instructed himself.

He leaned over the man in front of him and carefully refilled his empty coffee cup without asking permission in a desperate attempt to conceal his loitering. The man nodded in ignorant appreciation and kept scrolling through the slide deck.

David looked up again. Marcos was still watching him like a hawk. David quickly moved to another table.

"More coffee, ma'am?" David asked an attractive woman in her mid-forties as she feverishly pounded out a text message on her cell phone.

She shook her head, barely acknowledging him. He moved to the next person and offered the same question. After several seconds, he glimpsed at Marcos again. This time, however, when their eyes locked, Marcos started moving toward David.

David scurried in the opposite direction heading to the farthest table. Beads of sweat were now dripping down his wigged brow as he poured another cup of coffee for a portly gentleman wearing a three-piece suit.

"Excuse me?!" The gentleman admonished. "Try to keep it in the cup, bozo!"

David realized his pouring hand was shaking, which caused coffee to spill out onto the white, linen tablecloth.

"I'm terribly sorry, sir. I'll get some club soda."

"Don't bother." the man said with a dismissive wave of his chubby hand.

David turned and froze. Marcos was standing directly in front of him with his arms crossed. David could tell by his gaze that he was onto him.

However, before he had a chance to speak, the rude, portly gentleman stood up, elbowed David out of the way, and engaged Marcos with a hearty handshake. Consequently, Marcos had no choice but to divert his attention to the man.

Seeing his escape window, David swiftly relocated to the other side of the room, by the exit. He had done what Jacob had asked him to do, but now it was definitely time to go.

Chapter 68

Marcos's conversation with the portly man concluded and, seeing that the mysterious member of the wait staff was now on the other side of the room, he called over Sergeant Henderson.

"Yes, sir?"

"Call Simon and tell him I want to dismiss a member of the staff without making a scene."

So as not to raise any concerns, Marcos resumed his position at the podium to make an announcement.

"Ladies and gentlemen of the staff, we appreciate your support this morning, but I'm told Simon Seifert would like to see you in the hallway to discuss lunch." Marcos lied.

The staff made their way out the door, including the gentleman who was making Marcos uneasy.

As they were leaving, Marcos noticed Associate, Hunter Thompson, limp into the room and hurry to his reserved seat. Marcos would inquire later about the reason for his tardiness, the limp, and the bruising on his face.

Seeing that the District Leaders had resumed their seats, and now that Hunter was in attendance, Marcos continued with the rest of the morning agenda which included honoring the three "rising star" Associates who had been invited to the meeting as Marcos's guests. He formally introduced Damian, Hunter, and Tara to the group, encouraged them to stand and be recognized, and took a minute to laud their recent contributions to the Cohort's national agenda.

David stood quietly outside the meeting room door reflecting on what had just happened. Whispered conversations amongst the other staff members signaled to David that their abrupt dismissal from the meeting was abnormal.

David's reflection was interrupted by an unwelcomed question from one of the other staff.

"Are you new? I don't think we've met." One of the female staff extended her hand. David reciprocated the gesture but refrained from making direct eye contact.

"I thought we were going to be short-staffed this fall. Where did Simon dig you up?"

David robotically responded with his rehearsed backstory, which seemed to satisfy the woman's curiosity.

At that moment, the meeting room doors opened and Cohort District Leaders filed out in droves. *They must be taking a bathroom break before the next session begins.* David concluded.

Just then, he glanced down the hall and panic set in. Simon Seifert was jogging down the long corridor toward them. He looked both angry and frantic.

"Wait here, and have your badges ready to be scanned. I mean it!! No one move an inch!!" Simon sternly commanded as he stormed past the staff and into the meeting room. Marcos met him just a few steps into the room and immediately pointed at David.

Oh no! David had to disappear, and fast.

He darted down the short hallway and made a quick right turn into the long, luxurious hallway with the floor-to-ceiling windows on the outer wall to his left.

In a full sprint, David quickly arrived at the secret door leading to the back stairwell. He flung the door open and descended the flight of stairs, in seconds. He heard the door open above him and recognized Simon's shrill voice screaming after him.

"Hey, you!! Come back here!!"

There was no way he could make it to Jacob's secret office without exposing it. Instead, he opened the door to the floor he was on. Relief flooded over him when he recognized the interior décor of *Ballroom A*.

The large space was now dark, but the dim, natural light streaming in through the ballroom's windows allowed David to snake through the tables and chairs and fly toward the exit. As he darted through the Inn's lobby, he saw Jacob seated in front of the fireplace, solidifying his alibi.

David made a beeline toward him. Sensing David's alarm, Jacob shot to his feet.

"They made me! Simon's right behind me!" David alerted.

"Do they know it's *you*?" Jacob asked.

"I don't think they know it's *me*. But he's coming, he's right behind me, Jacob!"

"Here's a master key that opens all the guest rooms. *Run* to your room and the second you're in the room, take off your disguise and get in the shower. Go, now!"

Jacob pushed David away and casually resumed his seat in front of the fire. No one had seen them talking – this plan could work.

Just as David ducked out of sight, Simon emerged from *Ballroom A* completely out of breath and panting. His dirty-blonde head swiveled wildly around the lobby searching for the imposter. He ran to the front desk and screamed for the desk clerk who suddenly appeared from the backroom holding a half-eaten sandwich.

"Did you see a waiter come through here?!"

"No, I was in the back eating my lun—"

"Nevermind, idiot! Did you see *anyone*?!" He yelled at the young man. The desk clerk shook his head.

Simon saw Jacob and ran to him.

"Jacob, did you see a waiter in a white jacket?! It's important!"

"Sorry, Simon. Didn't see anyone. Who are you looking for?" Jacob hoped the distracting question would give David a couple more seconds to get to his room.

Simon didn't answer and continued to scour the lobby. Then he heard the sound of a door slam down the first-floor hallway. Like a rabid dog, Simon scurried back to the front desk. Jacob overheard Simon ask which guests were still in the rooms on the first floor.

"Just one. Stoneman, Room Six," came the response. Simon rushed down the hallway toward Room Six. Things were about to get interesting.

Chapter 69

Sarah jumped as she heard the door open and then slam shut. She nearly screamed when she saw a stranger in a waiter's uniform standing in front of her. The man removed a pink mouthpiece and threw it into the trash can by the door, along with his eyeglasses. Sarah's jaw dropped.

"David? What the—"

"Shhhhh!" David put his index finger over his lips as he grabbed Sarah's arm and pulled her into the bedroom.

"There's no time to explain. The concierge is chasing me."

"Simon? What do you mean he's cha—" Again, Sarah was interrupted.

"Tell him I'm in the shower. We're in trouble, Sarah. Just trust me!"

At that moment, there were three loud knocks at the door. David disappeared into the bathroom with his wig in hand. Sarah, trying to make sense of the situation, walked to the door and opened it a crack. It was Simon.

"My apologies, Ms. Mercer, but did a member of the hotel staff come into your room within the last few minutes?" Simon asked as he looked past Sarah.

"No. No one came in here." Sarah didn't know what was happening, but she trusted David. She was appalled by Simon's response.

"Well, ma'am, I'm afraid I have to search your room anyway. It's a security matter. Excuse me." He said as he barreled through the door and pushed Sarah aside.

"Hey! You can't just barge in here!" Sarah objected, but Simon paid no attention.

Simon peeked in the empty closet and dove to the floor to look under the bed. No sign of an intruder. The only room Simon hadn't checked was the bathroom. He heard the shower running, then it suddenly turned off. Sarah tried to warn David without being too obvious.

"David, the concierge is here. He insisted on searching our room for some mystery person." Sarah shot a reproving look at Simon.

Simon politely knocked on the bathroom door. "Mr. Stoneman, it's Simon Seifert. I'm terribly sorry, but I need a word with you right away, sir." Simon knocked again, this time more aggressively. Hearing no response, Simon flung the unlocked bathroom door open to find David dripping wet wearing just a towel wrapped around his waist. David feigned surprise.

"Get out of here, man!" David yelled, acting angry. Simon was mortified.

He glanced around the bathroom and, seeing no one, shut the door and continued the conversation through the door.

"I beg your pardon, Mr. Stoneman, but is a member of the wait staff in there with you?" That question caused Simon to turn beet red.

David opened the door, still fake fuming, "No! There's no one in here, you moron!" He said as he tugged open the shower curtain to reveal an empty shower.

"Happy?" David, still sporting his towel, stormed toward Simon who was frozen in place. David was inches from Simon's face.

"I'm reporting this invasion of privacy to the police. You'll be lucky if I don't sue you for this."

Simon looked down at the floor with his lip quivering, "I'm deeply sorry, sir, I just thought—"

David interrupted and pointed to the door.

"Leave my room now, so I can get dressed!"

As Simon speed-walked to the door, Sarah continued to scold him for his unprofessional behavior. Sarah's usually-sweet disposition turned sour in a hurry.

As he reached the door, Simon had heard enough. He suspected his tenure as the Inn's concierge was over anyway, so, he held nothing back.

"You know what, Ms. Mercer? You and Mr. Stoneman don't belong here anyway. This hotel is for *VIPs* only. You're just a couple of charity cases." He smugly replied as he opened the door.

But as he turned to leave, his eye caught something in the trash can. It looked like a mouthpiece and a pair of glasses.

The light from the hallway accentuated the fresh spittle dripping off the side of the gum-colored apparatus. Then it clicked.

Simon put his foot in the closing door and pushed it open again with two hands as he ducked back into the room. He had been duped.

"Mr. Stoneman..." Simon barked. He then pulled out a small radio which was fastened to his brown leather belt. He didn't hear the door shut behind him as it should have. Simon turned to find Jacob standing in the doorway, pointing a gun at him.

"Simon, if you say one word, I *will* kill you." Jacob stepped into the room and pressed the cold metal against Simon's head. Sarah was in shock.

"Dave?" Jacob hollered. David appeared wearing spare gym clothes from his suitcase, his hair still wet.

"Did you get some good stuff in the room?" Jacob asked. David nodded.

Simon's knees became weak. The Cohort's quinquennial meeting had been infiltrated by *David Stoneman* himself. Simon was as good as dead. In that moment he realized that his only possible chance of survival was to prevent Jacob, Sarah, and David from ever leaving the Inn alive.

Chapter 70

Damian sensed something was terribly wrong. The mid-morning break had now lasted over *twenty* minutes, which didn't make sense. Damian crossed his arms and read the room as he impatiently tapped his shoe on the carpet. He saw Sergeant Henderson near the podium being reprimanded by Marcos.

Tara could sense Damian was anxious.

"You look tense," she said as she sat next to him.

The cadence of Damian's foot tapping increased.

"Something's happening, Tara. I don't think it's good."

Judge Cathpert sauntered into the conversation sipping steaming black coffee. Hunter joined as well.

Damian didn't like Hunter. He couldn't trust a man who knowingly let his wife be captured and likely killed, all so he could become the managing partner of some law firm. Despite Damian's blind ambition, he would never sell out those closest to him like that.

"It appears our *meetin'* has been postponed. *Y'all* should've gotten the message on your tablet." Judge Cathpert said as he took another sip.

Damian and Tara exchanged glances. Something *was* wrong.

"On another note, do *y'all* know Hunter?

Hunter smiled and nodded – he knew Damian but hadn't yet met Tara. After catching a glimpse of her attractive physique, he was eager to do so.

"Hi, there. Hunter Thompson." He said with a playboy smile, despite having a busted lip and a black eye, as he extended his hand which Tara unenthusiastically shook. Tara was not interested in becoming the next mistress of a social-climbing Cohort Associate. She had her own plans which no overdressed Romeo was going to derail.

Nevertheless, Hunter continued his advances. "What role are you playing with us, gorgeous?" Hunter asked, again, ogling Tara. She reluctantly replied.

"I'm an Associate who worked with Mr. Roberts in Washington. He recently assigned me to support Damian at Menda Industrial. For a 'big deal' guy, they don't tell you much, do they?" Tara commented, intending offense.

Hunter's smirk turned upside down. He couldn't let that one go.

"I see…you're a *liaison* Associate. I get it. They just pass you around the Executive Council, right?" Hunter winked at Tara. She responded in kind.

"No, I do a bit more than that. I make sure the Cohort's nine-figure investment in overseas projects continues to generate that same return year-over-year. That's a lot more than your little law firm does, isn't it?"

Oddly, despite her repeated insults, it actually made Hunter want Tara more.

"Trust me, man. I already tried. She won't have any of it," Damian said as he rolled his eyes. Judge Cathpert chuckled and retreated to the restroom and Hunter floated to another conversation circle nearby.

Damian and Tara remained with their eyes trained on Marcos and Sergeant Henderson's heated conversation. At that moment, Sergeant Henderson's radio blasted with a loud alert. Concern flooded over his face. He raced past Marcos and out the conference room doors.

Marcos scurried over to Tara and whispered in her ear.

"There's a mole...the meeting's been compromised."

Chapter 71

Why is the golf pro holding a gun to my head?

Simon wondered as he raised his hands in silent surrender. Simon's purple, patterned sports coat now felt heavy on his unathletic shoulders. His armpits had sweat soaking through his mint green buttoned-down shirt.

"David, where's the lapel pin?" Jacob asked as looked around the room.

"It's in the bathroom," David responded.

"Pin it back on. The footage is being uploaded to the server in real-time. I want to capture this."

Jacob's statement nearly caused Simon to faint. Not only had the Cohort meeting been infiltrated, it had been *recorded*. His life was over – the Cohort would kill him within the week. The sanctity of the Rhett's Bluff Inn had been breached and on *his watch*. That was unforgivable.

"Who are you people?" Simon murmured; his voice shaky.

"Shut up!" Jacob barked as he pushed the gun barrel harder against Simon's sweaty forehead.

David retrieved the South Carolina flag pin and stuck it on the left side of his T-shirt.

Simon's fear suddenly turned to rage. His only chance of redemption would be to deliver the traitors to Marcos and then beg for mercy.

"You all have no idea who you're messing with. They can get to *anyone, anywhere!*" Simon said as he glared at Jacob with his hands still in the air.

"But it doesn't have to end badly. Let me negotiate a trade. The recording for cash. I guarantee they'll give you a ton of money for the footage."

Jacob used his weapon to lift Simon's chin.

"No...*you* have no idea who *you're* messing with. We've been tracking the Cohort for years. All we have to do is leak online what we already have and your organization crumbles. We have the power now, Simon."

Simon couldn't help but laugh, "You think you're watching *us?* We have people in every major government agency. The FBI, NSA, CIA, DOJ – all of them. Where do you think we learned about dead drops, microdots, and stenography? Our people in the intelligence community taught us how to do it. We're everywhere!"

At that moment, the door burst open and four armed FARCO operatives ran into the room. They moved into position, carrying M-4 assault rifles. Sarah screamed and David ran to stand in front of her. Some of the men looked familiar to David – then it clicked: they were some of the same FARCO operatives he had encountered in Washington the year before.

Like a human shield, Jacob grabbed Simon's collar and flung him between himself and the operatives. Jacob clenched the top of Simon's disheveled hair with his left hand as he aimed his sidearm at Simon's temple with his right. Then, he carefully peered out at the operatives.

David and Sarah slowly retreated to the corner of the room. The situation was silent and tense, but it was clear the operatives' attention was not on them, at least not yet. The leader of FARCO's Alpha Team spoke first.

"Mr. Blake, release Mr. Seifert, now!!" He yelled as the FARCO team collectively took one step closer.

"Not another inch, or he dies," Jacob responded with his gun still pressed against Simon's sweaty brow. Simon pleaded for the operatives to back off.

The team leader glanced at David and Sarah.

"Simon, who are they?"

David responded directly, "We're just guests at the hotel. We're nobodies."

"Names?" The operative demanded.

"David Stoneman and Sarah Mercer." David put his hand on Sarah and repositioned her even further behind him.

The operative smiled as he recognized David. "Good to see you again, Mr. Stoneman." He sarcastically said as he radioed Sergeant Henderson.

"Sergeant, this is Alpha Team Leader. We located Seifert, but he's being held at gunpoint by Jacob Blake. We also have two hotel guests involved in the situation – David Stoneman and Sarah Mercer. How should I handle? Over."

The pronounced static from the radio filled the room before Sergeant Henderson's response came through, loud and clear.

"Eliminate Seifert and Blake. Bring Stoneman and Mercer to the Lagoon Room."

"Roger that." The operative said as he put his finger on his assault rifle's trigger.

Simon couldn't believe what he had just heard. He had been a loyal Cohort Associate for years. He accommodated their every whim and kept their most guarded secrets. Simon pleaded his case to the FARCO team.

"No, no, no…I work directly for the Executive Council. Call Marcos Roberts or Judge Cathpert, and they'll tell you. These are the traitors and I delivered them to you." He implored as he lowered his hands. Jacob ducked further behind Simon, knowing what was coming next.

"Come on, guys, it's *me*…" Simon said as he put his hands on his chest.

"Engage!"

The gunshots were deafening in the small hotel room.

Simon took most of the gunfire and fell backward, dead. Jacob returned shots as Simon's dead weight collapsed on top of him. Jacob hit one of the operatives in his body armor but the barrage of bullets was too much. He was hit several times and Jacob's right arm went numb. The lead operative put a final bullet in his head to end it.

David was draped over Sarah on the floor. When he looked up, he saw the FARCO team hurrying toward them. One of the operatives extracted two hoods from a tactical backpack. The leader aggressively wrapped the hoods over their heads.

"Take me," David pleaded, "leave her alone! She has nothing to do with this!"

Sarah was screaming. And at that moment, David realized he was powerless to save her.

Chapter 72

M arcos had just received word the mole had been captured by FARCO.

He stood stoically behind the podium and calmly requested that the District Leaders take their seats for an important update. He chose his next words very carefully – he didn't want to lie, but he couldn't tell the truth. Luckily, his political background had adequately prepared him for such an occasion.

"Ladies and gentlemen, I have some unfortunate news. You should have received an email a few minutes ago explaining that our meeting has to be postponed." Marcos announced as he feigned disappointment.

"The weather experts tell us that even though Hurricane Mary has been downgraded from a Category 4 to a Category 2, the flood-related damage has created hazardous conditions around the hotel, which is worse than expected. As a result, local officials have *ordered* us to evacuate."

He continued as frustration swept through the crowd. "I wish there were something I could do, but if we don't acquiesce, they're going to start asking more questions, and we certainly don't want that." He paused and looked down at his expensive watch.

"We'll send the rescheduled details to you via encrypted email within the next couple of weeks. The good news is that every District Leader, and any family members or guests you may be traveling with, will be safely evacuated from the Inn's rooftop, via helicopter, within the next half hour."

Marcos looked to Judge Cathpert in the front row. The bony jurist gave him a nod of approval. The movie star District Leader raised his hand with a question.

"Can we leave by *boat*? My assistant chartered a boat to get me and my wife out."

"You're certainly welcome to explore other exit options, but I've been told the traditional waterways are too dangerous for travel."

That wasn't entirely true. Rather, an airborne exfil was the only surefire way to guarantee the District Leaders escaped without risk of intercept by whichever agency had infiltrated their meeting.

Marcos looked at Sergeant Henderson who pointed up to the ceiling. He held up his open hand with his five fingers signaling the first helicopter would be on the roof in five minutes. Marcos took that as his cue to wrap-up his remarks.

"The first helicopter will be on the roof in a few minutes, folks. It will be a first-come, first-served boarding. Please collect spouses and guests from your rooms and make for the roof immediately. We may, or may not, be able to accommodate luggage – that will depend on space." Marcos cleared his throat.

"Finally, despite the circumstances, and as we've done at the end of each meeting for decades, please join with me as we close by reciting the Cohort creed." All attendees stood to their feet, put their hands over their hearts and, for the second time, ritualistically delivered the Cohort's creed. Thereafter, the crowd quickly dispersed.

Marcos stepped away from the podium. Judge Cathpert was still seated in the front row along with Damian, Tara, and Hunter.

"So, *Prometheus*, you *gonna* tell me why we canceled this *meetin'* early? *Aah* know it wasn't because of the wind and the rain." Judge Cathpert asked his son-in-law.

Marcos sat down next to the judge.

"There have been multiple security breaches within the last twenty-four hours, Holton. First with the FBI agent at your house and now there's an imposter masquerading as a staff member. We had to shut it down."

"*Aah* can tell you that anyone stupid enough to try to sabotage our organization doesn't understand what they're *doin'*." Judge Cathpert crossed his arms over his frail frame and continued.

"It's *gonna* be hard for anyone to stop us now." He stated with confidence.

Marcos appreciated his father-in-law's optimism, but he wasn't so convinced. Judge Cathpert gingerly rose to his bony feet.

"*Aah* have to swing by my house and grab a few things. Tell my daughter it'd be nice for her to drop us a line once in a while." Judge Cathpert pointed at a FARCO operative camped near the door.

"Get a boat. *Aah* need *somethin'* from my place."

As Judge Cathpert ambled out of the room, Marcos collected his materials from the podium. It was time to go.

"Sergeant, I'm ready. Make sure your team knows I'm getting on the *first* chopper."

"Ten-four, *Prometheus*."

But before Marcos disappeared into the hallway, he had one final demand.

"Sergeant, find Simon and have him call my secure line. I want a full briefing on the imposter before I land in Washington."

"Yes, sir." Sergeant Henderson responded knowing full-well he had just ordered Simon's execution.

Damian stood uncharacteristically silent next to Tara and Hunter. He nervously bit his lower lip. His conscience was still weighing on him about how Bailey had been treated. He had brought her to the Inn, like a lamb to the slaughter. If she didn't agree to join them, they would certainly kill her. He felt he had to do *something* to help her.

"Does anyone know what's happening with Bailey?" He asked.

Hunter responded, "Yeah, she's still downstairs. Surely, you're not thinking about bringing her with us."

"Yes, I am. Menda Industrial needs her." Without waiting for Hunter's permission, Damian approached Sergeant Henderson who was coordinating the exfiltration with several members of the FARCO team.

"Henderson, take us down to the lower level. I want to give Bailey Thompson *one more chance*."

Sergeant Henderson begrudgingly left another operative in charge and led Damian, Tara, and Hunter down the back stairwell.

Chapter 73

David was dizzy and disoriented as he slogged along, not knowing where he was being taken. He had been beaten and dragged through a seemingly never-ending maze of hallways.

Constant rib jabs made it difficult for him to focus on anything but the pain. David could barely breathe through the scratchy material of the black hood which remained tightly wrapped around his aching head.

All at once, he was jolted to a halt and flung into a chair. His arms were yanked behind his back which caused his chest cavity to crackle. The ropes burned his wrists as the FARCO operatives tied him up.

David called out for Sarah – no answer. He yelled louder. Still, no answer.

The verbal outburst resulted in another hard punch to David's abdomen. He hacked and coughed as he reclaimed the wind which had been knocked out of him.

Someone grabbed the top of David's hood and ripped it off. He blinked several times as his eyes adjusted to the dim lighting of the Lagoon Room. The raised waterline of the windowed wall afforded virtually zero natural light, leaving the entire space dark and eerie. Everyone in the room donned military fatigues and was carrying loaded weapons. This was the second time he found himself sitting in a room surrounded by FARCO operatives – it was two times too many.

An older man with a chiseled jawline, bulging biceps, and military-style haircut, stood directly in front of him. His arms were on his hips and David felt like the man was staring directly into his soul.

The man looked familiar to David, but he couldn't place him. Still, David was having an intense episode of déjà vu which was interrupted when the man spoke.

"Hello, David, I'm Sergeant James Henderson. Do you remember me?" Sergeant Henderson's stern look softened. His countenance was almost warm. David didn't recognize the man from his run-in with FARCO the year before – how did he know him?

David simply gave the answer he thought would yield the best outcome.

"You look familiar, yes." David scanned the room for his girlfriend, but she was nowhere to be found. He panicked.

"What have you done with Sarah?!"

Sergeant Henderson silenced David by raising his hand. When he did so, the operative standing to the right of Sergeant Henderson pointed his weapon at David's head, daring him to speak again.

"Don't worry, she's close." Sergeant Henderson assured as he pointed to a tall FARCO operative who opened the door and dragged in *two* female hostages. One was Sarah, but David didn't recognize the other woman. Both ladies had duct tape wrapped tightly over their mouths and their hands were bound in front of them.

Anger welled up inside David. He directed his emotion toward Sergeant Henderson.

"If you hurt her, I swear I—" Sergeant Henderson interrupted.

"I don't think you remember me, David." Sergeant Henderson came closer and crouched to look David in the eye.

"You and I met many years ago when you were just a boy…I knew your dad."

David gulped, not sure he wanted to know more about his father's connection to this psychopath. Sergeant Henderson paused; his lips turned upward into a deviant smile.

"You see, David…your father was a Cohort Associate."

Chapter 74

The words sunk in like daggers. David remembered now. He *had* met Sergeant Henderson many years ago at his family's home near Lexington, Kentucky. Sergeant Henderson had been to their house several times to meet with David's father, Paul Stoneman.

David's dad was a decorated war veteran who spent his entire career in military service. He was the stereotypical military father who insisted on strict rules and rigid routines for his family. He was a good man and certainly would not fraternize with nefarious company, regardless of their power and influence. That's what didn't make sense to David.

"Bring in the others." Sergeant Henderson ordered. The FARCO operative opened the door and Damian, Tara, and Hunter entered. Sergeant Henderson continued.

"*You* were the mystery waiter at today's Cohort meeting, weren't you?"

David offered no response.

"Do you know what the Cohort is, David?"

Again, no response.

"Your dad would be proud of you, you know that?"

"Screw you!" David fired back, red with anger. Sergeant Henderson nodded at the FARCO operative standing to his right, who gladly put his fist across David's face. His head recoiled and warm blood poured from his busted lip.

The room was deathly silent.

"Why *me*?" David finally asked.

"I'm giving you one chance…"

"One chance to do what?"

"To join the Cohort." Sergeant Henderson replied.

Sergeant Henderson continued, "You're the guy who killed the Division Act last year. That was our legislation and you squashed it. That doesn't happen to us. So, we want you working *for us*, not against us." Sergeant Henderson smiled.

"There's a reason I didn't kill you in Washington when I had the chance."

He clasped his large hands behind his muscular back.

"Like all great military leaders do, I retreated, regrouped, and waited for the perfect time to strike again. Or, in this case, invite you to join us *here* this weekend."

"Invite me?"

Sergeant Henderson drew close to David, his voice lowered, almost to a whisper.

"Absolutely…what better time and place to meet than at the Cohort's quinquennial meeting? And what better way to ensure you would be in town than to terminate your buddy, Tommy Felton." He paused, hoping David would connect the dots.

David's heart sank in his chest.

"You killed Tommy so I would come to Charleston?" David's blood boiled as it dripped from his face.

Sergeant Henderson nodded.

"It worked, didn't it? Felton knew too much anyway, Dave. *She* knows too much also…" He exclaimed as he pointed at Sarah. Attempting to divert attention away from her, David changed the subject.

"You claim you knew my dad, but he would never befriend someone like you."

Sergeant Henderson chuckled, "I brought him in as one of the first members of the Cohort's security detail. He was really good. Then he and I were made Associates together. You knew he was a special operator, right? He was certainly tougher than me."

David's father rarely spoke about his time in the military. With his dad's muscular physique, quiet demeanor, and consistent whispered conversations in his home office, David had always suspected his father was involved in covert activities. However, he was never privy to any details and knew better than to ask.

Sergeant Henderson pulled out the picture of himself, David's father, Judge Cathpert, and Dr. Lyons, and held it up for David to see.

"As I said, we were part of the Cohort's original security detail; the group eventually became FARCO, with which you are already familiar, of course." Sergeant Henderson said with a grin. "I know egotistical politicians have claimed credit for FARCO's creation, but it was your dad and me who brought it to life, and *he* was the mastermind behind it."

Sergeant Henderson's demeanor turned serious.

"Your father lost his way, David. He began rallying people against the Cohort's cause. Against *me*!" Sergeant Henderson became angrier with every word. He folded the picture and returned it to his pocket before wandering over to the dark, murky windowed water wall. Just then, an alligator brushed by the glass, flashing its razor-sharp teeth.

"There was nothing I could do...the order came down from the Executive Council. Your father had to be killed."

"You lie!! My father died in a car accident!" David protested.

"Is that what they told you?"

David scowled at the military mercenary, "Is this some type of confession, Henderson?" David asked, suddenly remembering he was still wearing his lapel pin recording device Jacob had given him.

"I don't want to dwell on the past, David. I focus on the future."

Sergeant Henderson turned to the FARCO operatives and directed them to remove the duct tape from Bailey and Sarah's mouths. The two women gasped for air.

"All three of you have a simple choice – join us, or die." Sergeant Henderson calmly informed. Hearing no immediate response, he added a kicker.

"If you choose to join us, the Cohort Executive Council will grant each of you 'Associate status,' with immediate effect. You could be extremely valuable to the Cohort and you will reap great financial rewards for your support." Sergeant Henderson looked at each of the three prisoners separately before re-asking his question.

"So…what do you say?"

Chapter 75

Bailey considered Sergeant Henderson's ultimatum. *Join, or die.*

The thought was overwhelming. Sarah was struggling with the decision as well, and David knew why. The idea of never seeing her son again was too much for her. David gave Sarah a reassuring nod as tears rolled down her reddened cheeks.

David had already made up his mind. His father had taught him to do the right thing, even in the face of adversity. He would rather die than cower to these tyrants.

Sergeant Henderson broke the long silence, "Well, have you made a decision?"

"I have, and I bet you can guess what it is." David barked.

Sergeant Henderson sneered and glanced at a member of the FARCO team. The operative gave David another punch to the jaw. His head flew back and pain shot like electricity through his entire frame.

Sarah pleaded for them to stop. David raised his head and blinked his eyes as the figures in front of him slowly came back into focus.

After seeing how David was treated when he impolitely declined the Cohort's invitation, Bailey chose a different path. She couldn't save her kids from their monster father if she were dead.

"I guess I'll join. It's not like I have much of a choice, right Damian?"

Bailey found Damian hiding in the corner of the room with his hands resting in his expensive pants pockets. He shamefully stared at the ground. Bailey then turned her attention to Tara who was standing next to him.

"And you, cupcake!" Bailey hollered.

"From now on, I'm in *every* Menda meeting you're in, you got that?!"

Tara displayed a rare smile.

"Untie me, now!" Bailey ordered. Sergeant Henderson instructed an operative to do so.

Hunter approached his wife with his arms opened wide. His phony attempt at affection was pathetic.

"Baby, I knew you'd come around. I told them—" He didn't finish his sentence before Bailey put her left knee hard into his groin. Hunter hit the floor with a thud. As Bailey walked over him and toward the door, she added one more verbal jab.

"I want a divorce."

The FARCO operatives snickered, happy to see the arrogant lawyer writhing on the floor in both physical and emotional pain.

Bailey disappeared into the hall as Hunter waddled to catch up with her. Damian joined them, hoping to patch things up with Bailey before they returned to Atlanta.

Sergeant Henderson gave the signal for two FARCO operatives to follow them – he didn't trust Bailey. He then turned his attention to Sarah who still had tears rolling down her face.

"Cut her ties." Sergeant Henderson ordered. Once Sarah was free, he asked his question again.

"Well, Ms. Mercer. How about you?" Sarah looked at David. He nodded – she had no choice.

"Even with Stoneman out, we could still benefit from *your* influence in Washington. After all, you became famous last year, too." Sergeant Henderson gently lifted Sarah's head and twisted the emotional knife.

"...Ms. Mercer, if you don't join us, I'll have my team pay your son a visit at school. You won't recognize him after they're done with him. Do you want that?"

Sarah wept uncontrollably and crumbled to the floor.

"Leave her alone, Henderson! She'll join! Just leave her alone!"

David knew he had to make the decision for Sarah. He cared for her too much to let her think she had made the choice herself.

Unfortunately, proxy acceptance was unacceptable. Sergeant Henderson instructed two FARCO operatives to pick Sarah up off the ground. Her legs felt like rubber beneath her.

"WELL?!" The mercenary leader screamed into Sarah's face. He was done with the gentle approach.

"Okay," she whimpered. Sergeant Henderson ordered the FARCO team to take her out into the hall with the others. Thereafter, only he, Tara, and one other operative remained in the Lagoon Room with David.

David wouldn't be able to talk his way out of this one. He had thumbed his nose at one of the most powerful groups in the world, insulted the leader of their elite security force, and fed the CIA key information that could lead to the Cohort's international demise. He was either incredibly brave or insanely stupid.

As David accepted his fate, he felt a small glimmer of pride. A couple years earlier he would have jumped at an opportunity to fast-track his career and chase fame and fortune as a Cohort Associate, as Hunter had done. But David had evolved.

He had transformed from a lowly caterpillar into a beautiful butterfly and his evolution was finally complete. David had his priorities straight – as Henderson acknowledged, his father would have been proud.

David's self-reflection was interrupted by the sound of Bailey screaming at Hunter in the hall. The raucous irritated Sergeant Henderson, causing him to leave the room to deal with the situation himself. The remaining operative followed his boss into the hall as well. Only Tara and David remained. Tara stared at David, cold and unfeeling.

"You got in with the wrong crowd, lady." David admonished.

"They'll just kill you when they're done with you. You know that, right?"

Tara moved toward him. Her strides were determined, yet graceful.

She reached into her skirt's waistband and pulled out a knife and opened the blade.

This is it, David thought. *It's over.*

Tara held the blade at David's neck-level and moved the knife forward. The tip pushed up against his tanned skin, ready to plunge into his flesh. David closed his eyes expecting the cold steel to bite at any second. But the painful thrust never came.

He opened his eyes and saw Tara leaning over him and fiddling with the rope knot that kept him bound – Tara was helping him.

Chapter 76

J udge Cathpert was short of breath as he stumbled into the large foyer of his battered island home. The house was a disaster. Branches, rainwater, and debris had poured in through broken windows and totaled his home's first floor. The hurricane had turned the picturesque beach house into a war zone.

The expensive glass-blown chandelier which once hung elegantly in the entryway was now shattered and submerged under standing water. And the paintings on the walls, all originals, were bleeding color streaks as the lights flickered above him.

Judge Cathpert squinted down the entryway's narrow hallway and realized the back half of the house was in even worse shape than the front. However, he wasn't worried about his home. He was more interested in retrieving something extremely valuable from deep within his bedroom's closet.

The decrepit jurist climbed the dark wooden staircase to his second floor. His bony hands clung desperately to the frail banister as he approached the landing. He could feel his belabored heart pounding in his chest. His legs began to cramp, but he ignored the pain. He didn't have any time to waste.

He hurried to the master bedroom which was now soaked thanks to a large errant tree branch which had broken through the bedroom's window allowing the elements to pour in. Despite the mess, Judge Cathpert headed straight for the walk-in closet. He darted to the back corner and fell to his knees.

He stared at the state-of-the-art black security safe in front of him. The safe was large with an eight-gauge carbon steel door and a fourteen-gauge steel body. Judge Cathpert entered the secret pin number on the electric keypad. Relief flooded over him as he pulled open the safe's door.

An old, brown box was inside and on top of the box lay several yellowed family letters. The letters had been passed down for generations in the Cathpert family. The secrets those letters contained were too incriminating to even include in the Cathpert Family history book.

However, Judge Cathpert casually tossed the letters to the side and opened the box. Even in the deep, dark recesses of the closet, the shimmer of the gold was unmistakable.

Chapter 77

Although Tara had weakened the ropes, David was still bound in the chair. She couldn't cut all the way through before the Lagoon Room's door flung open once again. It was Sergeant Henderson and a FARCO operative returning from the hallway. The operative carried a battering ram.

Tara immediately put her knife back to David's throat, pretending to threaten him. She turned to Sergeant Henderson as he and the operative approached.

"He's been mouthing off. Let me finish him, Henderson. Just say the word."

Both David and Tara held their breath, praying Sergeant Henderson would not grant Tara's faux request. Sergeant Henderson stared at David for, what seemed like, an eternity. His genius mind was deep in thought. David employed reverse psychology.

"Do it, Henderson! Go on, coward! Tell *her* to do it. I know you want someone else to do your dirty work anyway." David dared. That comment triggered the desired response.

"No…an easy death just won't do. I have something better." Sergeant Henderson fired back with a devilish smile. He looked over to the room's wall of glass holding back the adjacent lagoon. He brushed Tara to the side and nodded at the FARCO operative who walked over to the glass wall. The military leader put his hand up signaling for the operative to wait. Sergeant Henderson drew close to David.

David was pushing his hands together hoping the ropes, which had been partially cut, would not suddenly snap and foil his escape plans. Sergeant Henderson loomed large over him. He scowled at David and the muscles in his jawline flexed.

"I trusted your father, David. And he betrayed us." Sergeant Henderson crouched down and continued. David remained silent.

"But I won, didn't I?" He said in an angry whisper. "I'm here and he's not!" The veins were popping out of his muscular neck.

"Now I have the pleasure to dispatch you, his pride and joy, from this earth. I just wish he could've seen me do it."

Sergeant Henderson stood, took a step back, and cocked his head to the side.

"Maybe after this I'll pay your mother a visit in Kentucky. She still lives on that horse farm, right?"

David considered breaking the ropes right then and lunging at the FARCO leader. He wanted to kill this man *with his bare hands.*

David hadn't spoken to his mother for years, but hell would freeze solid before he would let anything bad happen to her.

Sergeant Henderson continued, "Sarah, too. We're going to use her like a puppet in Washington. We'll make her publicly criticize you. It'll only take a few months before everyone in America thinks you're just another scumbag lawyer looking for your fifteen minutes of fame."

Tara was standing by idly, watching the psychological torture unfold. Sergeant Henderson continued his taunting.

"Once this island dries out there will be an investigation into deaths and damage as a result of nature's fury. That's what we're going to do with you, Dave…let nature have its way with you."

Sergeant Henderson nodded at the FARCO operative. He drew back the battering ram and swung it toward the glass wall which was holding back millions of gallons of lagoon water. With each forceful hit, the strong glass weakened and began to crack.

Sergeant Henderson held up his hand and the operative stopped. The room was silent. The only sound was the continued crackling of the glass wall as it expanded out to the edges, like a spider's web.

"That's good. Let's let him watch it crack before it breaks." Sergeant Henderson instructed as he, the FARCO operative, and Tara hurried out of the room. Tara glanced back at David with helpless eyes. There was nothing she could do – David was on his own. Sergeant Henderson was halfway out the door when he turned to lodge one last verbal arrow.

"Say hi to your dad for me." He snarled as he slammed the door behind him.

In what appeared to be David's final moments, he couldn't believe it had been less than a week since he received the news that Tommy Felton had died. Now, he was facing his own demise in the luxurious dungeon of a secret hotel. He was tempted to despair. He had failed the CIA, he had failed Sarah, and he had even failed his father.

Then, suddenly, with only the sound of cracking glass as a soundtrack, he had a feeling rise from deep within his broken spirit. *Not today*, he thought as he forcefully ripped his arms away from one another. *This isn't how my story ends.* With one mighty tug the ropes popped off and fell to the floor. He was free.

In that moment, the broken glass wall finally gave way followed by a deafening crashing sound. The entire lagoon poured into the small chamber. David sprinted for the door as he heard the rush of the water closing in behind him.

As the alligator's scales brushed against him, David finally found the bronze door handle and opened it with every ounce of strength left in his battered body. He shot through the doorway like a bullet.

The water's propelling force bashed him against the hallway's walls as he flailed like a rag doll. After the water had carried him dozens of feet down the hall, he was finally able to gain solid footing and run toward the back stairwell as the water thinned out at his feet. He looked behind him and saw the large alligator thrashing in the middle of the hallway, disoriented by its unfamiliar surroundings.

David had to get upstairs, and *fast*. He had to save Sarah and get off this island.

Chapter 78

The gold in Judge Cathpert's family safe was worth millions and served as the family's financial insurance policy in case the government ever froze their accounts or seized assets. The gold pieces came from an eighteenth-century shipwreck off the Florida coast, and the story of how the gold illegally made its way to the Cathperts was memorialized in the secret family letters.

Judge Cathpert dumped the gold into two black duffle bags. His father had once kept the gold in a bank owned by a Cohort Associate until the early 1990s. However, the bank's new ownership began asking too many questions and the gold had to be moved and the bank owner permanently silenced.

Ultimately, the treasure was split into three parts. One-third to Judge Cathpert; one-third to the Cohort's central treasury; and one-third was buried in a secret location on Kiawah Island. The buried gold was yet another fail-safe in case the other two-thirds were discovered, stolen, or seized.

One of the family letters included a map showing where the buried gold could be found. Judge Cathpert remembered it was somewhere near Kiawah's Night Heron Park, but he never had the need, time, or desire to conduct an extensive search and extract it.

Unfortunately, Night Heron Park was now under several feet of flood water, just like Rhett's Bluff. It would be impossible to unearth that gold for months, until the waters receded and the land dried out. In the meantime, Judge Cathpert was happy to take the gold in his safe and come back later for the rest.

The judge planned to slip onto a local fishing vessel, toss a gold coin to the captain to keep his mouth shut, and disappear in the Caribbean until things quieted down. His wife, Barbara, could fend for herself – after all, she had betrayed him and the family.

The thin jurist folded the family letters and placed them in one of the duffle bags. As he closed the bag, Judge Cathpert heard an unmistakable rattle coming from the closet's dark corner on his right. He turned just in time to see a diamondback rattlesnake spring at his arm and sink its venomous fangs deep into the judge's veiny hand.

Judge Cathpert shot to his uncertain feet and desperately whipped his bitten arm, causing the snake to fly into the bedroom behind him. The black and brown diamond pattern on its yellowed back almost looked regal on the wet white carpet. But, as a native South Carolinian, Judge Cathpert was well-aware of the snake's lethality and knew he had only minutes before the snake's venom took effect.

With his uninjured hand, Judge Cathpert flung the heavy duffle bags over bony shoulder, hurried down the hall, and quickly descended the stairs. As he glanced down the foyer's hallway and into the living room, he noticed the Cathpert family history book sitting idly on a small table near the back of the house where he had placed it after he had commandeered it from Special Agent Manheim.

The book contained too much incriminating information to simply be left behind – he had to retrieve it.

Despite the increasing pain and swelling in his hand, the judge ran and scooped up the book and held it under his armpit, still carrying the weighty bags on his other shoulder. Then, he slogged back to the front with his hands full and heart racing.

When Judge Cathpert opened the front door, he saw the FARCO operative bobbing up and down in the small motorboat in the rough water where he had left him. The operative rose to his feet when he noticed the judge.

"You need help, sir?" The operative asked.

At that moment, a surge of numbness shot down the judge's arms and legs and his vision began to blur.

"Just bring the boat close to the steps." He murmured as his heart began to beat more rapidly and his breathing became more labored. All results of the rattlesnake's deadly venom, no doubt.

The rain came in spurts but was thinning. In the distance, the once-dark clouds were turning a lighter shade of gray. Still, the view from the porch was unbelievable. The Cathpert's front yard had transformed into a murky green lake. Judge Cathpert cautiously followed his feeble feet measuring each step down while also balancing the weight of the bags.

The operative transitioned to the left side of the small motorboat, sat on the far side of the boat, and held on with both hands bracing for the jolt when the judge stepped in.

Judge Cathpert had made it to the third to last step. The water covered its surface and he could go no further. At that point, he was as white as a ghost.

"I got bit by a snake inside…a poisonous one." He finally confessed, realizing the gravity of his perilous situation.

The operative didn't know how to respond except to suggest they immediately retreat back to the Inn and get a helicopter to fly Judge Cathpert to the nearest hospital. But before the operative could radio the crisis in to Sergeant Henderson, the numbness in his limbs caused Judge Cathpert to fall forward.

He felt like he was falling in slow motion as his frail body smashed into the side of the boat. One of the duffle bags toppled into the boat causing the gold coins to scatter on its floor. The other bag disappeared into the water with a splash along with the family's book as Judge Cathpert clung for dear life to the boat's edge.

The operative pulled, but Judge Cathpert's thin arm slipped through his grasp and the judge went under the water.

He sunk in the water until his body hit the soft grass of his front lawn. He couldn't move his arms or legs to swim back to the water's surface and he could feel the muscles twitching all over his body. Judge Cathpert then lost the ability to control his throat muscles and could no longer hold his breath. Water poured into his mouth and lungs like a waterfall – he was drowning.

In that moment of immense pain and panic, Judge Cathpert felt regretful.

He regretted his lifelong blind loyalty to the Cohort and the litany of illegal activities which had monopolized much of his life. But most of all, he regretted he would not have the opportunity to apologize to his wife and daughter for decades of horrible behavior. He had lived a life of arrogance, corruption, murder, villainy, and greed. And in his final seconds, he was tormented by the realization that he was now powerless to change that awful legacy.

All at once, the green water around him slowly faded to black and the judge's world went dark forever.

Chapter 79

Sergeant Henderson darted into the flooded foyer of the Rhett's Bluff Inn. The water had risen high enough to seep through the Inn's grand front doors and cover the once-pristine floor.

"Where's the SURC?" Henderson demanded as he maintained his death grip on Sarah's arm. Another operative was handling Bailey.

"I radioed for it to be brought around, sir."

Out the Inn's back window Sergeant Henderson saw one of the helicopters gliding toward the Inn's rooftop.

"Have all Cohort Members been evacuated?"

"Yes, sir, Bravo Team Leader coordinated, sir. Received confirmation of complete exfil ten minutes ago, except for present company. That bird is for us. Should we take the hostages to the roof, sir?"

"No, the SURC is better for hostage transportation."

Sergeant Henderson pointed to Tara, Hunter, and Damian. "You three...head to the roof and take the helo to the rendezvous point. Alpha Team, facilitate their exfil; the rest are with me." Sergeant Henderson ordered.

"Should we exfil with the SURC on the river side, sir?" The operative asked.

"Negative. We'll dump the SURC at Bohicket Marina."

"But won't people be looking—"

"I wasn't finished," Sergeant Henderson snapped.

"With the roads flooded and the tree cover, we can get almost halfway to Bohicket under cover by following the main roads out. Less risk of possible intercept. Copy?"

"Copy that, sir."

"Let's move!" Sergeant Henderson barked. Hunter followed closely behind the operatives as they disappeared into *Ballroom A*, heading for the secret stairwell leading to the roof. Tara hung behind.

"I need a weapon," Tara told Sergeant Henderson. He looked her up and down.

"Why do *you* need a weapon, sweetheart?"

Tara was unphased by the condescending comment.

"Look, we know the Cohort has been compromised, but we don't know the extent of the breach. Damian's gun is back at our cottage. So, like I said...I need a weapon."

Tara's stone-cold stare caused Sergeant Henderson to acquiesce. He didn't have time to argue with her.

"Give her your sidearm." Sergeant Henderson instructed one of the operatives.

The man unholstered his pistol and begrudgingly handed it to Tara. She gripped it tightly and ran to *Ballroom A* to join the others.

At the same time, the SURC arrived outside the Inn's front door. Sergeant Henderson told the remaining operatives to load Bailey and Sarah into the boat. He hopped in as well. The wind and the rain had stopped and small rays of sunshine were coming through the dispersing clouds.

David had overheard the entire exchange from his hiding spot in the first-floor hall, just around the corner from the lobby. He had a decision to make. *Should I follow the SURC, or go to the roof?* While his heart wanted to race after Sarah in the SURC, his mind told him to go for the chopper first.

Peeking around the corner to ensure the coast was clear, he sprinted into *Ballroom A*. Despite his debilitating fear of heights, David was headed to the roof.

Chapter 80

Tara thrust open the doors to the roof to find an orange and white MH-60T Coast Guard recovery helicopter waiting for them. The long rotor blades were whipping through the salt air and the sound of the engine was piercing.

Several FARCO operatives stood guard as Damian and Hunter ducked and trotted to the aircraft. They hoisted themselves into the cabin and Damian peered out the helicopter's tiny window. Tara remained in the stairwell's open doorway. They locked eyes and he waved at her, signaling for her to join them.

Tara heard footsteps coming up the stairs behind her. She leaned over the railing to find David racing toward her two steps at a time. *He had made it out of the Lagoon Room alive!*

This was her chance. She held up her index finger to Damian indicating she needed one minute and stepped back inside the stairwell. She only had precious seconds alone with David and had to make them count.

As David scaled the last set of stairs, he stopped, dead in his tracks, when he saw Tara above him.

"Stay here for *thirty seconds* then open this door and run to the helicopter. I'll cover you. You understand?" Tara waited for David to acknowledge.

"What are you—"

Tara cut him off, "No time to explain, you just have to trust me."

David nodded. He didn't trust her, but he had no choice.

"I'm armed and I'll cover you," Tara shouted as she bolted out the door. She jogged to the Alpha Team Leader who was huddled with other operatives on the far side of the roof. Tara had to be convincing.

"There's a potential threat on the North side of the building. Federal agents are on the premises." Tara pointed as she yelled over the sound of the helicopter. The Alpha Team Leader looked confused.

"Nothing came through on the radio."

"This order came directly from Marcos Roberts! He called me on his cell and tipped me off that they were coming. Don't just stand there, get on it." Tara screamed. The men snapped into action, studying the North lawn below, searching for the threat.

All Tara needed was a few seconds and she had gotten them. She scurried to the helicopter's open door and climbed in to find Hunter, Damian, and one other FARCO operative sitting in the cabin.

She reluctantly took the open seat next to Hunter, near the front. She nestled up against a large orange container and a metal rescue basket, both of which are standard on Coast Guard helicopters.

One of the two pilots leaned back into the cabin. With his helmet on and tinted eye shades down, all Tara could see was the bottom-half of the pilot's face as he asked his question.

"We good to go?"

"No, there's one more," Tara responded.

"One more? Who are we waiting on?" Damian asked as he conducted a quick count of the passengers. In that instant, Tara saw the rooftop door swing open. David shot out of the dark stairwell and sprinted toward them.

Tara pulled the sidearm from her waistband and fired a round into the body of the FARCO operative sitting across from her. Hunter and Damian recoiled in shock. Tara turned the gun toward the pilots.

"Get us in the air, now!" She screamed as she pushed the barrel of the gun against one of their helmets. Hunter and Damian were dumbfounded. But before they could make sense of the situation, David hopped into the cabin, ready for a fight.

"Go, go, go – they're coming! FARCO is coming!" He yelled as he yanked the wounded operative out of his seat and flung him out onto the roof.

The aircraft began to rise. Hunter sprang into action and lunged his athletic frame at David attempting to push him out the cabin door. Hunter's strength surprised David and, for a moment, he thought he was going to fall. However, adrenaline kicked in and he was able to keep his balance.

Hunter had a firm grip on him, but David's quick jab to Hunter's ribcage caused Hunter to drop his left arm just enough for David to slide further into the cabin and away from the open door.

Tara repositioned to gain a better vantage point as she held the pistol with two hands and pointed it at the open cabin door. The helicopter slowly rose – five, ten feet in the air. FARCO operatives appeared in the rising doorway and grabbed feverishly to pull themselves into the cabin. Tara fired three successive shots, two of which hit the Alpha Team Leader. The chopper continued its ascent. Tara had successfully kept the other operatives at bay – they looked on, helpless, as the helo hovered above the Inn's roof.

One-hundred feet, one-hundred fifty feet. Tara aimed her gun back at the pilots.

"Head for the island's entrance and follow the main road. If I don't see Henderson's boat in two minutes, I'm shooting both of you. And no radio warnings either!"

The pilots acknowledged the directive. Hunter and David continued to wrestle.

They rolled onto Damian, who was cowering in his seat. Hunter was landing punch after punch on David with combinations of head and body shots. David could taste fresh blood in his mouth.

Sensing he had the upper hand, Hunter pushed David onto his back and straddled him to secure a superior fighting position. He drew his right fist back, ready to land another powerful blow. David put his arms up to parry the punch.

Then, David saw arms wrap around Hunter's strong neck. It was Tara. Hunter fell to the side with Tara clinging to him. He used his sharp elbow to jab Tara, which caused her to release her stranglehold. Simultaneously, both Hunter and David realized Tara had set her gun down on the seat to grab Hunter. Hunter crawled toward the weapon as David clawed at his torso. If Hunter got to the gun, it was over.

Suddenly, the helicopter, which was now hundreds of feet in the air, made a sharp turn which caused Hunter to fall backward. He flew toward the chopper's open cabin door and grabbed Tara's leg as he fell out of the aircraft.

She opened her arms and reached for David, panicked. In an act of supernatural courage and despite his lifelong fear of heights, David dove forward toward the helo's open door and locked arms with Tara, just in time.

Hunter was dangling in the air and tearing at Tara's clothes as he began to slip. Hunter's weight was pulling them downward and Tara kicked wildly to shake him off. In what seemed like slow motion, David saw Hunter finally lose his grip and fall toward the earth. The look of terror on his face was haunting.

The helicopter was high over the Inn as Hunter fell. He flailed his arms as gravity pulled him faster and faster. He landed with a thud on the Inn's roof. A pool of blood spread out from behind his head – Hunter was dead.

At that moment, David, still holding tight to Tara, realized her gun remained on her seat unattended. A chill flew down David's spine. *Damian.*

David closed his eyes tightly and hoped it would be quick. Tara was screaming for him to pull her up. Then he felt it. Two hands grab his ankles. Damian was *saving them.*

Damian pulled with all his might and was able to lift David and Tara to safety. Damian clutched the gun and pointed it at the pilots.

"Find the SURC now!" He demanded as the helicopter flew over Night Heron Park.

Tara was laying on the cabin floor. She was tough, but that experience caused her whole body to shake.

"*Veritas Vincit*, my friend." Tara said as she displayed a hand gesture that David knew to be the "peace" sign.

Damian returned the sign, "*Veritas Vincit*," he then turned his attention back to the pilots. David was puzzled by the exchanged. *Veritas Vincit?*

Tara inhaled deeply as she crawled into one of the open seats. After a second of silence, she stated the obvious.

"Oh yeah, David, I forgot to mention…Damian's with us!"

Chapter 81

B ailey and Sarah huddled next to each other as the SURC flew down a waterway that used to be Kiawah Island Parkway. The island was a ghost town. Debris from the luxury homes floated in the water like mini-icebergs.

But despite the hurricane's damage, Kiawah was still beautiful. Sounds of birds squawking in the lush green trees and the unique Kiawah smell gave the sense that the island would forever embody nature's serenity, even in the aftermath of a deadly hurricane. Eventually, the waters would recede, homes would be rebuilt, and the resort guests would return. But it would take some time.

The boat flew through the front gate's security checkpoint and whipped around the snaking road as the path opened to the vastness of the Lowcountry salt marsh.

The SURC was now out from under tree cover. The sky was a pleasant shade of robin's egg blue, with just a handful of gray clouds still swirling above. Hurricane Mary was gone.

Sarah and Bailey clung to each other as the SURC passed Mingo Point. Bailey overheard Sergeant Henderson repeat their destination to the FARCO operative driving the boat.

"Bohicket Marina is four clicks that way." Sergeant

Henderson pointed over the man's left shoulder into the distance, "You know where you're going?"

"Yes, sir. Copy that," the operative responded. They were approaching the place where Kiawah Island Parkway intersected with the original boundary of the Kiawah River.

Bailey evaluated possible escape options. The most obvious option was to dive into the water and swim for dry land. But that was too risky and the boat was moving too fast. She concluded their best chance of survival was to escape at Bohicket Marina. Until then, she would wait.

Sarah was thinking about her son, Mark. She shuddered at the thought that he would be harmed if she did not cooperate with the Cohort. She didn't know if David were dead or alive. But if he were alive, Sarah was confident he would come for her.

At that moment, Bailey and Sarah heard the sound of a helicopter above. They looked up and saw the orange and white Coast Guard chopper rapidly descending on them.

Chapter 82

Sergeant Henderson squinted and saw a figure standing in the helicopter's open doorway. As the aircraft continued toward them, he recognized that it was Tara. She was aiming a gun at them. *What?!*

"Take cover!" Sergeant Henderson yelled as two shots rang out. The rounds hit one of the operatives in the neck, and he collapsed on the boat's deck and bled out in seconds.

"Divert, divert, turn left!!" Sergeant Henderson screamed as the SURC driver hid behind the captain's chair and whipped the boat to the left onto the original boundary of the Kiawah River.

Sergeant Henderson unholstered his sidearm. He was ready for the fight. The driver was crouched, but still able to maintain eyes on the waters ahead. The burly operative was dead and another was leaning against the side of the boat, trying to secure a covered vantage point.

The two female hostages were lying flat on the deck with their hands over their heads.

Sergeant Henderson looked back at the helo and couldn't believe his eyes. Tara was holding Damian in front of her as a human shield. Regardless, one of the operatives fired a shot which barely missed Damian's head by a couple of inches.

"Hold your fire!!" Sergeant Henderson yelled.

Sergeant Henderson knew Marcos Roberts would have the entire FARCO team killed if they accidentally hit Damian, the Cohort's most valuable Associate.

Tara resumed her shooting. She hit the standing operative in the arm. He writhed in pain gripping his arm in agony. Bailey saw an opportunity and took it.

She jumped up and rammed the injured operative, pushing him toward the side of the boat. Unable to catch himself with his injured arm, the operative flipped over the side of the SURC and into the marshy water with a splash. Bailey then hit the deck, hoping Tara would continue her assault.

Sergeant Henderson aimed his sidearm at Bailey. He no longer cared about his orders; Bailey had crossed a line and he would make her pay. But before he could pull the trigger, Tara fired two more shots forcing Sergeant Henderson to take cover.

As the aircraft dropped closer to the boat, the SURC's driver employed evasive maneuvers and twisted and turned the boat in the murky water.

Another round of gunshots narrowly missed Sergeant Henderson's boots. Then he saw it.

It can't be, he thought as his jaw dropped. David Stoneman was now in the helicopter's open doorway with the rescue basket clip, in hand. He leaned forward and connected the clip to the helicopter's hoist. *This was a rescue attempt.*

With Damian out of sight, Sergeant Henderson peppered the side of the aircraft with gunshots forcing David back into the cabin. Sergeant Henderson couldn't do any more damage without the risk the chopper would go down and kill Damian.

Consequently, the helicopter moved into place twenty feet above the backside of the SURC as it skidded through the marsh. With the basket secured to the hoist, Tara instructed the pilots to lower the basket. They obeyed.

I'm going for it, Bailey thought as she ran toward the dangling basket which was suspended in mid-air. Tara provided covering fire, causing Sergeant Henderson to stay hidden in the front of the boat. The helicopter dipped just long enough for the basket to be within reach of Bailey's outstretched hand. Then, she jumped…and made it!

Bailey clung to the metal basket with both hands and held on for dear life. She used every ounce of strength to pull herself up and in. Bailey turned and called out to Sarah.

"Come on!! You're next!!"

Chapter 83

Tara was running out of ammunition and couldn't continue covering fire for much longer. A shot here and there was all she could afford. Sergeant Henderson was still hunkered down, but Tara could see he was reloading his weapon.

From inside the helicopter's cabin, David was watching the scene unfold and, despite his fear of heights, he knew what he had to do to save his girlfriend.

"Get me closer!" He yelled as the helicopter dipped once again. The basket was so low it nearly hit the back of the SURC as it flew through the marsh. David jumped down onto the stern of the SURC. When he hit, he rolled and pain shot up through his calves. He crawled to the dead burly operative and grabbed his loaded rifle.

Once he retrieved the weapon, David angled it at the operative driving the boat.

"Face forward and keep driving!!" David shouted. The operative put his left hand in the air and nodded in agreement.

David then motioned for Sarah to get behind him as he trained the weapon toward the front of the boat, fully expecting Sergeant Henderson to pop up any second and begin shooting.

David had a plan, but it would require *perfect* execution. He turned to Sarah and told her what he wanted her to do. Sarah looked at him like he had lost his mind.

"Are you sure?!" She questioned as she looked at Bailey who was still dangling in the metal basket.

"Yes…go in five, four, three, two, one. Now!" David rose to his feet and shot multiple rounds in Sergeant Henderson's direction. Sarah ran and jumped off the back of the boat toward the hanging basket as David had instructed. Bailey reached out and wrapped her arms around Sarah's shoulders. Sarah's feet were inches from the whipping water below and she could feel the water's stinging spray on her ankles. Bailey and Sarah pulled toward each other and Sarah was finally hoisted into the basket.

David ceased firing and looked back, relieved his girlfriend was safe. She had made it; now it was his turn. He shot a look at Tara who was still hanging out the side of the helicopter. Tara pointed to her weapon signaling she would provide covering fire for him.

She aimed at the front of the SURC and pulled the trigger. Nothing. She pulled it again. Nothing. David's heart sank – she was out of bullets.

Time was up. Sergeant Henderson peeked over the captain's chair. His weapon fully loaded, he opened fire at David and paused when he realized Sarah and Bailey were sitting ducks in the hanging basket. All he needed was one clean shot to hit David where it counted – his girlfriend.

David returned fire and, again, Sergeant Henderson ducked behind the captain's chair.

Think, David demanded of himself. *Think*.

Then it hit him. There was only one way to distract Sergeant Henderson long enough for David to make a run for the basket, but he would only have *one chance* to pull it off.

David motioned to Tara to have the helicopter lowered one last time. She relayed the directive to the pilots, who dipped the basket once again. David turned to find Sergeant Henderson taking aim at Bailey and Sarah who were hanging helpless behind him, like fish in a suspended barrel. It was now or never.

David held on to the side of the SURC with one arm, and with the other arm, fired his final round into the leg of the operative driving the boat. The bullet landed squarely in the back of the operative's thigh which caused him to jerk the SURC's steering wheel, and yank back on the throttle he was clutching so tightly. The SURC immediately stalled in the water.

The sudden, unexpected jolt caused Sergeant Henderson to fall hard against the deck with a thud and his weapon flew from his grip. The helicopter continued its fast forward trajectory. *This was it.*

David dropped the gun as the hanging basket flew toward him with breakneck speed with Bailey and Sarah still inside.

To avoid hitting the SURC, the pilots pulled up and to the right – the basket followed. Seeing the sudden shift, David ran to the right side of the stalled SURC, put his foot on the edge of the boat, and leaped with all of his strength. His outstretched arms reached for something, *anything*.

Just as gravity began pulling him toward the earth, he felt the basket's metal hit the palms of his open hands. He squeezed. Immediately, his right hand lost its grip. David felt his other hand slipping as well. The centrifugal force of the ascending helicopter felt like heavy weights on David's shoulders. He was sure he was going to fall to his death. His worst fear was becoming a reality.

Just as he accepted his fate, he felt four arms grab him – it was Sarah and Bailey.

"We've got you!" Sarah exclaimed. In seconds, they pulled him into the basket.

As the helicopter floated high above the salt marsh and away from danger, David looked back and saw the SURC below, buoying in the water. Even at a distance, David watched Sergeant Henderson limp to his feet and gaze up at him. David knew, deep down, he had not seen the last of Sergeant James Henderson.

Chapter 84

Tara's weapon was empty, but the pilots didn't know that. She waved the gun in their faces and demanded they get the bird on the ground in a safe location.

"Where do you want us to go?" The senior pilot asked.

"Charleston Airport. Now, give me a phone."

The pilot acquiesced. Tara sat in one of the cabin's seats and called a secret number. Her conversation was cryptic and short.

"We're headed to CHS now. ETA, twenty minutes. *Veritas Vincit.*" She said as the call ended.

David heard that same Latin phrase Tara and Damian had used earlier. He still had many questions, but now was not the time.

"Our people are meeting us at the airport," Tara relayed to Damian.

"Security and transportation will be waiting when we land. If questioned, the cover story is we are tourists from Cincinnati who got caught in the storm and were rescued. Got it?"

Tara required verbal acknowledgments from everybody as she collected and secured David's South Carolina lapel pin which had been recording the whole time. She then stuck her head into the cockpit and gave the pilots an ultimatum: forget they saw anything, or be shot. They happily chose the former.

Chapter 85

Sergeant Henderson puttered the SURC through the marsh. He doubled-back in an attempt to locate the wounded FARCO operative who Bailey had pushed into the water. But he found nothing and presumed him dead. He contacted the rest of the FARCO team for an update – it was all bad news.

The operative who had been driving the SURC was still nursing his wounded thigh. He had lost a lot of blood and was pale.

However, Sergeant Henderson's mind was not on the well-being of his man. The Cohort had been compromised and he would, no doubt, be blamed for it. And, while Sergeant Henderson didn't scare easily, the thought of taking the fall and incurring the wrath of the Cohort's Executive Council was terrifying to him.

"Sir, are we still going to Bohicket Marina?" The wounded operative managed as he clung to his leg.

"Yes. The back way as we discussed." Sergeant Henderson coldly responded. "Get up and drive. I need to coordinate the next steps." The injured operative dutifully hobbled to his feet, wincing with each step as he took the SURC's controls.

Sergeant Henderson pulled a secure phone from a metal box that rested near the captain's chair. He had to tell Marcos Roberts the prisoners had escaped. He then dialed the most private number in his phone's contact list.

Marcos answered his Cohort cell phone in his deep voice.

"Yes?"

"*Prometheus*, this is Henderson. I want to give you an update, sir. To summarize, Damian Little has been kidnapped. While it's unconfirmed, we believe that his consultant, Tara, is working *against us*."

"What are we—" Sergeant Henderson cut Marcos off.

"Forgive me, sir, but there's more. Alpha Team just radioed to tell me Judge Cathpert was killed by a poisonous snake at his home and Hunter Thompson fell from a helicopter and he's dead too."

There was no response. Sergeant Henderson looked down to see if the line had been disconnected. It had not. He heard a long, frustrated sigh on the other end.

"Sergeant, you're telling me that after I left the Inn, the longest-tenured member of the Executive Council died, along with one of our up-and-coming Associates, and our *most important* Associate has been taken hostage by another Associate? Is that right?"

"Yes, sir, that's correct...and there's one more thing." Sergeant Henderson nearly choked on the words as they left his mouth.

"The three prisoners escaped as well."

Again, deafening silence. *Prometheus's* next words were horrifying.

"You and your team have failed us this week, Sergeant…"

That admonishment cut Sergeant Henderson to his core.

"Is there any *good* news to report?" Marcos finally asked.

"Yes, sir. I understand Judge Cathpert was, uh, killed while trying to recover gold from his home. Fortunately, while Cathpert was killed, most of the coins were recovered by the operative who was with him. We can add that money to the Cohort treasury in Washington."

"Well, that certainly helps. What's the status of the Inn?"

"A lot of storm damage, and the Lagoon Room is a total loss, sir."

"Make sure your team cleans out any incriminating evidence. Take care of it, Sergeant. You have a lot to make up for."

"Copy that, sir."

The line went dead. Sergeant Henderson planned to dump the stolen SURC at Bohicket Marina, rendezvous with his remaining FARCO team members, and comb and sanitize the Rhett's Bluff Inn to ensure everything appeared "storm-related." The flood waters, wind damage, and alligators would help to cover the Cohort's deadly tracks, but they had to act quickly before the local authorities arrived.

After years of service, this quinquennial meeting was supposed to be Sergeant Henderson's final operation.

However, his plans had been sidetracked, yet again, by David Stoneman. This time, however, he didn't have a money-hungry lawyer or a crooked politician to take the fall – it was all on *him* and this monumental career failure infuriated him.

Decades earlier, David's father had nearly eliminated the Cohort with his turncoat principled stances and lofty ideals. Now, his son was unknowingly on the brink of finishing what his father had started. If David learned *the truth* about his dad, Sergeant Henderson feared David's interference, to date, would pale in comparison to what he could do next. Only time would tell.

Chapter 86

The commandeered helicopter touched down on an unflooded section of the Charleston International Airport. Once the chopper landed, agents swarmed the cockpit and handcuffed the pilots.

"They'll never talk," Tara muttered as they carried the men away, "they'll die before they talk."

"A couple million dollars under the table to the right Cohort Associate and they're home free. For all we know, the guys who just arrested them are Associates." Damian added.

Bailey, Damian, David, and Sarah exited the helicopter and piled into a white passenger van. A driver and an additional security guard were seated in the front. *This was no ordinary transport.*

After a few minutes of driving, Damian gave Bailey the news that Hunter was dead. She was actually relieved; her children would be safe and she could put this whole ordeal behind her.

The van had an escort vehicle which followed as they coasted down the South Carolina highway. "Where are we going?" David asked as he tried to read the road signs through the van's tinted windows.

"Greenville. Roughly four hours upstate," came Tara's short response.

"Why *Greenville*? I need to get back to Washington. My son could be in danger." Sarah pleaded.

"We have men monitoring your son at St. Albans. He's fine." Tara responded as the security guard in the front passenger seat reached back and handed Tara a tablet.

"When can I get to Atlanta?" Bailey asked.

"Soon. We have people watching your house too. A private jet is fueling at the Greenville/Spartanburg Airport as we speak. That's your ticket home." Tara said, studying the information on the tablet. She swiped the screen with urgency as if she was looking for something specific. Then she found it.

"Is this your father, David? Paul Stoneman?" Tara asked as she turned the screen toward David.

It was an old picture, but it was him.

"Yeah. Why do you have a picture of my dad?"

Tara looked at Damian and continued.

"Do any of you know what you were just a part of?"

No one said a word.

"You just disrupted one of the most exclusive meetings *in the world*."

The van remained silent.

"So, are you CIA, or what?" David finally asked.

Tara smiled and again looked at Damian who returned a confident smirk.

"Not quite. I'm CIA, just like Jacob, and Damian is a recruited CIA asset. We're so deep cover that only a handful of people even know about our agency affiliation." Tara took a breath and continued.

"But our CIA responsibilities were just *a part* of our work here. As such, it was too risky for me or Damian to be wired in the Cohort meeting, like you were, David. If someone found out, then the entire operation would be compromised. And sorry to say this but… if *you* were caught, our cover would still be intact and the op could still move forward." She paused for a moment as if she were searching for a simple way to explain a complex issue.

The Cohort has been on the CIA's radar for years, but we couldn't get much traction with our investigation because certain members of the intelligence community were working for the Cohort and against us the whole time. Destroying evidence, deleting files, sending us on wild good chases, and even killing witnesses. Every time we would come close to a smoking gun, the evidence would simply disappear. That's the power of the Cohort – they're everywhere, and can get to anyone.

Tara had turned completely in her seat and set down her tablet commanding everyone's full attention.

Our intel says that, early on, the Cathpert family had connections in England with members of a secret group called *The Society of the Elect*. The Cathperts brought a more radical faction of *The Society* to America – the Cohort – and promised to finance the group with their ill-gotten treasure which came from centuries of colluding with pirates. In return, they received an emeritus seat on the Cohort's Executive Council, which was assumed by Judge Holton Cathpert after his father died. Operating in the shadow of the American Mafia, the Cohort developed in the twentieth century by adding new Members and engaging non-members, called *Associates*, who would execute their plans at the local level. The Cohort eventually grew large enough in America to where Judge Cathpert suggested they develop their own security force to protect the organization's interests. He then recommended two of his military buddies as the first leaders of that security team – David's father and Sergeant James Henderson.

A chill flew down David's spine as Tara spoke.

After a while, David, your dad realized the Cohort had plans to deconstruct American society and build a new world order run by the Cohort leadership. This radical ideology would, no doubt, shatter the entire infrastructure of the United States. Existing religious, economic, social, and political institutions would be destroyed. Your father knew he couldn't stop the organization by himself, nor could he just walk away without risking the life of his wife and young son - *you*. So, he secretly formed a competing group that sought to undermine the Cohort's sinister plans…he called it *the Coalition*.

The Coalition? David couldn't believe it. The man he saw as a detached, overbearing military father was actually carrying the incredible burden of leading a resistance to counteract the treasonous plans of a domestic terrorist group.

"Damian and I are both members of the Coalition," Tara confessed. "There are *thousands* of us now."

"Your father's legacy survives, Dave," Damian added. Tara turned to Bailey.

"We were playing a double-blind strategy against the Cohort using Menda Industrial. And, for obvious reasons, we had to keep you in the dark, Bailey. Frankly, we thought you may be a Cohort Associate yourself. We knew your husband, Hunter, had been turned, but we were not sure about you until this week."

Bailey nodded. *Finally*, it all made sense. She had a question.

"Does that mean Townsend & Moore works for the Cohort?"

"Quite the contrary," Damian responded with a beaming smile.

"Hunter's boss at the firm, Matthew Phillips, has actually been one of *the Coalition's* lead attorneys for years." He paused for a moment.

"It was Matthew's digging that proved Hunter was tipping FARCO off to potential whistleblowers and having them killed. If Hunter were still alive, he would be in handcuffs right now."

Tara grinned at Damian and added an additional detail, "Oh, and Bailey? You'll be happy to know, Menda Industrial is *not* laundering money for the Cohort, as you might have suspected. Instead, it's generating revenue for *the Coalition* with the help of the CIA!"

Chapter 87

An hour flew by as the group peppered Damian and Tara with questions. Sarah was exhausted and had fallen asleep against the window. However, the two lawyers were wide awake and eager to continue their cross-examinations.

"So, is Menda Industrial a cover for the Coalition or a front for the Cohort?" Bailey asked.

"That's tricky. The answer is *both*." Damian responded.

"Give us more…"

"We positioned Menda to be the main contractor for major Cohort-related construction projects around the world. The Cohort thought Menda was their primary vehicle to launder money from certain international markets, and *on paper* it is. With Tara's help and influence with Marcos Roberts, I was able to secure my position as Menda's CEO. That's when things got exciting." Damian looked to Tara to add more context.

"Because the Cohort has moles inside the intelligence community, we couldn't just put any undercover CIA officer in as the Menda CEO. Instead, we recruited Damian as a civilian asset. Jacob Blake thought we were recruiting him as a *CIA asset*, but we actually recruited him for *both* the

CIA and the Coalition – he was a double recruit."

Tara continued, "My relationship with Marcos Roberts allowed me to support Damian as *a consultant*. As you can imagine, Bailey, I had to remain cold with you in the office just in case you were working with *them*."

David rubbed his stubbled chin and squinted, trying to absorb the information.

Tara's smile widened, proud of her next statement, "The best part is that Menda Industrial and all of its assets are, in fact, *owned by the Coalition*."

The words hung in the air like a morning mist.

"How?" David asked.

Again, Damian and Tara locked eyes. The pride of their deception was written on their beaming faces.

> Menda Industrial is owned by a private trust which was established by the Cohort to hide its financial transactions. Damian convinced the Menda board of directors that *he* should be the sole trustee of that trust, giving him nearly unlimited power to control the company's money, assets, and trade secrets. Just a few days ago at Menda's quarterly board meeting, the Menda board unanimously approved Damian's new strategic plan. But really, buried in the fine print, they approved the transfer of all Menda's cash and assets to *Coalition-owned* companies. So, the Cohort's cash cow company now owns *nothing*. It's now just a hollow shell. It will take them *months* to figure out what happened and even when they do, they won't be able to report it because it will bring

to light *their* illegal activity. Damian plans to resign as CEO when we get back to Atlanta and Bailey should also resign as General Counsel to protect herself as well. Both of you will be offered new executive roles with Coalition-owned businesses.

Bailey was seriously impressed, but a little embarrassed. Even as Menda's chief legal counsel, she had been thoroughly confused by the maze that made up the company's international corporate infrastructure. Apparently, it was intentionally dizzying for a reason. When she returned to Atlanta, she would review her ethical obligations on how to quickly detach from Menda in order to salvage her law license.

Still, Bailey was confident that no amount of corporate ju-jitsu could fudge the company's accounting books without someone seeing serious red flags. She asked another question.

"How does the Cohort *not know* they're being duped? Surely, they would see the money being siphoned out of their accounts."

"That's where the CIA comes in," Tara responded. "We generated forged financial statements for Menda Industrial. The Cohort leadership can only see the amount transferred *into* the company's account, but the CIA hid what went out. On paper, Menda is making money hand over fist. But really, they're broke."

Tara turned to David.

"One more thing…similar to the Cohort, your father insisted the Coalition establish a creed by which we live: *Veritas Vincit*. It's Latin for *truth prevails*, and the phrase's origin dates back to well before the Coalition was founded. If we can't say it, we simply hold up two fingers, like the peace sign, to signal that phrase to each other. It's also a way for us to identify other Coalition members in the community." Tara held up the hand gesture.

"As the good book says, 'you shall know *the truth*, and the truth shall set you free.' That's what we believe. That's what your father believed, too, David."

Chapter 88

The white van pulled into an abandoned parking lot near the Greenville/Spartanburg Airport. The driver and security guard exited the vehicle and locked the doors behind them.

Sarah was still snoozing with her head propped against the window. Bailey and David were wide awake, thinking about their life-changing conversation with Damian and Tara.

As Bailey waited, a barrage of memories played in her mind about her career. Shady backroom settlements, hushed cover ups, and crooked lawyers haunted her psyche. *The Cohort's signs were all there. How could I have missed them?*

Bailey would never again be able to stand in line at the grocery store, sit in traffic, or attend an event without looking around and wondering who was a Cohort Associate. She didn't know who she could trust. That was what terrified her the most – they were all hiding *in plain sight*.

The security guard opened the van door, which startled Bailey and woke Sarah.

"We're good to go. Mr. Stoneman and Ms. Mercer are going to Washington. The rest of us are headed to Atlanta." The driver announced.

"You okay?" David asked Sarah. She nodded and rested her head on his shoulder. David put his arm around her and turned to Tara.

"What's next for us, Tara?"

"Well, David, you have a choice."

"What's the choice?"

"There's no easy way to say this…" She paused for a second, trying to find the right words.

> You know too much about the Cohort. It won't take them long to find out you all made it out alive. Based on their past practice, they will immediately try to dismantle your life. Then, they will hold your former life hostage unless you start working for them. You simply cannot escape them by yourself.

Tara's words stung like a thousand knives, but rang true. Apparently, the struggle was far from over. Bailey responded.

"Look, I just found out that the father of my children was a murderous psychopath. And when I get home, I have to make up some elaborate lifelong lie about what happened to him so my kids don't end up in therapy for a decade or on some assassin's kill list." She paused.

"So, the last thing I need is more dramatics. Just tell us what we need to do to return to some semblance of normalcy!"

"Fair enough," Tara responded. "Door number one: you can go into a witness protection program and assume fake identities to keep you and your family safe." She continued.

"Door number two: you can go about your life as if nothing happened, and hope for the best."

"Is there a third door?" David asked, hoping it was better than the first two options.

"Yes…you could work with the Coalition and help us bring down the Cohort."

David and Bailey sat silent.

"Door number three!" Sarah confidently announced.

All eyes turned to Sarah.

"Are you sure, Ms. Mercer?" Tara asked.

"I'm not going to hide any longer and I *will not* live the rest of my life in fear. My son and I have been through too much, and it stops now!"

Something had changed in Sarah. She was stronger and more courageous than ever. David was proud of her. The last few years had presented a variety of unpleasant situations for Sarah and her son, Mark. She now realized all that turmoil had flowed from the Cohort's hands and she was finished playing their deadly game.

"What about you two?" Damian asked as he looked at Bailey and David.

"Same," Bailey responded, inspired by Sarah's bravery. She, too, was not going to be strong-armed into living like a prisoner. David, however, was hesitant to commit – he didn't even totally understand what he was committing to.

"I'm not sure…"

"No problem. We don't employ intimidation tactics, threats, or blackmail – that's what the Cohort does. Just let us know when you've made your decision, David."

At that moment the driver chimed in, "Plane is fueled and ready." He announced.

"Good. I think it's safe to say that I've overcome my fear of heights." David joked as he hugged Sarah.

"Let's go home."

Chapter 89

Bailey was in the backseat of a black sedan as it pulled into her upscale Druid Hills neighborhood. Her driver had been waiting for her at the Dekalb/ Peachtree (PDK) airport and informed her that her SUV was already parked safely in her driveway with the keys sitting on the dash. The man indicated the transportation convenience was courtesy of the Coalition.

Bailey was so exhausted that she dismissed the obvious grand theft auto offense. She was just glad to be home.

It was dark outside, but most of the lights in the house were still on. As the car stopped in the driveway, Bailey's children pressed up against the large window on the home's third floor, eagerly waving their hands with big smiles.

The driver pointed to a chair on the front porch. It was her luggage, which she thought had been left in her cottage on Captain Maynard's Island. Her cell phone, purse, and keys were also sitting on top of her suitcase.

"Again, courtesy of the Coalition," the driver announced as he gave Bailey the peace sign.

She thanked him and watched the black sedan disappear into the night. Bailey collected her thoughts and her things as she ambled up the front steps and into the house.

"Hello?!" She hollered as she stepped onto the red Persian rug in the entryway.

She could smell a roast cooking in the kitchen and heard footsteps racing above her. Then, she saw her kids, Emma and Daniel, fly down the grand staircase. She teared up, full of emotion.

Hearing the commotion, Alice came in from the kitchen and stood in front of the wooden dining room table silhouetted by the light from the chandelier. She crossed her arms and smiled warmly as Bailey gave her kids lots of hugs and kisses.

"Dinner's almost ready, Mrs. Thompson. Will Mr. Thompson be joining us?" Alice innocently inquired.

"Yeah, where's daddy?" Emma asked, looking up at her mother with eager eyes.

It was time to share the difficult news. Bailey crouched down and looked her daughter in the eye, then she motioned for her son to come closer too. Before she could say a word, Bailey began to cry. The concerned look on her children's faces was devastating and the news was only bad. Through her tears, she was able to manage a few sentences.

"Your father passed away this week, kids…I'm so sorry."

"What?! How?!" Alice gasped in disbelief. Emma and Daniel's eyes welled with tears as the words soaked.

"Daddy joined me on my work trip and had an accident at the hotel." Bailey lied.

Alice ran to her side to console her. They all stood together in the large entryway and wept.

After two hours of emotional distress, Bailey grabbed a quick shower and dozed on the couch with Emma and Daniel nestled on either side of her, fast asleep. Sobs, breakdowns, and half-answered questions caused Bailey to turn on one of their favorite streaming shows as a temporary distraction.

The kids were drained and didn't even make it through one episode before they both fell asleep in her arms. Bailey carefully relocated them to opposite sides of the leather couch and covered them with blankets. She then walked into the kitchen where Alice was loading the dishwasher.

Bailey thanked Alice for her help over the past few days and gave her permission to head home. Alice offered to stay and support, but Bailey respectfully declined. She needed time alone with the kids.

The horrible truth was that Bailey was glad Hunter was gone. Of course, she had to put on a sad, mourning widow act in public but she knew the truth about her late husband. It was in her children's best interest to remain blissfully ignorant and live a lifetime thinking their dad was a model citizen.

Bailey had contrived a far-fetched story of how Hunter had died falling from the rescue helicopter as they were trying to escape the storm – a horrible *accident*. She would commit this false version of events to memory as if they had actually happened, and repeat it for the rest of her life.

Chapter 90

It was late and Bailey's large home was cold and quiet. Despite the hour, she began calling close friends and family to tell them the 'sad' news about Hunter.

After an hour of difficult phone conversations, Bailey finally climbed the stairs to her third-floor home office. As working professionals with around-the-clock schedules, Bailey and Hunter had invested in a home office setup, complete with multiple computer monitors, a scanner/printer, and, of course, a necessity for any lawyers' office – a document shredder.

Bailey turned on the computer. As a habit, she desired to respond to work emails which had, inevitably, piled up.

However, it was unclear whether Bailey was still employed by Menda Industrial. She would call Damian in the morning to find out. Oddly, Bailey felt more comfortable now that she knew the truth about Menda Industrial. At least she was in the loop.

After Bailey skimmed dozens of emails, she peeked at the time on the clock. It was nearly midnight, and a big yawn caused her to consider turning in. As she rose from her desk, a new email alert drew Bailey's attention. It was marked *urgent*, and the subject line simply said: *Your Children*.

Upon closer examination, a chill flew down Bailey's spine – the email was sent from one of her own personal email accounts that she hadn't used for years. Without taking her eyes off the screen, she sat back down and read the email.

Bailey,

As you read this, your children are being taken from the couch where you left them sleeping soundly. If you alert the authorities, you will never see Emma or Daniel again. We'll be in touch with what we want you to do next.

There was no signature line, only a lightning bolt symbol. Bailey sprang from her desk and sprinted down two flights of stairs. Her heart was pounding and fear overtook her. She raced into the living room where she had left her kids. The television was still on, but as she circled the large leather couch, she nearly fainted – they were gone.

Chapter 91

David stared out his home's bay window and into the darkness of his front lawn. He sat quietly at his empty dining room table, alone.

The moment they touched down in Washington, Sarah dialed Mark's cell number. She had to know he was okay. The tense situation softened when she heard his voice. He was confused as to why several 'serious-looking' men had been following him around the school's campus for the past twenty-four hours. But Sarah gave a simple, fabricated explanation which Mark blindly accepted.

After the call ended, Sarah insisted she go visit Mark, in-person and David encouraged her to do so.

David had a lot to think about and was okay being alone for a couple of hours. Consequently, David took a taxi home and allowed Sarah to keep the black car service provided by the Coalition. Like Bailey, their luggage was waiting for them on David's front steps.

David got up from his dining room table and walked into the library which sat off an adjacent hallway. His book collection had grown over the years, but his gaze moved beyond the books to a dusty shelf in the corner upon which sat a handful of old, discarded family photos.

He focused on one photo, in particular, of his mother and father when they were first married. His father was wearing his formal military attire, and his mother looked stunning in her long, white gown.

It had been a long time since David took a few quiet moments to reflect on his parents. He had not spoken to his mother in *years* and in the last conversation they had she was nagging him to get married and start a family. That was ironic coming from her.

David's father's death was especially difficult for her. Dating dozens of zeros and consistently finding the bottom of liquor bottles was hard for David to bear. His mother's personal trainwreck was just one of the reasons David had left home.

He now had a new perspective on why she had dealt so poorly with her husband's death. David's mother had to know about the Cohort and the Coalition, and likely lived in a state of secrecy and fear as a result. That situation would be enough to drive anyone to the edge of sanity. At that moment, David felt the desire to reach out to his mother. It had been *too long*.

Suddenly, an emotion rose up inside of him. He realized he could not stand idly by and continue to let tyrants destroy families like his family, Bailey's family, and Sarah's family. The nation his father had fought so hard to defend was under attack from a ruthlessly effective domestic foe. Whether he liked it or not, this fight had come to his doorstep. Really, it had been there for decades.

Unfortunately for the Cohort, David was not one to back down from giants. On the contrary, he ran out to meet them on the battlefield, undaunted and unintimidated. Like the Division Act the year before, the Cohort was David's *next* Goliath.

In that quiet moment in his home's library, the phrase 'the land of the free and the home of the brave' took on a new meaning for David. He had to make a choice. A choice to exhibit courage and stand for something greater than himself, or to let the giant win. His entire life was angling at a God-given purpose – one which he could no longer ignore. And he had the opportunity to honor his father's legacy in the process.

David retrieved his cell phone and dialed the contact number Tara had given him. Even though it was late, she picked up after the first ring. He cut right to the chase.

"Tara…I'm in!"

Chapter 92

Marcos Roberts was running late for a meeting with his boss, the President of the United States. It was early as Marcos raced from the White House's Palm Room onto the West Colonnade, past the Rose Garden, and, finally, into the historic Oval Office.

The President was sitting behind the Resolute Desk skimming through a thick stack of *Top-Secret* documents. A classified military operation in South America required his immediate attention and he had been receiving real-time updates from the staff of the Situation Room and the national security advisor.

POTUS was in excellent shape for a man in his sixties. He had short, thinning white hair, combed neatly to one side, and donned a navy suit with a patriotic red and blue tie.

The President glanced over the reading glasses which balanced on his full nose as Marcos rushed in, out of breath. Marcos's attempts to conceal his dishevelment were futile.

"Rough night, or bad traffic?" The President joked as he returned to his page-skimming.

The complications of Hurricane Mary had delayed Marcos's trip back to Washington. Even the White House chief of staff was not immune to travel difficulties caused by Mother Nature. It was around 2 a.m. when he finally made it to his home in Potomac, Maryland.

Marcos had casually discarded his travel suit over a spare bedroom chair and passed out the second his head hit the pillow.

A few hours later, he was awakened by the loud buzzing of his phone. In the darkness of his bedroom, he squinted at the small screen. It was a text message from POTUS confirming Marcos was back in town and asking him to come into the office that morning. Despite his exhaustion, when the President asks you to come in on a weekend, you obey.

There wasn't time for a shower and certainly no time to pick out a fresh wardrobe. Consequently, Marcos threw on the same outfit he had worn just hours earlier. It was the easiest option in a crunch. A decision he was now regretting as he stood in the presence of the leader of the free world wearing a wrinkled suit.

"I understand the hurricane ruined your vacation plans... sorry to hear that. No one deserves time away more than you, Marcos." The President acknowledged.

"Thank you, sir. Never can predict the weather." Marcos quickly moved on to more pressing matters.

POTUS and Marcos spoke for several minutes about options on how to handle the issue in South America. The President favored one of Marcos's more diplomatic approaches, as usual.

"That's why I call you first, Marcos!" The President roared as he slapped his exhausted chief of staff on the back. "You help uncomplicate difficult situations." Marcos feigned a smile, secretly longing for a tall cup of hot coffee or a nap.

Marcos and the President's relationship went back more than a decade. Marcos was just a lowly staffer on Capitol Hill when the future President flew onto the political scene in a landslide gubernatorial victory in Illinois. Marcos was one of his boots-on-the-ground leaders who pledged undying allegiance to him and his political future.

After two gubernatorial terms, the Governor wanted the big seat and hired Marcos as a leader of his presidential campaign. That was two years ago, but it seemed like yesterday.

The President rose from his desk and glanced out at the White House's South Lawn as the morning sun cascaded into the room. Unsure whether the President needed him for other matters, Marcos loitered in the center of the Oval Office waiting for his boss to speak.

Marcos had a busy day ahead of him. In addition to catching up on ordinary White House business, Marcos also had to worry about the impact Hurricane Mary had on the Cohort's quinquennial meeting – it was essential that it be rescheduled as soon as possible. The Members expected it and Marcos's reputation as Cohort President hung in the balance.

By now, the local South Carolina authorities would be scouring the barrier islands, searching for survivors, and assessing storm damage. However, if Sergeant Henderson and the FARCO team did what they were supposed to do, all Cohort-related evidence would be long gone.

Marcos headed toward the exit on the opposite side of the Oval. As he approached the door, POTUS stopped him.

"Hey, Marcos, care to walk with me for a second?"

Marcos obliged. After a few steps along the West Colonnade, the President spoke.

"You know, I thought about you all getting caught in that storm down there. Looked pretty bad." The President said as they made the right-hand turn along the historic walkway.

With that comment, the President stopped and turned to his chief of staff. He leaned in and his demeanor changed.

"Listen, *Prometheus*, Henderson briefed me an hour ago. I know what happened."

"Sir, we've discussed this. I have to keep you in the dark regarding *any and all* Cohort matters so you'll have plausible deniability. That's what we agreed."

The Cohort had waited for a century to put one of their own in the White House. Only three people knew POTUS was a Cohort Member – Marcos Roberts, Sergeant Henderson, and the late Judge Cathpert. Now, that list was down to two.

Searching for his cell phone, Marcos reached into his jacket pocket and felt something metallic. He removed the shiny gold coin and flicked it at his boss. The President eyed the piece and grabbed it out of the air as it glistened.

"Cathpert's gold?" The President asked as he studied the coin in his palm.

"That's right. Cathpert didn't make it, sir."

"Henderson told me. I never liked that bastard, anyway."

The President clutched the gold piece tightly in his right hand.

"Even with this week's snafu, I think we're still ready to greenlight *Phase Two*, aren't we, *Prometheus*?" The President asked.

"Yes, sir – we're ready!"

"Good. Start making the calls…it's time!" The President ordered as the two men disappeared into the People's House.

THE END

Printed in the USA
CPSIA information can be obtained
at www.ICGtesting.com
LVHW050305081224
798606LV00004B/902